Hana Hsu

AND THE

Ghost Crab
Nation

Hana Hsu
AND THE
Ghost Crab Nation

SYLVIA LIU

RAZORBILL

RAZORBILL

An imprint of Penguin Random House LLC, New York

First published in the United States of America by Razorbill,
an imprint of Penguin Random House LLC, 2022

Visit us online at penguinrandomhouse.com.

LIBRARY OF CONGRESS CATALOGING-IN-PUBLICATION DATA
Names: Liu, Sylvia, author.
Title: Hana Hsu and the Ghost Crab Nation / Sylvia Liu.
Description: New York : Razorbill, 2022. | Audience: Ages 8–12 years. |
Summary: In a near future where most adults are connected to the multiweb through
neural implants, a twelve-year-old uncovers a corporate plot to genetically manipulate
her classmates, and her scientist mother may be involved in the conspiracy.
Identifiers: LCCN 2022001304 | ISBN 9780593350393 (hardcover) | ISBN
9780593350416 (trade paperback) | ISBN 9780593350409 (ebook)
Subjects: CYAC: Genetic engineering—Fiction. | Technology—Fiction. |
Family life—Fiction. | Science fiction. | LCGFT: Novels. | Science fiction.
Classification: LCC PZ7.1.L585 Han 2022 | DDC [Fic]—dc23
LC record available at https://lccn.loc.gov/2022001304

Manufactured in Canada

1 3 5 7 9 10 8 6 4 2

FRI

Design by Tony Sahara
Text set in Averia Serif Libre Light

To my parents, Bernard and Terry,
and my sister, Vivian,
for being there from the start

1

One day, I will fly with my birds.
—H. H. June 6, 2053

Hana was late—and nowhere she was supposed to be.
She hurried through the junkyard, sidestepping
the pits and sharp edges of scrap plastic and tire rims.
She wrinkled her nose at the sour rot and waved away the
cyber flies. Her eyes darted back and forth, scanning past
the scavenger kids picking through the trash, on the lookout for her own prize.

She was here for a reason—she had to find the perfect
piece for the pigeon automaton she was making for Lin.
A few hours from now, her older sister would get meshed
at the Enmesh Day Ceremony. Like all thirteen-year-olds,
Lin would join the world of adults—her neural implants
would activate, and her brain would be connected to the
multiweb, online at all times.

The moment that happened, everything would change.
Hana would be left behind. Until it was her turn to be
meshed a year from now, Hana wouldn't be able to compete with Lin's meshed friends, and she just knew Lin

would forget about her. She already kind of had.

The last time Hana and Lin had made bird bots together was when Ba was alive. They both used to tuck notes with their wishes inside the metal bellies and clever trapdoors, but now only Hana sent the bots to the wind, rattling off to who-knew-where, Lin too busy to bother with such "childish" things. It was Ba who'd always insisted on adding a pièce de résistance, the finishing touch that showed a bot was made with love.

That was what she was looking for—a special piece for Lin's present. Finishing the bot for Lin was the best chance to reach her sister and hold on to what they had together.

At the top of a trash pile, Hana wiped her brow. The Atlantic breeze brought a welcome scent of salty air. A car buzzed overhead, flying toward City Center in the distance. Hana's heart made like a hummingbird at the sight of the gleaming buildings and hovercars swarming like glittery insects. In a few hours, she'd be there in the thick of the excitement, watching her sister get meshed and enjoying her own Start-Up festivities.

Her comm vibrated and rang.

Āiyā. It was Ma's ringtone, a techno oldie from the 2020s. She didn't need to hear Ma say, *Hana Hsu, get home right this instant,* so she swiped it off. Since Ba died a year ago, Ma had thrown herself into her genetic research, a rocket shooting to the stars while burning

Hana to cinders in her wake. And now Ma expected her to jump at her call? No thanks. Besides, she'd be home soon, so there was nothing for Ma to worry about.

A glint in the trash caught her eye. Hana scrambled down to it. Peeking from the rubble was a small, round item with gears and hands, an antique watch like the ones Ba used to collect.

It was perfect—as if Ba had reached across from the other side to give her a gift on this special day.

Hana reached for the treasure.

A hand darted across her view and snatched it away.

"Hey." She looked up and her stomach clenched.

The girl towering over her was solidly built, with spiky almost-white hair and ice-blue eyes. She wore a grimy tank top, cargo pants, and scuffed-up boots. An octopus tattoo crawled up her left arm and a crab was inked on her right wrist. The scavenger kids at the junkyard had never bothered Hana before, treating her like an eccentric visitor. Why, of all days, did she have to be picked on today?

Hana decided she couldn't show any fear. "I saw it first."

"Too bad, cuz I got it first." The girl dangled the watch from its cracked band and inspected it with a smug smile. She looked a few years older than Hana, maybe fifteen or so.

Hana's heart thumped, but she glared at the girl. There

was no way she was going home without the watch. "Why do you want it? I thought y'all only want pricey things, like nickel and tin."

The girl raised an eyebrow. "A Vista Vap telling me what I want? That's rich."

Hana prickled at the slur but swallowed a retort. No point in getting her butt kicked today. "I'm sorry. I was curious."

"Curious? Haven't you heard curiosity killed the crow?" The girl pocketed the watch.

Hana's heart sank. She didn't have time to find another part, and she really had to get back home.

The girl narrowed her eyes. "What are you doing in the Bottoms?" Her lips twisted into a smirk. "The Dump's no place for a nice kid from the Vistas."

Nice kid? Hana ignored the jibe. "I make things. Automatons."

"Like robots?"

"Not really. They're mechanical, like windup toys," Hana said. "I mean, they're not toys."

"How can you have bots without a power source?"

This girl actually seemed curious. She couldn't be all that bad if she was interested in automatons. Hana reached into her messenger bag and pulled out her almost-finished bird. "I call them bots for short, but they're not really robots. See? It works with springs and gears."

The girl tossed her a sharp look. "I've seen those before." She reached for it. "Let me see that."

Hana clutched the bot close. What had she been thinking, showing this girl her bird? This wasn't one that Hana planned to share with others—this was for Lin. And even the ones she'd sent out in the world weren't meant for this girl either. She'd had some silly idea a kindred soul would find her notes, but this was no such person. This was a tattooed stranger who looked like she beat up people for fun.

The girl's eyes flitted from the automaton to Hana. "Getting jacked tonight?"

"Jacked?"

"You know, brain-jacked? Meshed?"

"Not this year. I'm only twelve." Hana couldn't wait to be meshed, to be like her sister and Ma, though the girl's junkyard slang made it sound less appealing. "But I'm a Start-Up," she added, unable to hide the pride in her voice.

The girl narrowed her eyes. "Careful with that."

"What do you mean?" Being a Start-Up was an honor.

The girl shrugged. "Not everything's what it seems."

Hana frowned. She'd never met anyone who hadn't wanted to join the elite Start-Up program. But this girl wasn't like anyone she'd ever met. She drew herself up and held out her hand. "May I have the watch?"

The girl's icy eyes bore into hers, and she broke into a

grin. "All right." As she reached into her pocket, the girl's gaze blanked out—the telltale sign of an incoming call on her neural network. She scanned the horizon warily. "You better get out of here. It's not safe."

A piercing whistle rang out.

"JingZa!" a boy with matted brown hair yelled as he ran by.

"Huàidàn!" the girl cursed.

Other scavengers grabbed their packs and scattered.

A junkyard sweep by the JingZa, the private security guards of the I Ching Corporation. Gut-cramping fear twisted Hana's stomach. Scavengers weren't technically allowed to scrounge at Corporation-owned junkyards, but she'd never heard of them enforcing the rules. She'd never once seen a member of the JingZa here.

The girl took off.

Hana stared for a moment, then followed her—better to stick with someone who knew what to do.

They scrabbled over faded plastics, their feet skittering over the uneven ground. The tattooed girl was faster, but Hana lunged after her.

The JingZa came into view, three trash piles away. Two men in mesh exoskeleton suits and the distinctive I Ching red helmets made quick work of the first junk heap. Not surprising, with their extra-powered legs.

As they ran, the girl yelled over her shoulder, "Stop following me. The 'Za want me, not you." She peeled away.

The girl ran ahead, pulling something from her pocket. She paused by an old tire, gave Hana a pointed look, and stuffed the thing into the hollow of the tire, then clambered up over the ridge and disappeared.

Hana raced down the trash pile in the opposite direction. Frantically scanning the area, she spotted a gap in the garbage and scrambled in. She wedged herself in a cavity full of shadows, held up by metal beams. Scrunching into a ball, Hana tried to control her ragged panting.

Heavy steps sounded nearby.

"Don't let them get away."

"One of them has it."

Hana stilled herself as best she could, wondering what "it" was that the I Ching goons were after.

She could not get caught. I Ching was one of the most powerful Corporations in the world and had its tentacles everywhere. And to complicate things, Ma worked at I Ching as a high-level scientist. If Hana ended up on its radar, she'd for sure get her mom in trouble. Even worse, the JingZa, like all corporate police, picked people off the streets and held them hostage until they paid "fines." It was a more civilized way to deal with lawbreakers than the old police and court systems, but Hana had heard of people who couldn't afford to pay the fines, or families who had to give up their homes just to raise the money. Hana had to keep quiet and out of sight.

Her comm rang.

Super loudly.

Hana fumbled to silence Ma's ringtone.

But it was too late.

A rough hand dragged her out of her hiding spot. Blinking, she found herself face-to-chest with one of the JingZa, a man with too many muscles bunched all over his body.

He lifted her by the elbow, almost dangling her in the air. "What do we have here?" His breath smelled like onions.

Hana's vision narrowed and everything slowed. This was so not how this day was supposed to turn out. "Excuse me, I'm lost," she stammered. Her best hope was to play little lost Vista girl.

"We'll see about that." The man twisted close to scan her iris.

This was no good.

She looked away to avoid being scanned and kicked his shin as hard as she could. With a grunt of surprise, the man loosened his hold on Hana, allowing her to wrench away and run.

Hana shot through the narrow clearing between the garbage mounds, past stacks of hubcaps and metal pieces. A metal bar stuck out of the trash, and Hana grabbed it with all her might.

It slid out. The pile of junk above it shifted and tumbled behind Hana and blocked the officer chasing her. One of the pieces scraped her arm painfully as she surged forward, narrowly avoiding the rest of the falling debris.

A shout came from above. "Forget that one," the officer cried. "We want the ones with the crab tattoos."

The one chasing her took off after his partner.

Hana doubled over, catching her breath. Out of the corner of her eye, she spotted the tire the girl had stopped at. She must have left her the watch. Glancing around, Hana reached into the tire's hollow and swept her hand inside, trying not to think of spiders. Her fingers landed on a metallic object the size of her thumb.

She pulled it out.

An e-scroll lay in her palm, the metalloid cylinder glinting in the sun.

Her heart hammered. Was this what I Ching was after? There was no way she should take the scroll. The whole thing screamed danger, maybe even crime. She should leave it here and go home.

But she remembered the pointed look the girl had given her. It had to be a silent plea to take it and keep it safe. Her curiosity got the better of her.

She closed her hand around the scroll, stuffed it in her pocket, and ran.

2

Hana booked it down the old train tracks until she reached the edge of her neighborhood, houses jammed together on the Vista hills. Heart still pounding, she scrambled up the hill, past scratchy bushes, and ducked through the gap in her backyard's chain-link fence. She hissed as the fence brushed her freshly scraped arm and headed to the shed tucked in the corner of their backyard.

Her workshop. She'd hide the scroll here. With a press of the sense lock, the door gave way with a soft whir. Hana dropped her bag and sagged with relief, surrounded by the familiar jumble of half-built bots, tools, and spare parts.

She took out the e-scroll and unrolled it until it snapped into a flat, lightweight tablet. A foreboding came over her. Scrolls were mostly a novelty item used for hand-held games for unmeshed kids, but this didn't feel like a game. Hana tapped the screen, and letters rolled up, self-adjusting to her reading speed.

ggctcattat ataagttatc gtttatttga tagcacctta ctacttgggt
aaccgtggta attctagagc taatacatgc tgaaaatccc gacttcggaa

gggatgtgtt tattagattc aaagccaacg ccccccgggg ctcactggtg
attcatgata accgctcgaa tcgcacggcc ttgcgccggc gatggttcat

The letters continued their march until she paused them with a tap on the screen. For some reason, they seemed familiar. Hana touched the menu bar to see if the scroll contained any other files, but it just held more of the same letters repeated over and over. She reached for her comm to look up the strange code.

The comm rang again with the blasted ringtone.

"Yeah, Ma. Láile, láile, I'm coming!" Hana hung up before her mother could yell at her. She snapped the scroll shut, then rummaged through a box and chose a blue jay bot with sardine-can wings, snicked open its trapdoor, and pushed the scroll into its belly. She shoved the bird under the others and grabbed her bag.

Hana ran the dozen steps through straggly weeds to her back door. Their two-story synth-clapboard house was one of the few single-family homes in the Vistas, one they lived in thanks to Ma's high-powered job. The screen door clattered behind her, and she kicked off her boots onto the haphazard pile of shoes.

Her grandma sat at the kitchen table shaping dumplings, her fingers flying as she pinched the packets of dough and watched her favorite telenovela on the screen wall. Popo had insisted on making her out-of-this-world panfried dumplings for Lin's celebration party tonight.

Hana would never need a sensory boost to savor the juicy meat filling or enjoy the just-right chewiness of the dough.

"Hi, Popo." Hana gave her grandma's shoulders a small squeeze. Seeing Popo always made her heart go puddly and warm.

"Hello, Meimei." Oh, good. Today Popo knew who she was, calling her by the family nickname, Little Sister.

Popo was the only adult Hana knew whose brain wasn't connected to the multiweb. Most adults had gotten meshed as soon as the tech came out in the late 2020s, especially older people who wanted to be mentally sharp. But Popo always said she didn't like the idea of changing her brain with chemicals and wire mesh. Sometimes Hana wished Popo *had* gotten meshed, because then she'd remember things better.

At the whiff of junkyard on Hana's hand, Popo wrinkled her nose and flashed a puzzled look. She grabbed Hana's hand and gave a small shake of her head, her eyes soft and watery. "Āiyā. You could use a long bath."

Hana smiled queasily. What era was Popo lost in now? No one took baths anymore unless they were super rich and could afford to waste that kind of water. "Shouldn't you get ready for the ceremony?" Hana asked.

"Not me. I've got to finish these dumplings. I don't want to go . . ." Popo scrunched her brows as if to catch a fleeting thought. "I'm not one for crowds."

Hana slid her hands from under her grandma's. "You

should wash your hands. You don't want to know where I've been." She helped Popo up from the chair and walked her to the sink.

"You are a kind girl," Popo said. "You remind me of my granddaughter, Hana."

A pang shot through her. Popo had lost the thread again. She planted a kiss on her grandma's cheek.

"You're late again." Ma stood at the doorway, buttoning the mandarin collar of her formal I Ching tunic, a long plum-colored shirt embroidered with golden DNA strands.

"I'm sorry." And Hana really was. She was rattled from her narrow escape, and she didn't even get the watch. Plus, now she had a strange scroll hidden in the workshop to worry about.

Lin rushed in, hair dripping down her polymer robe. Grabbing a blister pack of water, she squealed at her best friend, Cassie, who holo-hovered above her comm. "Can you believe these are the last few hours we'll have to use a comm?"

Cassie replied with an equally piercing shriek.

Hana winced. The one benefit of Lin getting meshed was that Lin and Cassie could talk through silent brain waves after tonight.

"Lin, you haven't gotten dressed yet?" Ma snapped. "It's an important night for you." On top of graduating from Start-Up, Lin was a squad leader in the Showcase

Challenge, featuring her class's newly boosted powers.

It was hard to follow in the footsteps of a superstar sister who couldn't help excelling at everything.

"Yep, yep. On my way." Lin finished her water and hopped over their cat, Apollo, on the bottom step of the stairs.

"And you"—Ma turned to Hana—"get cleaned up. We leave in less than an hour." Spotting Hana's scrape, Ma grabbed her arm. "How many times do I have to tell you to stay out of the Dump? It's dangerous there. Go spray some RealSkin on it. This is why I don't want you making those silly bots."

Hana pulled away. "It's just a scrape." She ducked her head to hide the angry tears threatening to leak out. Ma didn't get her anymore. The bots were her connection to Ba, not some silly toys.

Popo thrust a bowl between them. "Sesame candy, Sophia?"

Ma's face softened and reached for a piece. "Thanks, Mom."

"Take one for Walter too."

Ma's face paled. After a pause, she said in a strangled voice, "Sure," and plucked another from the bowl. Ma always went along when Popo forgot Ba was dead. "Hana, please get ready," she said in a tired voice.

Ma's eyes lost focus as a call came in on her neural network. After a brief silent conversation, she glanced sharply at Hana. "Did you see anything unusual at the junkyard?"

Hana gulped. Surely Ma couldn't be talking about the security sweep. Or could she? In a panic, Hana shook her head. "I didn't notice anything." She didn't like lying, but she didn't want Ma to know how close she'd come to being arrested.

Ma gave her a sharp look. "I don't want you at the Dump anymore. There may be dangerous scavengers there. Go get ready. I've got something to deal with." Ma spun on the well-worn heel of her black leather boot and disappeared into her office off the foyer.

Hana stared at the closed door. Ma always had something more important to deal with. Lately, it seemed Ma only ever paid attention to the multiweb.

She stomped up the stairs to her and Lin's room. When she got meshed a year from now, she'd be able to talk with Ma brain-to-brain, and maybe then Ma would finally see her.

And everything would be better.

3

Hana set the shower for two minutes. She stood under the spray of soapy water, questions roiling through her mind.

Who was the tattooed girl at the junkyard?

What was the e-scroll with the strange code?

Was I Ching after the scroll, and what should she do with it?

The shower done, a blast of warm air dried her. She sprayed RealSkin on her arm, which brought instant relief, the red welts smoothing over as the patch blended with her light brown skin. Hana put on the bodysuit that was delivered earlier to be used for her training year. It was fitted but not too tight, made of a silica and tungsten bioweave. The suit, along with virtual reality glasses, earbuds, and haptic gloves, would immerse her in the multiweb in her training sessions, giving her a sense of what it'd be like to be meshed a year from now.

Hana entered the bedroom she shared with Lin. Her sister stood in front of the interactive holomirror fixing her white tunic. Though Lin was a year older and half a head taller, sometimes people mistook them for twins, with their straight black hair, round faces, and similar features. But while Lin's hair waterfalled down her shoulders, Hana's stuck out in messy tangles.

Lin touched the base of her neck gingerly. She'd been implanted with the mesh bioware a week ago to allow her brain cells to meld with it. It would go active tonight.

"Did it hurt?" Hana asked.

"Nah. It was like getting bit by a horsefly, painful for only a moment."

Hana winced at the thought, then held out a hair tie. "Braid my hair?"

Lin gave her a quizzical look. "Sure." It'd been a while since they'd done anything together.

Hana sat on the bed's edge while Lin brushed her hair in quick, short strokes. She closed her eyes, pushing down the memory of Ba brushing her hair before school.

"What's Start-Up like?" She'd been interested in Lin's Start-Up year, but Lin hadn't bothered to share much. When Hana found out a month ago that she'd been chosen to be a Start-Up along with a thousand other twelve-year-olds in the City, she was thrilled, but Lin was too busy to fill her in on what it was like. It had been a huge accomplishment to be chosen by the Council of Corporations, to obtain the grades and teacher recommendations needed to be selected, but Lin hadn't been impressed. After all, she'd done it first.

"It's a lot of fun." Lin parted Hana's hair and began to

braid. "In the fall, you'll go to one of the district Start-Up schools a couple hours a day after regular school. You'll meet new people and play virtual reality games and compete against each other to see how well you use your boosts."

Hana felt a spark of hope. She could use a friend to fill the giant Ba-size hole in her life. Before he died, her family had been more than enough, but now she was lonely. Ma stopped laughing and hardly came home from work, Lin found the multiweb and her new friends more interesting than Hana, and her bots were her only friends. "What's the point of Start-Up school really?"

"You know what they say," Lin said. "Start-Ups are the best and brightest. When we're meshed, we get special chemical and protein boosts, for intelligence, strength, or enhanced senses. But with great ability comes responsibility, so we need training."

"I know the propaganda," Hana said, "but why do we need a year of training?"

"It's only a few hours a day after school. And honestly? I think it's for us to get to know the other future corporate leaders."

"Where will you intern?" Lin, at the top of her Start-Up class, would have first pick of the corporate internships they'd do for the rest of middle and high school, the first of many stepping-stones to power and leadership. Since governments were hollow figureheads and the major

Corporations ruled in most countries around the world, the only way to make a difference was to be on the corporate fast track. And Start-Up was the best way to get there.

Lin's hands paused. "Duh. I'm going to work at I Ching and boost my AI like Ma. Look how successful she is, in charge of science and tech at one of the most powerful Corporations, and she does so much good."

"You don't want to work in diplomacy, like Ba?"

Lin's grip on Hana's braid tightened painfully. "No thanks. Ba's job as a hostage negotiator got him killed."

Hana twisted around, glaring. "It wasn't his fault one of the Nile warehouse employees held the others hostage. He saved them."

"But not himself. If he hadn't been there, he wouldn't have been caught in the crossfire," Lin said bitterly, but then her face softened. "But you're right. I shouldn't blame him."

Hana bit her lip. They rarely spoke about Ba's death, which had hollowed out their lives. "I wish he were here today," she said.

Lin squeezed Hana's shoulder. "Me too." Lin let out a long sigh and switched to the other braid. "Ba would want us to keep going and help the world. With my artificial intelligence implant, I can work on big problems, like stopping sea level rise. Plus, I'll be like Ma with my intellect boost. We'll be on the same wavelength."

Lin had a point. Ma had been thrilled when Lin chose the AI boost. "You sound like Ma," Hana said. "If I had AI, I'd try to bring Popo back to reality."

"You know what Ma would say. Think bigger to solve bigger problems," Lin said.

"Popo not knowing her own family is a big-enough problem." A familiar feeling of powerless anger welled up.

"Maybe." Lin tied off the braid.

This was the most conversation they'd had in a long time, and it both buoyed and drained Hana. They could've been talking like this for the past year instead of Lin running to Cassie and Hana burying herself in her automatons.

Lin leaned over and reached for her comm.

Oh no. Lin was about to be sucked up and lost to Cassie again. Hana wanted to hold on to the connection she'd missed so much. She had to do something kuài—quick. "I have something for you," she said impulsively.

She grabbed her bag and rooted through it for the pigeon automaton. It was missing the watch—the pièce de résistance, and she hadn't even put in a note yet, but she couldn't wait.

Hana handed it over, breathless with anticipation. She knew Lin would love it. She had to. Hana needed her best friend back.

Lin glanced at the bird bot. "Cute. Thanks." She tossed

it onto her nightstand. "Let's go before Ma gets on our case." With a swish of her hair, she left the room.

The hole inside Hana opened jagged and wide.

She'd blown it. If only she had waited until she had the watch and written the note. It might not have made a difference—but maybe it would've reminded Lin of all the times they'd made bots with Ba, and it would've been like he was here with them again.

Anger flared up at the thought of the tattooed girl from the junkyard snatching the watch from right under her nose. Even if Lin wouldn't have noticed anyway, it wasn't fair that Hana wouldn't have a chance to find out. Unless she was able to get the watch back from the junkyard girl somehow. Her thoughts flashed to the e-scroll hidden in her bot. If I Ching was really after the scroll, it wasn't safe to keep it. As soon as she could, Hana would try to find the girl and accomplish both her goals—get rid of the e-scroll and recover the watch.

And if her sister wasn't coming back to her—at least, not yet—she would have to go to Lin. Becoming a Start-Up was one step closer to getting meshed and connecting with her sister again—and she couldn't wait.

4

Hana's spirits zoomed along with the maglev train as it sped toward City Center, away from the Vistas and past the tin-roof shacks of the Bottoms, the slums that spread amoeba-like throughout the City. The train was packed, people pressed shoulder to shoulder, all heading to the Enmesh Day Ceremony. Because Ma was a high-level I Ching official, Hana and her family were invited every year, along with the other important Corporate families. Otherwise, only the families of the City's thirteen-year-olds about to be meshed and twelve-year-olds honored as Start-Ups came in person, while everyone else streamed the festivities. Hana couldn't get used to how visible she was this year in her bodysuit, as strangers repeatedly smiled at her or congratulated her with gōngxǐs.

Hana bounced her knee rapidly. Start-Up was finally here, but the events of the day weighed on her. In the morning, she'd try to find the scavenger girl to return the e-scroll and get back the watch, and then she'd be free to focus on her exciting year to come.

"Are you nervous?" Ma asked.

"It's not that. I . . ."

"You'll be fine." Ma's focus returned inward, as usual.

Hana slumped. She'd hoped this was one day Ma would get out of her head and be with her daughters, but apparently not. She checked her comm to see if the junkyard raid had made the news.

6.6.2053. *Enhanced Honey Bees on Strike, Replaced by Cyber Bees.* When Honey Bees rebelled against their neural mesh implants, Dowsanto developed cyber bees, robotic bees to replace them in the crucial role of pollinating 30 percent of the nation's food crops.
>>> **Bite-Size News**

6.6.2053. *Scientists Warn of Environmental Tipping Point.* After over eighty years of warning about climate change, scientists now debate whether to fight it with tech and human ingenuity or flee in search of new and better worlds. >>> **Crowdsource News Network**

Hana swiped off the comm. The raid should have been noteworthy. She'd spent plenty of time around the junkyard, and she'd never once seen a member of the JingZa before today. Something important must have happened to make them show up. But the Corporations controlled so much of the news—if they didn't want info out about the raid, it was as if it never happened.

The train approached the chaos of City Center—the high-rises, drifting billboards, and kaleidoscope of hover-cars. Their train hissed to a stop at the third floor of the cantilevered Convention Center. Ads crawled up the glass walls, advertising the Big Five Corporations that controlled worldwide society—I Ching, Nile, Plex, Maskbook, and Pear. Floating billboards cycled through hundreds of flashing enticements, individualized for those who were meshed.

Hana's pulse quickened. Part of her loved coming to City Center for the bursts of colors and sounds, while the other part felt totally overwhelmed. Sometimes, Hana worried being meshed would be like this all the time. But it would be worth it.

They stepped off the train into a crowd of hundreds funneling down the wide ramp to the Convention Center foyer, the sun streaming through the glass walls and glinting off the bodysuits of the Start-Ups. The scrumptious smells of steamed buns, fried dough, and bacon kabobs from food carts wafted through the air. Popo would've loved the bāos, even while telling everyone they weren't as good as her own.

Hana's throat tightened. Last year, Ba had rushed from cart to cart, telling them they had to try this or that. She turned to Lin. "Do you remember . . ." But Lin had surged ahead to get ready with her class.

Hana squashed down the heavy feeling. Today wasn't

about the past—it was about her future. Entering the great hall, she brightened. Thousands of jelly chairs, egg-like pods with spongy surfaces that kept people still while immersed in the virtual world, filled the cavernous space facing a stage. A latticework of metalloid struts held up the domed roof. Hundreds of people milled around, and others settled into the jelly chairs, getting ready for the shared simulation. By the start of the ceremony, the Convention Center would hold almost ten thousand people.

An usher handed Hana earbuds, multisensory glasses, and gloves. On this day each year, everyone under thirteen was given the latest tech for one day to simulate what it was like to be meshed. As a Start-Up, she got to keep the gear for the rest of her training year.

She put on the earbuds and glasses, a transparent eye mask. Instantly, her surroundings transformed. The ceiling became a sky filled with pillowy pink and golden clouds. The jelly chairs became wooden folding chairs on a grassy field facing an outdoor stage.

Hana let out a delighted laugh. Pennants flapped in the breeze, kites danced, and jugglers on stilts threw crystalline balls as lively fiddles and breathy flutes filled the air.

In her side vision, info scrolled by. Anything she focused on opened floating vids and captions. The first few times Hana used the glasses in previous ceremonies had been dizzying. Now she knew to use her eyes to click and call up info or her gloves to swipe at the holoscreens.

Hana glanced at her sister, whose arm was around Cassie. Her stats popped up.

> **LIN HSU.** Thirteen years old. Resident of Vistas, Old Virginia. Enmesh Class of 2053, Start-Up intern, I Ching. PARENTS: Sophia Hsu, mother (employed by I Ching). Walter Hsu, father, deceased (formerly employed by Pear). SIBLINGS: Hana Hsu, Enmesh Class of 2054. She/her.

A man dressed in a gold-and-green-checkered court jester suit motioned Hana to join the rest of the Start-Ups by the stage.

Hana turned to Ma for a last-minute hug, but she was a few yards away, standing close to a dark-haired man in an old-fashioned suit. Ma gripped the man's elbow in an overly familiar way, their heads bent close in silent conversation.

Warmth rushed to Hana's face. Was Ma seeing this man? He had sharp features and an intense look about him. Ma shouldn't be allowed to like another man so soon after Ba's death. She tried to pull up his info, but nothing came up. She tapped her glasses, and more nothing. That was odd. Scowling, Hana trudged to the stage.

Someone jostled her—a boy with dark brown hair and caramel-colored eyes, also wearing a Start-Up bodysuit. He was looking at Ma and the man with a puzzled expression.

"Watch it." She shot him an annoyed look. His info scrolled up, but she flicked it away.

He frowned. "You were in my way."

Whatever. She got in line with the others waiting by the stage. Officials snapped a blue silicone wristband on each of them, marking them as Start-Ups, and directed them back to reserved places in the front rows.

"Ooh, now we're tagged—trapped in the machine," someone behind her said.

Hana turned. A girl with a long brown ponytail and a conspiratorial smile winked at her. Hana returned a smile tentatively. The girl looked part Asian and had a restless, friendly energy. Of course, Hana blanked on saying something witty, so she awkwardly made her way to a chair instead. As she sat, she read the girl's info.

CHARLENE COHEN. Twelve years old. Resident of Treelawn, Old Virginia. Enmesh Class of 2054. PARENTS: Annette Goto, mother (employed by Nile). Saul Cohen, father (employed by Nile). SIBLINGS: Laila Cohen, Enmesh Class of 2052 (Start-Up intern at Plex). She/her.

A brief unease flickered. Both of this girl's parents worked at Nile, I Ching's main rival. She hoped that sort of thing wouldn't matter when it came to making friends at Start-Up.

"Welcome, Enmesh Class of 2053," the mayor of City Center announced. When she focused on his tightly woven hair, Hana's glasses informed her he'd used Shea Elixir. A glance at his face opened an ad for Bronzer Plus to Get That Extra-Shimmery Look for That Special Someone.

The mayor gave the same speech every year and Hana usually tuned him out, but now she paid attention, her mouth suddenly dry.

"Today marks the twenty-fourth year of the neural net revolution," he said. "Every year, I like to take a moment to remember the fateful day in 2029 when scientists made a breakthrough in merging the human brain with computers. By using nanotechnology, they created a neural lace that could be injected into the brain. This bioelectronic mesh merges with the brain's cells, creating a wireless connection to the multiweb. In laypeople terms, we became 'meshed.'

"As a result, we have access to all known information," the mayor continued, "and brain-to-brain communication is a snap. Today, along with others around the world, we celebrate Enmesh Day for the thirteen-year-olds in our district, including the group that has spent a year training in the Start-Up program. They will be our future leaders. But first, we welcome the next class of Start-Ups."

Hana leaned forward. This was her moment.

The mayor paused dramatically. A sparkly glow radiated from him.

"This year we are doing things differently for the Start-Up class."

Puzzled expressions all around. Hana opened her homelink app in her glasses and direct messaged Ma. *Do you know what's going on?*

Ma's reply came back almost instantly. *Pay attention, Hana.*

"Normally, Start-Up training is nine months of after-school sessions coinciding with school schedules," the mayor said. "This year, we are moving Start-Up training to the summer and condensing it into three months."

Murmurs spread through the crowd.

The mayor held up a silencing hand. "The schedule change is due to new advances in enmesh technology."

Hana's heart leaped. She'd be meshed in a few months instead of a year! Being meshed would mean getting closer to Ma and Lin and landing one of the coveted Corporate internships sooner. She wondered what the catch was.

"Because it's our first year on a fast-track schedule," the mayor said, "we will only enmesh those who do well at our tests during the new Start-Up summer school. Only half of the group will get meshed early. The rest will have to wait until next June."

Hana's heart thudded. She had to be in that first group. Whatever the tests were, she would ace them. She couldn't stand the thought of another year being cut off from Ma and Lin, not now that it was possible to join them in three months.

The mayor spread his arms. "Start-Ups, let us begin."

The clouds closed in, casting the field in shadow and a brief chill.

The moment had come. Like a surfer waiting for the perfect wave, Hana faced a mountain of possibility about to take her on the ride of a lifetime.

"Start-Up class, welcome to your summer of discovery."

A few heartbeats later—*BAM*. Hana's suit was powered on.

A buzzy feeling surged through her. Together with the glasses and earbuds, every sense heightened. The pink clouds parted to let in streams of light, and a warm summer breeze washed over her. The reds became redder and the blues more neon. Music thrummed through her whole body.

It was amazing.

Around her, the other Start-Ups broke out in grins or sat up straighter, as if zapped. She caught the eye of the girl in line, who pumped her fist and flashed a smile. The boy she'd run into before had a slightly quizzical expression. Their eyes met briefly, and she looked away.

"Now to the main event," the mayor announced.

It was Lin's time to shine.

"We will connect the Enmesh Class of 2053 to the multiweb," the mayor explained. "Immediately following will be the Showcase Challenge. Remember, you can comment and like the action via the public feeds, but all private messaging is disabled."

Hana wondered what the Challenge would be this year. Each year, the ceremony featured an action-packed adventure that let the newly meshed Start-Up students show off their new boosts—physical agility, AI, or enhanced sensations. The audience, either meshed or wearing glasses, experienced the simulation along with the Start-Up grads from their jelly chairs. The audience could choose to stream the experience of any Start-Up student, as the students all broadcasted them.

When she was younger, she'd taken off her glasses to see if the students were really running around onstage, but they all stayed sunken in their jelly chairs, immobile like the audience. This year, she wouldn't miss a moment, and she'd start with Lin's feed. Getting into her sister's head might give her a clue on how to excel at Start-Up in the next few months.

Hana tried to send Lin a last-minute good luck ping, but private messaging was already turned off.

"Now we will turn on the implants." The mayor's voice, warm as honey, echoed through Hana's earbuds.

A hush descended.

"Welcome to the neural net, Enmesh Class of 2053."

Lin and her fellow Start-Up grads onstage, as well as the other thirteen-year-olds scattered around the audience, stiffened in a collective jolt as their neural connections were activated. Most broke out into smiles. Some shifted and squirmed.

It was done. Lin was now part of the adult collective. She was enmeshed.

"And now," the mayor said, "let the Challenge begin."

5

For a moment, Hana still sat in the folding chair of the grassy field simulation, watching her sister and the others on the wooden stage. Then the entire scene rushed toward her like someone vacuuming a giant silk fabric—the people, flags, mountains, and clouds sucked in and shrank into nothingness.

A thrill buzzed through her. She found Lin's feed and tapped into it, and a new scene exploded outward. Pieces of sky, waves, and wooden boats engulfed her into a new reality as she streamed her sister's experience. The bodysuit, glasses, and earbuds immersed her into the Challenge—she experienced it all as if she were Lin herself.

Her—Lin's—legs almost buckled under as she gripped the railing of a large Chinese junk, its dragonwing sails caught in a stiff breeze. Lin's classmates were spread out on the ship and two others like it, tossed like toys on the turbulent sea. As their bow sliced through the silver-tipped waves, ominous clouds roiled above.

A slew of info scrolled up the side of Lin's field of vision, aided by her newly implanted AI. *You are the captain of the* Hai Long *with a crew of sixty-seven sea fighters and crew. You face imminent attack. Chances of a pirate sortie: 25 percent. Unknown sea creature: 32 percent. Typhoon: 10 percent. A combination of the above: 37 percent.* Frantic messages zipped across her feed. *Captain Lin, what are the orders? Captain Tyler hailing you.* A feed of hundreds of likes, hearts, and zaps streamed at the bottom of her field of vision; comments and advice poured in; and debates between audience members broke out.

Hana—in Lin's head—recoiled. How in the world did Lin keep track of this barrage of info? Lin opened a window for each of the other captains' avatars. A wave crashed onto the junk, splashing her with a bracing cold spray. Hana couldn't believe how the ice water stung, so real.

"Captains Tyler and Amirah." Lin swayed as she wiped her face. "My best guess is we'll face a sea creature." She yelled to her crew, "Prepare for an attack!" The teens spread out, some climbing the rigging and others spooling out line and gathering weapons.

The onslaught of info was too much. Hana switched into the head of a boy climbing the tall middle mast. His field of vision was refreshingly clear of any data, and she realized he'd gotten the physical boost. She felt him speed up the mast to the top spar. The wind whipped through his hair and salt spray stung his eyes.

An angry churning mass of water powered its way to

the boat, and the ocean itself became a charging beast. Out of the fury came a bulbous form, with rippling skin in silvers and purples. Massive tentacles three times the length of the boats towered and dripped over the junks.

"Kraken!" the boy yelled.

Hana felt the boy's cold sweat trickle down her neck and the hairs stand up on the back of her head. An order from Captain Lin came into the boy's field of vision: *Surround the kraken and attack the vulnerable spot near its eyes.* The boy scrambled down the mast, his every move easy and fluid.

The junk rocked in the foaming water.

A giant tentacle crashed down. The boat shuddered and floor planks cracked. Another boy tossed him a line looped in a lasso. Together they flung the line and caught a flailing tentacle. It yanked them twenty, then thirty, feet into the air. He swung and scrabbled to cling to the tentacle.

Others from each of the boats dangled in the same wild dance as the kraken twisted and heaved.

Dizzy, Hana switched views again. She streamed Lin's friend Cassie, standing at the bow of the boat, and wondered what kind of boost Cassie had gotten. Once in Cassie's head, Hana knew—enhanced senses. On a scale of one to ten, everything was a solid fifteen. Drops of water pinged with exquisite precision. The ocean shone a hundred shades of sea-gray and night-gray. Thousands of messages and emojis from people livestreaming her feed zipped and danced.

The kraken swelled up like a balloon, its tentacles high above the junks and thundering down again. The bone-deep judder knocked Cassie off her feet. The world spun as the junk splintered into crunching pieces, shouts and screams all around.

Hana had to get out of Cassie's head. Feeling all the sensations was too much. She switched back into her sister's feed. Even though she had been overwhelmed earlier, at least now she was ready for the rush of data, and that made it easier to deal with. Lin's AI ran through a dozen simulations of possible responses.

The boat listed to one side—

And the scene glitched.

And froze.

Hana sat up with a jolt, heart pounding. She was back in her jelly chair in the Convention Center. The domed ceiling loomed above with its skeletal beams, no longer a stormy sky. Gone too were the kraken, the boats, and the fight. Even the fairgrounds were gone, leaving only the eerily silent center with the Enmesh Class and the audience sitting in their jelly chairs, all locked in the simulation.

Hana was the only one booted out of the Challenge.

She'd never felt more alone, eyes wide open while everyone around her was zoned out.

Hana blinked—

And found herself back on the junk.

She was no longer in Lin's or anyone else's head. The battle against the kraken took place furiously, but Hana witnessed the scene from a slight distance, like a hovering ghost. She no longer streamed Lin's AI-assisted feed, or the boy's physical boosts, or Cassie's sensations.

A crab scuttled sideways across the deck. It winked at her—or at least it looked like a wink.

Hana gazed at the kraken, which seemed to look straight at her, the whites of its eyes big rings and its whole body trembling. The kraken's eyes held a keen intelligence and a deep loneliness. She felt a sharp pang of sympathy.

At that moment, Hana knew.

The kraken was scared. Its thrashing wasn't that of a monster bent on destruction, but of one trying to escape.

She had to let Lin know, but access to private household networks was shut down. Hana tried their homelink anyway and found it active. Odd—it hadn't worked at the start of the Challenge, but really, this was one of the least odd things about her situation.

Lin! Leave the kraken alone. It's defending itself. Hana sent the message.

Lin's attention snapped to her. *Hana, how are you contacting me?*

That's not important. The kraken is lonely and scared. It's not a threat.

Hana could see Lin consider her words and finally nod.

She was slammed back into Lin's feed, which displayed an AI-generated Sun Tzu quote from *The Art of War*. *"If you know the enemy and know yourself, you need not fear the result of a hundred battles."*

Lin consulted with the other captains and sent a brain-to-brain order to all students: *Fall back. Everyone, fall back.*

The kids on the kraken leaped off. The ones dangling on the lines let go. Others bailed the leaking boats.

The kraken reared up, its body almost entirely out of the water. It came down with a huge splash, soaking all with a mini tsunami. The kraken twisted and disappeared beneath the waves, the junks spinning in its wake. The kids stood at the railings of their battered boats, gaping.

The Challenge was done.

6

Hana's mind spun as she came back to the Convention Center. The chaos of the high seas battle, the kraken's loneliness—everything—had been intense. But getting pushed out of the Challenge and coming back in as herself was the truly mind-boggling part.

The students came off the stage to meet their families. As they chattered and posted about their experiences, Hana called up the replay in her glasses. She focused on the moment she glitched out and frowned. None of the vids showed a break in the action, nor did any show the crab. Even her private conversation with Lin appeared as if Lin had simply paused to think.

"Well done, Lin." Ma squeezed Lin's arm. "How did you come up with that insight about the kraken?"

"It just came to me," Lin said, giving Hana a hard look.

Hana could tell her sister had questions. Well, she did too, but now wasn't the time to get into it, so she nudged Lin instead. "You're such a superstar."

Lin narrowed her eyes and flashed a smile. She was good at regrouping, that was for sure. "How is it fair I had to go through a year of Start-Up and you'll breeze through in a summer?"

"It's not a done deal I'll be in the early group."

"Oh, you will be," Lin said dismissively. "You're a Hsu." She scanned the crowd. "I've got to find Cassie." And off she went.

Hana turned to Ma, but she had walked ahead too.

Maybe Hana had imagined it all—the glitch, the crab. But no. She *had* talked to Lin and made a difference in the Challenge. She'd seen the kraken for what it was. She'd never heard about someone being kicked out of a simulation. How was she?

She'd go online later to research it, but for now, she trailed Ma back to the train.

⁕

The Hsu house buzzed with excitement, the party in full swing. Hana wended her way among her neighbors, Ma's coworkers, and Lin's friends.

"Thank you . . . Yeah, I'm excited . . ." She slid out of a random hug.

It was a balmy June evening, the bioluminescent trees and fireflies casting a magical glow over their tiny backyard. The motion-sensor trees were standard in the streets, but Ma had planted theirs as part of her lab's research into eco-friendly outdoor lighting. Hana wanted to talk to Lin about what had happened, but Lin and her friends had settled into jelly chairs to play games with their newly meshed brains. The adults swayed in rented dance bubbles or chatted silently over their neural links, either with each other or with friends in other cities.

Hana felt like the only one stuck in the here and now. Her suit and glasses had been powered off after the ceremony, not to be activated again until Start-Up on Monday.

"Hana, my favorite Start-Up!"

She turned to find Primo Zed, one of Ma's oldest friends and colleagues, a distinguished-looking man with salt-and-pepper hair, coming over with a wide grin.

Hana matched his grin and stepped in for a bear hug. "Shushu." Primo wasn't her real uncle but he may as well have been family. Primo and Ma had gone to college and grad school together and worked at I Ching for many years. They seemed to have an informal competition to see who rose higher in the ranks of Corporate power. For the last three years, he was the headmaster of City Center's Start-Up school, a prestigious launching pad to even more powerful Corporate positions. To Hana, though, he was their lifelong family friend and rock who had helped keep their family together after Ba died.

"Sorry I missed this month's family dinner," Primo said. "I'm so excited to have another Hsu girl come through Start-Up. We've got great things planned for this year."

"I'm excited too," Hana said.

"Great to see you." Primo and Hana exchanged another hug. "I've got to talk to your mom."

Hana made her way to the kitchen, where Popo arranged a plate of dumplings.

"Hi, Popo." She plopped down at the table and grabbed a dumpling with a pair of chopsticks.

"Here you go." Her grandma scooted over a small plate with soy sauce and vinegar.

Hana dipped the dumpling and took a bite. "Mmm. This is so good. I love you so much." She looked up from the dumpling and grinned at her grandma. "I love you too, Popo."

Popo chuckled and scooped more dumplings onto her plate. "Chī, chī. Eat, eat."

In between bites, Hana said, "You should've been there today. It was wild. I might be able to get meshed by the end of the summer—"

Popo's eyes flashed. Her chopsticks clattered from her hand onto the plate, splashing the sauce.

"Are you okay?" Hana sprang to her feet and took ahold of her grandma's elbow.

Popo gripped Hana's wrist. "Anwei warned me the time would come. I should've listened to him. Now it's too late."

"Who's Anwei? What's too late?"

"Hana." Popo's eyes bored into hers. "Do not fall for the

lies they will tell you." Tears welled up. "It may be too late for Lin, but you need to fight it."

Hana shook her head, reeling from the sudden urgency in Popo's voice. "I don't understand. What lies? What should I fight?"

Popo blinked and reached for a towel to wipe the spill. "Have I told you how I learned to make these dumplings?"

Too late for Lin. It sounded like Popo was talking about getting meshed. The junkyard girl's words echoed. *Not everything's what it seems.* She needed to figure out what Popo was saying. "Who's going to lie to me?"

"As a child, I loved eating Chinese food, but I always asked my mom to make American food—burgers, grilled cheese, things like that," Popo said. "Back in the 1990s, this country wasn't Chinese-influenced like it is today. I wanted to be like my friends and not bring weird lunches to school."

Hana sighed. Popo's mind had moved on before she'd been able to get any real answers, but maybe there was a hidden meaning behind this childhood story. Ever since I Ching had taken over the enmesh tech, Chinese culture had become widespread, and now Chinese food and sayings were peppered throughout most cultures. Hana had never lived in a world where Chinese culture wasn't popular, and she couldn't imagine what it would be like to feel like it wasn't cool. Now everyone was into C-dramas, ate xīfàn for breakfast, and did things like fight over who paid for dinner.

She made herself focus on Popo's words.

Popo continued, "At grad school, I had to feed myself. I realized the food I wanted most was home-cooked Chinese meals. I called my mom so many times, I learned how to cook by phone."

Nope, Popo's mind had simply wandered into her memories. Hana reluctantly set aside the puzzling warning. "I'm glad for me you learned to cook by phone."

Popo laughed and Hana spent the rest of the evening stuffing her face with dumplings and listening to Popo's stories of her youth.

She tried to brush off what had happened. But she couldn't stop wondering what Popo meant.

Do not fall for the lies they will tell you.

7

When you get meshed,
can they watch your dreams?
—H. H. June 7, 2053

The next morning, Hana woke up early. She needed to head over to the junkyard to find the scavenger and return the e-scroll, and while she was at it, try to get the watch back. She would add it to the bot and try again with Lin. But more importantly, she was unable to shake the fear that I Ching security really were after the scroll, and that they might track it somehow. The sooner she got it out of her workshop, the better.

Hana got dressed and tiptoed down the stairs, careful to avoid the creaking third step. Apollo balanced on the banister and yowled a brief protest. "Want some food?" Apollo wasn't enmeshed like some cats, so he didn't have a translator app embedded in his brain, but he knew the word "food." He darted to the kitchen, where she fed him fish pellets and grabbed an apple from the fruit bowl for herself.

Popo had left the screen wall on again, the news bytes scrolling by.

> **6.7.2053.** *Nile and I Ching Rivalry Heats Up.* The long-standing rivalry between corporate behemoths I Ching, leading info, tech, and neural net company, and Nile, the nation's premier security, logistics, and manufacturing Corporation, is reaching corporate cold war levels. I Ching accuses Nile of stealing its research on *Ophiocordyceps*, the zombie ant fungus, and Nile accuses I Ching of stealing its work on the cat parasite *Toxoplasma gondii*. **>>> AutoAI Updates**

> **6.7.2053.** *I Ching Authorities Close In on Hackers.* I Ching discovered and rooted out the hacker collective known as Bezorio attempting to infiltrate the City Center servers. **>>> I Ching News Service** MINDLESS MINIONS! 💀 YOU HAVE BEEN HA-HA-HACKED 💀🕷️ . . . 🜨

As Hana watched, the news item was chomped to bits by a hungry yellow circle. She giggled. It was rare to see a real-time info hack. Usually, any alterations to the news were subtle or instantly fixed by the corporate AIs patrolling the multiweb. The screen wall never truly turned off—even in standby mode, it was always listening and gathering info to sell them more things—but she swiped it back to the pineapple wallpaper pattern, the closest to off she could get.

Hana stepped out into a nice summer day—the usual gray skies, wispy clouds, a slight breeze, and a bird's morning song.

She ducked into the workshop and gathered her scavenger bag. She pulled the blue jay bot from where she'd hidden it and retrieved the scroll to inspect it again.

ggctcattat ataagttatc gtttatttga tagcacctta ctacttgggt

aaccgtggta attctagagc taatacatgc tgaaaatccc gacttcggaa

gggatgtgtt tattagattc aaagccaacg cccccccggg ctcactggtg

attcatgata accgctcgaa tcgcacggcc ttgcgccggc gatggttcat

Hana took out her comm to see if a Plex search would reveal anything, but she quickly thought better of it and put it back down. Multiweb searches were monitored by the Corporations. If this info was stolen or wanted by I Ching, any search would raise red flags.

The code scrolled on and on, too long to copy by hand; neither could she copy it to her comm nor the cloud. That would also likely be flagged. If only Ba were alive, he'd know what to do. Hana reluctantly shut off her comm and placed the scroll back in the bird bot and tucked it into her bag. Although she was intrigued by its mystery, it was better not to get involved.

As she left the workshop, something moved in the corner of her vision by the bushes. She scanned the yard.

Just the tinny buzz of a bee.

Hana ducked through the fence and down to the train tracks.

When Hana reached the part of the junkyard where she'd been caught by the JingZa, her breathing grew shallow, and her heart pattered double time. Pretending to search for scraps, she kept a lookout for the tattooed girl.

"Well, well. What do we have here? A Vista Vap!"

Hana looked up and her mouth dried out.

A wiry boy with hair gelled into angry brown spikes stood over her. Next to him was a girl with a similar do, though her spikes were longer and flopped into her eyes like triangle curtains. The girl was about Hana's age and the boy a year or two older.

Hana backed away slowly.

"Not so fast, Vap." With a couple of quick strides, the girl moved beside her.

Hana's thoughts raced. The scavengers had never bothered her before yesterday. Something had changed. What could she use as a weapon? She thought of Ba's antique Swiss Army knife she carried. Half its attachments were missing, including the knife, but the tiny screwdriver might work.

She moved her hand to her pocket, while edging away from the pair.

"You're far from home." The boy smiled lazily.

"I was just leaving." Hana's heart thumped.

"Find any good pickings?" The smaller girl picked up a short metal bar and banged it against a rusty frame. *CLANG.*

Think, Hana. If she had something good, she could trade her way out of danger, but all she had was the blue jay with the scroll in it, which she could not lose. "No, not today."

"So you weren't leaving. That makes you a liar." The boy sneered.

Her whole body tensed. Maybe she should make a break for it.

The two closed in, exchanging evil smiles.

"Show us what's in the bag," the boy said.

Flanked by the two, Hana gave up her brief fantasies about using a weapon but gripped the bag in a desperate effort to bluff them. "There's nothing here."

The boy ripped the bag from her hands, causing Hana to tumble forward.

Please, not the bot.

He barked a laugh as he held up her blue jay bot. "This

is cute," he drawled, making "cute" sound like two words. He tossed the bird to the other girl. "Here ya go, Tish. Happy birdy to you."

The girl snatched it and made a mock curtsy. "Why, thank you, Guille. You shouldn't have." Inspecting the bird more closely, her eyes widened. "Did you make this?"

Hana nodded, trying to remain nonchalant, like she didn't care if this girl had a mysterious coded scroll in her hands that could bring the JingZa any minute.

"Nice work, Vap." The girl dipped her head and scurried away. Her heart sank as the girl took off with the bot and the hidden scroll inside. Even worse, she was now alone with the boy.

He tossed the empty bag at Hana's feet. She scrambled to collect it. As she straightened, he closed the space between them, grabbed her wrist, and leaned in.

She gritted her teeth. "Let me go." She tried not to breathe in the sour smell of his sweat. They were about the same size. She had gotten away from the JingZa the day before. No way was this skeevy, mouth-breathing guy going to ruin her day.

Hana wrenched her arm up, breaking the boy's hold, and shoved him as hard as she could. She turned to run, but the boy was quicker. He grabbed her and slammed her against the junk pile, his face twisted into an ugly grimace. "Huge mistake."

Heart pounding, Hana edged her fingers to her pockets.

She would have to use her broken screwdriver after all.

A voice interrupted them, hard as cryo-ice. "Leave her alone, Guille."

They both looked up.

The girl she'd run into yesterday stood slouched with an almost-bored expression. A flush of relief came over Hana. She'd never been happier to see a familiar face.

"What's it to you, Ink?" the boy asked. "You like Vaps now?"

"Yeah, right," the girl—Ink—replied. "I love 'em. You're an idiot. Get away from her."

The boy raised his arms and backed up. "Didn't mean to scare your friend. Just having some fun."

"Have fun somewhere else."

The boy made a rude gesture and shoved off.

Hana turned to Ink and her grateful smile faded.

Ink's heavy-lidded expression was blank, her octopus tattoo twitching on her crossed arms. "You have something of mine," Ink said.

"I thought you left it for me. I have it—I mean, I had it. I was bringing it back to you." Hana's words tripped over each other. "The girl who was with that guy ran off with the scroll. It was in my bird."

"Bird?"

"My bird bot."

"Your bot." Ink blew out an exasperated breath. "Where did she go?"

"That way." Hana pointed.

"Let's go, then." Ink took off.

Hana hesitated only a moment before following. At the top of the ridge, Ink called to a nearby kid, "Did you see someone run by?"

"It was Tish. She went thataway." The boy went back to spearing trash.

Ink rolled her eyes. "I know where Tish hangs. I'll find her later."

Hana caught her breath. "Thanks for saving me back there. I'm sorry I lost the scroll."

Ink frowned.

Hana hesitated at her expression, but worked up the courage to ask, "What was so important about it?"

Ink squinted in the direction where the girl had disappeared. She considered Hana for a long moment. "There's someone you should meet."

Meet someone? If Hana knew what was good for her, she'd leave now. But Ink had saved her from a beating, or worse. And she felt responsible for losing the scroll. She saw an opening to ask for what she wanted. "Do you have the watch from yesterday?"

Ink's face flickered with annoyance. "Right. It's at my pad. Come with me and I'll get your watch back later." Ink moved expertly down the garbage mound.

It didn't feel like a great idea, but Hana followed. At the

bottom, they walked along a path of sorts between the piles of garbage. "I'm Hana, by the way."

Ink didn't answer.

Hana stole a wary glance at the imposing girl. "Where are we going?"

"You'll see."

They reached a trash heap with a large metal sheet leaning against its side. Ink dragged the sheet away, revealing a gap. "Come on." Ink squeezed through and disappeared into the crack.

Hana hesitated for only a moment before slipping in after her. Inside the tight space, Ink flicked on a light stick that self-adjusted to a soft glow and led her down a narrow passageway. Hana's breath grew shallow at the thought of the mountain of debris balanced above them. "I had no idea this was here."

"There's a lot you don't know," Ink said.

The tunnel widened slightly, and she ducked to avoid being poked in the eye by a protruding metal bar. The path sloped deeper into the ground, the smell older and mustier. They came to a corridor lined with dim motion-sensor lights wedged in battered sconces.

Hana had a good sense of direction. She figured they were under the patch of forest between the Vistas and the shanties of the Bottoms.

"Can I ask you something?" Hana said.

"No," Ink said without pausing or turning around.

Hana suppressed a smile. She could respect someone who didn't bother to be polite. "Why did those kids attack me? The scavengers around here never bothered me before."

"Yesterday happened." Ink gestured at Hana's Start-Up wristband, the one that had been fastened on at the ceremony yesterday. "You weren't a Start-Up before."

"What difference does it make? Everyone gets meshed, right?"

"We get jacked, but no one from around here gets into Start-Up."

Hana slowed. Maybe it was time to bail. For one, Ink was some junkyard rat. Two, she dealt in secret and possibly dangerous codes. Three, she was leading her through a tunnel under a pile of garbage. But, okay, four, she'd saved Hana from that boy. And five, Hana wanted to see where this tunnel led, the lure of the mystery overcoming her doubts.

She followed Ink.

They came to a rusty ladder that led to a wooden cover. Ink pushed it open and hoisted herself up.

Hana poked her head out too.

8

Dappled light danced through the trees towering above her. A clean smell of wood and fallen leaves. Chirps of frogs and birdsong. Hana's internal compass had been right. They were in the wooded area between the Vistas and the Bottoms.

Ink replaced the tarp, twigs, and leaves that had hidden the exit. "This way."

They walked through a gap in the trees that barely qualified as a path. As they tramped through the woods, their steps crunched the branches and pine needles, rhythmic and hypnotic.

They came to a shallow, meandering stream. Next to it was a large, flat rock. On the rock was an elderly Chinese man, standing with his back to Hana and Ink. He wore a pair of baggy gray pants and a loose-fitting T-shirt that had seen better days. His arms hovered over the water, as if warming himself by a fire.

"Hello, Ink." He turned around and smiled. "Is this your friend who makes the bots?"

Ink sniffed. "I wouldn't call her a friend. This is Hana." She gestured to the old man. "Meet Wayman."

"Nice to meet you, Mr. Wayman." Hana wondered how this odd pair knew each other.

Wayman hopped down from the flat rock, spry for someone whose hair was almost all white and whose face was a map of fine wrinkles. He seemed to notice Hana's surprise at his agility and said, "Qigong, it keeps me young." His face was vaguely familiar, but Hana was pretty sure she'd never seen him before.

He held his hand out palm up, in the usual greeting of a teacher or elder.

Out of habit, Hana placed her palm facedown on his.

Wayman turned her palm over and inspected it with interest. A crab tattoo like Ink's wound around his wrist.

"Hana," he said. "What is your family name?"

"I'm Hana Hsu."

Something flickered across the old man's face. He nodded. "Double *H*." He let go of her hand. "So you make things?"

"Yes."

"Small, mechanical things?"

"How did you know?"

Instead of answering, Wayman rummaged through a satchel on the ground. He pulled out a dragonfly automaton and flipped it over to show the initials *HH* scratched into it.

Hana's stomach did a flip. The dragonfly was one of her favorites. She'd let it loose a few months ago when she was missing her dad hard. Ba had loved dragonflies, and she'd sent this little guy with a note to say hello to Ba, wherever he was.

"For the past year or so, my people have found these mechanical creatures in one part of the junkyard. They got more sophisticated over time," Wayman said.

Hana had let the bots she made loose in a small park in the Vistas that overlooked the Bottoms in the distance. She thought they had flown into the woods, which felt mysterious and safe. She had no idea her bots could travel that far and land in the junkyard. She cringed at the thought of scavenger kids picking them up there.

Wayman handed the dragonfly to her. "Ink told me she'd met someone yesterday who made automatons, so I figured you must be the one. I'm glad to meet the maker of these machines."

Hana gave the dragonfly a happy squeeze. Holding it was a homecoming she didn't know she needed, finding this small piece of Ba. She flicked the hidden switch to reveal the belly cavity. It was empty. A deep flush warmed her face. Had Wayman read her notes? She would die if Ink had seen them too.

"Hana, I am a friend," Wayman said. Somehow the way his kind eyes shone made her believe him a bit.

Hana cradled the dragonfly.

"Ink tells me you have the scroll."

Hana scrunched her face in a pained expression.

"I . . . I'm sorry. I lost it. It was in a blue jay bot I made."

Wayman's face clouded.

"Tish took it at the junkyard," Ink said. "I'll get it back from her."

Wayman gestured to the rock. "Sit. We'll have some tea." He removed a thermos and tin cups from his bag.

Ink remained standing. Hana sat cross-legged on the flat part of the rock. She tucked the dragonfly into her bag, happy for the warm space it made in her heart.

Wayman poured the tea and handed her a cup.

Hana cupped it with both hands and sniffed: a strange mix of sweet and flowers. "What's in this?"

"A family recipe. Dried chrysanthemum flowers and other herbs. It's a restorative mix."

She didn't normally take drinks from strangers, but Wayman sipped his and Ink tossed hers bottoms up, so Hana took a small sip. It had a delicate flavor and was instantly soothing.

"What was on the scroll?" she asked.

"It has a code on it," Wayman said.

"A code?"

"It's a genetic code," Wayman said. "Everyone has genes inherited from their parents, made up of DNA. The genetic code is a blueprint for life—instructions that control who we are, what we look like, how we act."

"They're written in letters!" Now Hana remembered

Ma's lessons on genetics and realized why the code on the scroll had seemed so familiar.

"Yes, DNA strands are made up of millions of smaller units called nucleotides. There are four types, which have the initials *C*, *G*, *A*, and *T*."

"The *C*s, *G*s, *A*s, and *T*s on the scroll are parts of a genetic code," Hana said.

"Exactly."

"Why are they important?"

"We don't know. That's why we need to get ahold of it."

"You and Ink?"

"Yes, Ink and myself, among others. We call ourselves the Ghost Crab Nation," Wayman said. This sounded bigger than Hana had imagined.

Crabs, again. She flashed back to the crab that had winked at her on the deck of the boat in the kraken simulation. Something about the way he said "Ghost Crab Nation" plucked a string in her heart. The idea of a nation of crab people was strangely comforting.

"We live in troubling times," he continued. "Some of the Corporations have dangerous plans. If we can get ahold of that DNA code, we'll have an idea of what they're up to." He narrowed his eyes. "In fact, I have a confession to make. I'm interested in you not just because you make clever automatons. The truth is, we could use your help, Hana."

"Why me?"

"We need young people about to enter Start-Up."

"Why don't kids from around here get picked for Start-Up?" Hana asked.

Ink snorted. "Only rich kids are even in the running—future rulers and all. Start-Up is not the meritocracy they advertise. You must have connections and come from the right families to even be chosen. The whole system's rigged."

The way Ink described Start-Up was so different from what Hana had been taught all her life, that hard work and good grades were the way to get into the program. Hana had never thought of herself as rich, but compared to Ink, she supposed she was. "Kids here get meshed at thirteen, though, right?"

"Yes," Wayman said, "but if they're not in the official school system, they don't go through the enmesh program. They use underground channels, so their neural meshes aren't regulated or always safe."

Hana felt bad she'd never paid attention before. Her brows drew together. "Are you meshed?"

"No, I'm philosophically opposed to it," Wayman said, "but that's not the issue at hand."

"What does Start-Up have to do with this?"

"We're not entirely sure. We've learned that secret factions of the two largest Corporations, I Ching and Nile, are involved in something nefarious, and our sources think it may involve one of the Start-Up schools. We got intel that a man known as 'the Fixer' was planning to smuggle some data out of Nile research labs to deliver to I Ching, so Ink intercepted it before the Fixer could get to it."

Hearing about people at I Ching and Nile secretly working together went against everything Hana knew about the two companies. I Ching controlled much of the info streams in the multiweb and the enmesh tech, while Nile produced most of the tangible things people needed, from food to manufacturing to security services. They were like powerful rival governments, especially since actual governments were only ceremonial. It was astonishing to think of their workers collaborating.

"How would I help?" Hana asked.

"You could pay attention and keep your eyes open while you're at Start-Up," Wayman said.

"You mean like a spy?"

"Something like that. The Corporations have their tentacles in Start-Up. Both I Ching and Nile have placed new teachers at your Start-Up school and they will make big changes this year."

"Like how some Start-Ups will get meshed early," Hana said slowly.

"Exactly."

Hana didn't like the sound of this, but she knew nothing about this man, however kindly he seemed. She wasn't sure she could trust him. "You can't ask someone else going to Start-Up?"

"It's not easy connecting with Start-Up kids. There are about a thousand in the whole metro area but only three hundred in your Start-Up school, the one we're looking at," Wayman said. "You're also different. Most of your peers are addicted to the virtual world, even without the neural links. You, however, build tangible things and work with your hands."

Something loosened in her. Somehow, this odd old man got her in a way no one else did. But the fact that he knew about her bot-making meant his group might've been watching her. Meeting Ink no longer felt like a coincidence.

Hana put down her tea. "My mom works for I Ching. I don't want to get involved." She stood up to go. "I'm sorry I lost the scroll to that girl Tish."

Wayman steepled his hands under his chin. "How about this? Don't decide yet. Come back after school and I could train you."

"For what?"

"Qigong."

"Why qigong?" She knew this was a mind-body meditation and exercise thing Ba used to do, involving breathing and moving qi, the body's energy. *Woo-woo stuff*, Ma used to say.

"In this age of neural mesh and artificially enhanced

brains, you'd be surprised at how powerful the natural mind can be," Wayman said. "The key to harnessing the full power of your mind is through breathing and meditation, the cornerstones of qigong."

Learning qigong would be cool and it would make her feel closer to Ba, but the offer was too weird, coming from this stranger. "I've got to go."

"A word of warning," he added. "Once you enter Start-Up, do not trust everything you see or hear."

Popo's words echoed. *Do not fall for the lies.*

"Remember, their tech is a two-way street. The glasses will record all your searches and they'll activate the GPS tracker on your wristband."

Hana's mind whirled. "It was nice to meet you, Mr. Wayman."

It wasn't quite a lie, but it didn't feel like the truth either. Meeting Wayman and Ink was like lifting a veil, revealing the underbelly of her world that she wasn't sure she wanted to see. If they were right, then Start-Up might be hiding dangerous secrets.

9

*Now that I know someone may read this,
do I dare say what I feel?*
—H. H. June 8, 2053

The next morning, Ma glanced up from the kitchen table. "Where are you going?"

Hana paused, hand at the door. "The workshop." She'd spent a restless night pondering Wayman's words. She needed Ba's empathetic heart, and burying herself in gears and tin plates was how she could be close to him.

"The workshop." Ma's voice grew brittle. "I wish your dad had never set that up." Popo was the one who had taught her son-in-law, Hana, and Lin how to make bots, but it was Ba's idea to build their special workspace.

Hana clenched her jaw. How could Ma be so cold about her dead husband? She used to be so different, always quick to laugh or smile. "I'm going to work on my bots."

"Your bots." Ma let out an exasperated breath, then smoothed her features. "How about we go to the historical mall? We can get you new clothes for Start-Up."

Hana couldn't remember the last time Ma offered to

spend time with her. Of course, she was doing it to tear her away from the workshop, to cut her off from her memories. They faced each other, the pile of shoes strewn between them. The screen wall silently cycled through a Dowsanto ad for its new cyber bees in the wake of the Honey Bee strike.

Wayman's warning about I Ching came to mind. She could try to find out what Ma knew about the e-scroll, and maybe they'd even talk for once.

"Okay," she said.

Approaching the mall entrance, Hana skipped up to Ma. "Can we . . ."

Ma, immersed in a conversation in her head, walked briskly ahead and reached the sliding doors.

Hana's heart plummeted. What had she expected? Ma was never tuned to the present, much less to her. She hurried to catch up to Ma.

Ye Olde Shoppes re-created a shopping mall from the early 1990s, so no comms or neural networks worked here. When Popo began to lose her memory, the family brought her here to help her remember better. So strange to think that in 1994, her grandma was twelve, the same age as Hana now.

When Hana and Ma crossed the threshold, all

connections to the multiweb were cut, and a distracted look crossed Ma's face. "Did you say something, Hana?"

Finally, Ma was offline, and maybe they could actually talk.

"I just wanted . . ." Hana didn't know how to bring up any of what Wayman had told her, so she said instead, "Can we go to the thrift shop?" The clothing stores in the mall sold print-on-demand vintage '90s fashions. Hana liked that era's grunge style, with its soft plaid shirts, Doc Martens, and muted colors. Popo had laughed when Hana asked if she'd been into grunge. "I shopped at Contempo Casuals," she'd said, pointing to the replica store. Hana had laughed too, trying to imagine her grandma in a babydoll dress.

After buying Hana a plaid shirt, Ma suggested ice cream at Ben & Jerry's. Hana got the historical White Russian, and Ma ordered Chocolate Fudge Brownie, still going strong after more than sixty years.

Hana's taste buds danced with the first bites of cream and sugar. Maybe the sugar would put Ma in a talkative mood. "What was Start-Up like when you were my age?"

"We didn't have Start-Up." Ma dug into her ice cream. "It was 2029 and I was sixteen when people first got neurally connected. We went straight to brain implants. It was like the Wild West, survival of the fittest."

"What do you mean?"

"Companies fought to control the tech and software. It wasn't like now, where Pear created the tech and I Ching owns the neural networks." Ma put down her spoon. "Back then, people were enmeshed by different companies and in different ways. The wealthy got good ones. Poor people had to scramble to get what they could afford."

That sounded like what Ink and Wayman had described—junkyard kids had to settle for substandard neural links while the others got the latest tech. Maybe things hadn't changed so much after all. Hana put down her spoon too.

"Everything is better now." Ma's expression clouded. "It was . . . messy for four or five years. You know about the Infotech War. That was when your grandpa died." As people got meshed, national boundaries blurred, and traditional governments lost power. During the Infotech War, large businesses fought to control the powerful new enmesh technology, with I Ching coming out on top and the Big Five emerging as the ruling Corporations.

Mention of her grandpa caught Hana's attention. Ma and Popo hardly ever talked about him, so all she knew was that he'd died soon after Ma finished college. "What happened?"

Ma carefully spooned some ice cream into her mouth before responding. "Your grandpa was part of the Anti-Tech movement."

"What? How come you never told me before?" Hana had no idea her own grandfather had been part of that radical fringe group that wanted to stop progress. "What was Grandpa's name again?"

"Anwei."

Anwei warned me the time would come. "Popo mentioned him a couple of days ago. Was she part of the AntiTechs too?"

Ma sat back. "They both hated the idea of getting enmeshed, but they disagreed on tactics." Her voice hardened. "It turned out he had a secret underground life that got him killed."

Hana stared, equally curious and aghast. "What happened?" Popo was her funny, telenovela-watching grandma—it was hard to think of her with a past, and her grandpa was someone she'd never met, long dead.

"He ran a lab where I worked after college, but he also secretly worked with the AntiTechs, putting himself in danger." Ma said bitterly, "His principles were more important than his family."

"How did he die?"

Ma ran her fingers through her cropped hair. "The AntiTechs attacked one of Pear's factories, and there was an explosion . . ."

Hana brought her hand to her mouth. Poor Ma, to be left fatherless, just like her. And to think Grandpa, like Ba, also died due to corporate violence. "I'm sorry."

"It was a long time ago," Ma said in a clipped voice.

Hana was surprised to hear the pain in Ma's voice. Ma had been so cold when she complained about Ba and the workshop, but now Hana wondered if it was to cover up the grief, and her heart went out to Ma.

"From then on," Ma continued, "I threw myself into the enmesh tech, knowing I could do more good on the inside than fighting it like my parents. I wanted to make the world a better place, so I stuck with what I did best, studying genetics and biotech."

Ma collected their cups. The rest of Hana's ice cream had melted. She was still processing the fact that her grandpa was so opposed to getting meshed he'd died fighting the Corporations. It must've been so hard for Ma to get meshed against her parents' ideals.

But Ma was right. Getting meshed would solve a lot of Hana's problems. She'd have a world of knowledge to figure out how things worked. She'd be close again with Lin and Ma, and she'd be able to make a difference, interning at a lab working on memory recovery to help Popo.

They sat down on the ledge of a fountain where spouts of recycled water jumped from one square pool to another. "Have you ever researched ways to help Popo regain her memory?"

A shadow crossed Ma's face. "I did, but that's not happening anymore. In the past, we looked at promising treatments like metabolic enhancement and genetic editing, but almost everyone her age is enmeshed and their brains are repaired automatically." Ma's voice hardened. "There's no funding for unmeshed brains, and she made the choice to not get meshed."

Hana didn't know what to say. It seemed like Ma was blaming Popo for her illness. But maybe she was just upset, like Hana was, that Popo seemed to be slipping away from them.

Now that Ma was opening up to her, it was time to find out if Ma knew about the e-scroll. Wayman had said the scroll had something to do with I Ching, and Ma had seemed to know about the junkyard raid on Enmesh Day, so Hana couldn't help but wonder if she might have heard about it from her work. But Wayman's warnings held her back from coming right out and asking. She leaned over the fountain and trailed her fingers in the water.

"Ma?"

"Yes?"

"Do you ever worry I Ching might use tech in a way that could hurt people?"

Ma shot Hana a curious look. "People can use tech for good or evil. We have an ethics board that considers every project. Take your hand out of that water. It looks like it hasn't been cleaned since the 1990s."

Hana wiped her hand on her pants. "If someone was doing something dangerous at I Ching, you'd know about it, right?"

Ma gave Hana a hard stare. "I Ching is a large place. As comptroller of biotech and neurosciences, I keep an eye on all research—from cybernetics to nanotech to genetic engineering, but I don't follow every project." Her eyes softened. "Everyone at I Ching has humanity's long-term interests at heart. Our entire philosophy is to work on large and vexatious problems."

Hana could tell Ma truly believed what she was saying. And there was no reason for Ma to lie to her. She trusted Ma more than a couple of strangers from the Bottoms. Hana was about to start an exciting new phase of her life—she would throw herself into Start-Up, the stepping-stone to all the great corporate internships and colleges, and the key to getting closer to Ma and Lin.

"Are you excited about Start-Up?" Ma said. "I'm really proud of you."

Hana beamed. If she could bottle this rare approval from Ma and take it with her everywhere, she'd be set. "I really want to be in the group that gets meshed early," she said, "but I don't know if I'll make the cut."

"You can do it. You're as smart as your sister, and look how Lin sailed through Start-Up and is a summer intern at my lab." Ma stood up. "We should go. I've been offline long enough."

As soon as they left the mall, Ma blanked out, connecting back to the multiweb.

They rode the crowded train home in silence, and

Hana stowed away her questions. She felt she understood Ma a little better and couldn't wait for Start-Up to bring them even closer. She wouldn't spend another moment thinking about Wayman's or Ink's strange warnings and request for help.

10

*It's Start-Up Day, the first day of
the rest of my connected life.*
—H. H. June 9, 2053

A steady stream of students walked from the maglev stop or hopped off hoverbuses on their way to Start-Up school. Some kids shoved each other playfully, while others chatted in little knots. Hana's stomach fluttered at the thought of being among a few hundred of the most promising kids her age.

She came to the entrance of the two-story building clad with solar glass and billboards scrolling corporate ads. The one playing now showed Maskbook's slogan, INFORMATION IS KNOWLEDGE, on flipping tiles, alternating with images of the new Start-Up class. At the door, a couple of kids with wiry hair and dark brown skin, obviously twins, jostled each other. One swiped his wristband and said, "Hey."

"Hey," she replied, and held out her wrist to the scanner. Her wristband tingled to let her know it had powered on.

In the lobby, Headmaster Primo Zed greeted students

in a white suit, his edges glowing with the telltale sign he was in hologram form. He winked at her. "Nǐ hǎo, Hana."

Hana broke into a smile, comforted to see her family friend. "Nǐ hǎo, Shushu—I mean, Headmaster Zed."

"Welcome, Start-Ups," he said to the students in the lobby. "I'm Headmaster Primo Zed. Follow your wristband to your class, and your teachers will join you shortly. In the meantime, settle in and get acquainted with your fellow students."

A translucent map of the hallways hovered above Hana's wristband. She followed a glowing line to her classroom, set up with modular tables and chairs. About thirty other students were spread out among them, with no teacher in sight. A screen wall ran more ads.

A set of lockers lined another wall. When Hana approached them, a locker chimed, announcing itself as hers. She swiped her wristband to open it and stashed her bag. She closed the locker door and jumped. The boy who'd bumped into her at the ceremony stood next to her. His caramel-colored eyes were framed by long lashes.

"You," she said.

"Figures." He let out a snort.

They exchanged wary looks. Hana moved away and wondered what she was supposed to do now. A bunch of the kids had parked themselves at a screen wall broken up into individual touch screens. Most played *Way of the Warlords*, the most popular multiplayer game. A tiny girl with a braid almost to her waist, the twins she'd seen earlier, and others tapped at the wall.

Hana didn't feel like playing the game. She had nothing against *Way of the Warlords,* but there had to be more interesting things to do on the first day of Start-Up. She walked over to a table stacked with old-school games like board games, cards, and xiàngqí—the Chinese version of chess. Standing nearby was the friendly girl from the ceremony. She wore the same brown ponytail and mischievous look.

"When do you think they start the brainwashing?" she said.

Hana smiled. "I don't know. Soon enough?"

"I'm Charlene. I saw you at the ceremony." The girl tugged the end of her ponytail and grinned. "My friends call me Chuck."

Hana wondered what she should call her. "I'm Hana. Do you know what we're supposed to do?"

"Yeah. My older sister was a Start-Up two years ago and told me all about it."

"My older sister was a Start-Up last year and didn't tell me anything," Hana replied.

Chuck snorted and nudged Hana. "Good thing you have me. You need to know two things. One, we're being watched all the time. Even now, they're watching to see what we do."

"Really?" Hana thought that was creepy. She knew screen walls paid attention to people in order to sell things but didn't know the school monitored students with them too. "What's the second thing?"

Chuck grinned. "Lunch is the best part of the day."

Hana laughed. "Do you want to play a game?"

"Yeah! I love this old stuff," Chuck said. "I mean, I also love *Way of the Warlords*, but I can go old-school too."

"Me too." Hana beamed. Start-Up was turning out to be not so bad. Chuck seemed to be just her type of person.

Chuck rummaged through the games. "Ooh, we can play a strategic game like Go or xiàngqí." She gave Hana a conspiratorial nudge. "Or we could totally mess with them and play charades."

Hana returned Chuck's quick smile. It'd never felt this easy to talk to someone outside her family before. She spotted a mesh bag with old Chinese coins and a small book with a distinctive logo. "Oh! Do you want to—"

"Do an *I Ching* reading?" Chuck finished her sentence. "Is the sky gray? Um, yeah!" She pulled Hana to a nearby table.

Oh, great. Seated there was the strange boy from the locker.

"Hello." Chuck held up the bag. "Want to join us in an *I Ching* divination?"

He frowned. "Is that some kind of corporate game?"

"Nope, this is the original *I Ching*, a kind of fortune-telling, totally different from I Ching the Corporation. We can see what's in store for us at Start-Up. I'm Chuck, by the way." Her easy grin coaxed a smile from him.

"Tomás." He glanced at Hana and skipped the smile for her.

"Hana." She gave him a half wave, wondering what his problem was.

Chuck shook out the coins and passed three to each of them. "All right, we need to think about what we want out of Start-Up to come up with a question." In ancient times, people did *I Ching* readings by throwing yarrow sticks, but now people tossed three coins six times. Depending on the combination of heads or tails, they drew either a straight line or a broken line for each toss. Drawing all six lines made up a pattern of lines called a hexagram, each with a different meaning that they could look up in the book.

"I want to get meshed early," Hana said.

"Me too," Chuck said. "I can't wait until I'm meshed so I can do all my wushu moves in full immersive mode in *Way of the Warlords*. And my parents . . ." Her face clouded briefly, but then she smiled. "What about you, Tomás?"

Tomás seemed surprised, as if he wasn't expecting to be included in the conversation. "I don't know if getting meshed is such a big deal."

"What?" Chuck said. "Just wait and see. So"—she rubbed her hands together—"clear your mind and ask your question. The coins will do the rest."

Hana closed her eyes. She had a lot of questions. Would getting meshed solve her problems—connect her to her family? Would there be room in her future for her bots? And most importantly, what did she need to do to get meshed early? She tossed the coins six times, drew the hexagram, and consulted the book:

"I got the Tower." Hana checked the book and read, "'To see and be seen, yet not make contact.'"

"'The Tower's about preparation and observation,'" Chuck read.

Hana wondered what that meant for her time at Start-Up. Maybe it was a sign that she *should* pay attention to what was happening here.

"Mmm. I don't know what your question was," Chuck said, "but you're isolated. You'll need help. I'll rescue you from your tower, Rapunzel, if you ever need it."

Hana couldn't help laughing. "I don't need rescuing. What about you?"

"Okay, I need to come up with a question." The same fleeting expression of sadness came over Chuck again, but she shook her head as if to clear it. She threw the coins and made her hexagram:

"I got the Family." She read, "'Forming foundations that cannot be shaken and being sincere in word and duty.' Ha! That's me: loyalty, duty, and sacrifice!"

Tomás snorted softly. He threw his coins and made his hexagram:

"What's that?" he asked.

Hana read, "'The Raven: The way is broken. Advice should be well heeded.'"

Tomás pushed the coins away. "This is a stupid game."

"What was your question?" Hana asked. The Raven was ominous, but Popo always told her it was better to go into dangerous situations with her eyes open. Even though people treated *I Ching* as a game, Tomás didn't have to be such a jerk about it.

"None of your business."

"Touchy!" Chuck said. "I think the oracle's trying to tell you something."

"I think the oracle is a crock of . . ." Tomás's gaze moved past them to the classroom door.

A thin man in a short tunic entered the room. He walked among the students playing at the screen walls, tapped them on the shoulder, and whispered to them. Some looked up in confusion and others with curious interest. Each one he spoke to left their stations and walked out of the room.

The man came over to their table and bent near Chuck. "Come with me, please."

A startled look. "Me?" she said.

"We need you at the infirmary."

Chuck stood up and shrugged. "Catch you later, gators." She followed the others out.

The lights dimmed and then brightened. A short woman built like a small tank stepped into the room. She had a buzz cut and granite eyes and wore a black suit. "Good morning." She stood ramrod straight with her legs shoulder-width apart and her arms behind her back. "My name is Adhira Malhotra."

Hana sat up. This was the moment she'd been waiting for—Start-Up would finally begin. Chuck had better come back soon, or she'd miss it.

"Put away your games and I will brief you on the Start-Up tests."

But instead, Ms. Malhotra suddenly blanked out, apparently listening to an incoming message through her implant. Her face twisted with annoyance. "You'll have to excuse me. Follow your wristbands to the changing rooms to gear up and meet at the virtual reality room, and another instructor will give you the orientation." She hurried out the door.

Hana frowned. Start-Up seemed awfully disorganized.

11

The changing room was a flurry of rustling and excited murmurs. Chuck and the others who'd left the classroom earlier joined them. Chuck's face was flushed.

"Where'd you go?" Hana asked.

Chuck rolled her eyes. "They said I wasn't up-to-date on my nano pills." She shrugged. "I could've sworn I'd gotten the medtech at my last checkup."

"What a pain." Hana gave a silent thanks that her super-organized mom never forgot routine health updates like nano pills, which delivered tiny bots into their bodies to monitor and repair their cells.

The tiny girl with the long braid chimed in, "I thought I'd gotten my nano pills too. I'm Christa, by the way." Christa looked like she could be blown over by a strong gust of wind.

"I'm Chuck. I guess we screwups have to stick together." Chuck and the girl giggled.

Hana pulled on her gloves and snapped on her glasses, which immediately connected to the multiweb. Info on all the girls bombarded her view. She'd already seen Chuck's info at the ceremony and now read about Christa

Maynard, who lived in Treelawn, the same neighborhood as Chuck, and whose parents worked at Maskbook.

Hey, girl! A message from Chuck scrolled across her view, followed by a passel of bouncing bunnies.

Hana grinned and sent back a chorus line of dancing flowers.

They headed out of the locker room and met the boys in the hall on their way to class. Tomás's info came up.

> **TOMÁS ORTIZ**. Twelve years old. Resident of Vistas, Old Virginia. Enmesh Class of 2054. PARENTS: Marisa Perez, mother, deceased (formerly employed by Pear). Pedro Ortiz, father ███████. SIBLINGS: none. He/him

How odd. His dad's info was blacked out, something she'd never seen before. Her chest tightened when she read about his mom, knowing how hard it was to lose a parent. Tomás also lived in the Vistas, but she wasn't surprised they hadn't run into each other, since no one ever hung out in the streets.

As Hana walked through the hall, her feed labeled everything: MAINTENANCE, MULTIPURPOSE ROOM, SCREENINGS. Glancing at the vents brought up a map of the airshaft above, an animated tunnel spiderwebbing its way through the building's guts and venting out to the roof.

Chuck nudged her. "Come on, don't you want to get to the VR room?"

Still looking up at the schematics, Hana followed. When she arrived at the classroom, her new teacher stood at the door. He was a thin man with red hair and a beard split into two points. He wore skinny pants and a lightweight scarf, vintage clothes popular with adults trying too hard.

"Greetings, Ms. Hsu." His info was curiously basic.

MARTIN ZOBLE. Instructor, Start-Up school (employed by I Ching). He/him.

"Hello, Mr. Zoble." They exchanged the standard teacher-student greeting, the same hand press she'd shared with Wayman in the woods, his hand faceup and hers facedown.

Inside the room were rows of virtual reality machines—translucent egg-like pods with spongy seats, fancier versions of the jelly chairs used at the ceremony. A shiver of excitement ran through her.

Mr. Zoble entered the room.

Chuck tugged at her ponytail. "This is the best day of my life."

"Welcome to Start-Up," Mr. Zoble said. "As you heard at the ceremony, we are doing things differently this year."

Wayman had said, *They will make big changes this year.* But Hana shook that thought off. She wasn't going to think about Wayman anymore.

"At Start-Up you will compete against each other by

testing the leadership boosts through virtual reality games and taking classes on leadership, history, and informatics. We will keep a running score of your standing among the three hundred students in this school, and only the top half of the class will get enmeshed at the end of the summer," Mr. Zoble said. "The rest of you will be dropped from the Start-Up program and you'll be enmeshed when you turn thirteen along with the rest of the general public, with no special boosts or privileges."

Hana blinked. The mayor had said there would be an early group, but it hadn't sunk in that if she failed, she'd be out of Start-Up completely. She'd be the loser sister and a failure in Ma's eyes, cut off from the internship and college opportunities that came with being one of the elite.

"Remember, being a Start-Up is a privilege. Your wristbands will track your activities and whereabouts for the next few months. You're expected to behave as model citizens and leaders. Removing the wristband is an infraction that can get you kicked out of the program."

Unease pricked at Hana, but she tamped the feeling down. She didn't plan on having anything more to do with Ink, Wayman, or the scroll, so she didn't have to worry about being monitored.

"The pods are like the jelly chairs you're used to," Mr. Zoble continued. "You will be immobile while you experience virtual reality wearing bodysuits and glasses. When you're actually enmeshed, your brain will physically bond with a neural lace, but for now, the VR pods mimic the experience.

"I'll review the three leadership boosts available to Start-Up graduates. The first is grafting artificial intelligence, or AI, to your brain," Mr. Zoble said. "You'll think faster, make better connections, and see the bigger picture. Most of our corporate leaders have enhanced their minds with AI."

Hana chewed her bottom lip. As far as she could tell from Ma's harried life, seeing the bigger picture only made her work harder and deal with bigger problems. But getting AI would let Hana understand Ma better, and she'd be eligible for internships at the top Corporations, which would put her on a path to a future job to work on fixing Popo's memory.

"The second boost enhances physical abilities," Mr. Zoble said. "Your neural mesh, with the right chemicals and nanites, can produce faster reflexes, stronger muscles, and better coordination. Our elite Corporate security forces have these boosts."

Chuck elbowed Hana. "I could go for that."

"I know, right?" With a physical boost, Hana could've taken on the junkyard bullies on Saturday, or the JingZa guards the day before.

"Or, finally, you can increase your sensory inputs, letting you taste, feel, and hear things at heightened levels, and becoming leaders in arts and entertainment," Mr. Zoble said.

Based on streaming Cassie's experience in the kraken fight, Hana didn't think she could handle the sensory overload.

"Over the course of Start-Up training, we will test you on how well you use each boost. All tests will take place in *Way of the Warlords*."

Hana and Chuck traded grins. Other kids whooped. In *Way of the Warlords*, people lived and socialized in an ancient Chinese society of emperors, warriors, scholars, and monks. They could go on quests or trading missions, fight, or live and work as they pleased. Because it was such a popular game, almost everyone had accounts and avatars.

"We will score you on how well you use the boosts, as well as your judgment in facing each challenge," Mr. Zoble continued. "Your first test is open-ended to show you what it's like to be enmeshed. At some point, you will face an unexpected situation. You can use one boost— and only one—to help you, and which one you choose and how you wield it will determine your score."

In the margins of her field of vision, Hana could toggle tabs to switch between the boosts, PHYSICAL, ARTIFICIAL INTELLIGENCE, and SENSORY. The challenge sounded amorphous, but she was ready. She had to be.

"Select a pod and I'll meet you inside the game."

The students scrambled to the VR pods. Hana found one near Chuck. Their teacher gave them pointers, but they quickly figured out how to use them. Hana settled into the jelly seat and smiled grimly. She needed to be at the top of the class to not fail out of Start-Up. And that meant she needed to ace this test.

12

Hana blinked, momentarily disoriented. She stood in a clearing surrounded by woods, tall trees crowding in. This was not her usual entry point for *Way of the Warlords*.

Hana's avatar in the game was sixteen, the default age given to players. She hadn't bothered to change it when she started playing the game. She ran her fingers over the nubby cotton of her tunic. Her leather vest hung heavy, and she wiggled her toes in her well-worn boots. It all felt so real. Feeling these sensations was a hundred times more intense than playing on a screen wall or comm.

Others around her jumped up and down or ran in circles. Their avatars ranged from kids to ancient gurus in all sorts of armor and wild-looking skins. A girl and a guy wore matching purple superhero suits with the handles WONDER TWIN ONE and WONDER TWIN TWO. Hana guessed they were the tall twins from her class. One nice thing about the game was people didn't have to stick to historically accurate outfits or their perceived genders.

"Oho, you must be Hana!" A blue-haired teenage girl wearing blue-black armor that shimmered in the sun greeted her with a high roundhouse kick. She was over a head taller than Hana and ripped. The avatar's handle, WIND WALKER, appeared in the upper left of Hana's field of vision.

Wind Walker tugged one of her blue braids and grinned widely.

"Chuck?" Hana asked.

"Yep." Chuck had added about six inches to her height and wore a face with strong cheekbones and wide-set eyes. She looked to be about sixteen but had the same puppy-dog energy as she did on the outside.

"You like?" She spread her arms and spun round. "I'm a warrior monk." She brought her palms together in greeting. "My mom's always on my case for picking Chinese warriors instead of Japanese ones, like ninjas." She made a face. "Like I'm a traitor to her culture or something. I can't help that wushu is my thing." She looked Hana up and down. "You were easy to pick out. You look practically the same, but older. Where's the imagination, girl? Also, sweet handle, Magpie."

"I stick with what I know." Hana and Chuck pressed palms. Chuck's hands felt calloused and warm. "Sweet skins."

"Yeah, you can't buy these." Chuck showed off her tunic and armor, weapons clanking. "I had to earn them in quests and in kung fu training. And here's the best part." With fingers in her mouth, she let out a piercing whistle. A giant crow with three legs swooped down and landed on her outstretched hand. "Meet my friend Yatagarasu."

Hana let out a delighted laugh. "I can't believe you have one of the three-legged crows. They're so rare."

"You don't *have* them. They decide if they want to be with you." Chuck stroked the crow's wings. It cocked its head and flew off. "I have a way with animals."

Hana was sure Chuck was the coolest person she'd ever met.

In the middle of the clearing, Mr. Zoble wore the robes of a high court mandarin, his beard now snow white and coming to a point down his chest. "Students, you have forty-five minutes. Your assignment is to play the game as you normally would, whether it's going on a quest or living your *Way of the Warlords* life.

"At some point, you will face an unexpected situation, and you can use only one boost to help. You will be awarded points on how well you react and whether you successfully evade danger. Remember, each challenge will add to your running score."

He dissolved into a silvery mist.

Hana turned to Chuck. "I don't like being judged. We don't even know what we're going to face."

Chuck shrugged. "No use worrying until it comes. Want to go on a raid with me? I've been planning a mission to save a kidnapped prince." Her eyes darted up to her right. "Never mind. My warrior monk squad isn't online. Let's do something else."

"Do you want to see my workshop and store?" Hana said. Her favorite part of *Way of the Warlords* was her shop, where she built and sold automatons. Part of the reason she'd kept her older avatar was because it made running her business easier.

"You work at Artisan Village? I love shopping there for weapons."

Hana stifled a grin at the sight of this muscle-bound blue-haired warrior bouncing up and down like a little kid.

"What do you make?" Chuck asked.

"You'll see." Hana sent her the coordinates. A hovering arrow directed them down a path leading out of the clearing.

They passed Tomás in a loose-fitting white shirt and gray pants tied at the waist. He sported the standard avatar of a new player: his real face in a sixteen-year-old body. His handle was PEASANT4762. Players rarely kept the default settings. A few sessions of being ordered around or conscripted into servitude usually motivated people to create a different avatar. And at their age, it was super rare to find anyone who hadn't played the game before.

The sixteen-year-old version of Tomás towered over Hana and stood eye-to-eye with Chuck's avatar. So this was how the matrix calculated he'd look in a few years. Hana hadn't noticed those cheekbones before.

"Tomás." Chuck jabbed him playfully. "What's up with the peasant look?"

"I don't play *Way of the Warlords.*" Tomás gave what Hana had come to think was his usual scowl.

"Are you serious?" Chuck said. "What's up with that?"

Hana eyed Tomás. "What *do* you play?"

"Nothing. I'm not a gamer."

"What do you do for fun?"

"What's this? Twenty questions?"

Hana rolled her eyes. "Come on, Chuck, let's go."

"Should we ask him to join us?" Chuck asked. "He looks lost here."

Tomás glared at both of them.

"No." Hana headed down the forest path. Chuck was the first person she knew from the outside who Hana had ever wanted to show her workshop. Tomás was definitely not the second.

Chuck gave Tomás an apologetic smile and shrugged.

Normally, Hana would skip the walking parts of the game and click to the next scene, but she wanted to feel everything. As they walked through the bamboo grove, hollow stalks clacked and leaves rustled. The sound of the twigs cracking under their feet surrounded them.

Hana and Chuck arrived at Artisan Village, a jumble of wooden thatch-roofed shacks and stone cottages. A central square housed a busy market with stalls selling Buddha statues, trinkets, rugs, spices, and more. Vendors and buyers crowded the stalls, haggling or hanging out. Hana pushed her way through the market toward the side street.

A loud crash and yells erupted in the stalls.

Four bandits in their late teens shouted and weaved through the market, carrying sacks of stolen things. Following on their heels were the market guards, in leathers and waving wooden sticks.

"Stop! Thieves!" a large guard yelled. People scrambled out of her way as she swung her fighting stick in a wide arc.

They all—bandits and guards—came straight at Hana and Chuck.

"Run!" Hana yelled. The two sprinted from the oncoming chaos. Hana led the way, ducking between two stalls and into the street. Spotting the alley that led to her workshop, she put on a burst of speed. "This way!" Their flying feet threw up clouds of dirt behind them.

They slipped into the narrow alley. Panting hard, Hana slowed, but Chuck gripped her arm.

"Hana! Behind you!"

The bandits ran full tilt into the alley, their pursuers close behind.

Hana and Chuck pressed themselves against the alley wall.

The bandits whirled to face the guards, who came at them with wooden batons. One of the girl thieves snatched a stick and rushed to meet the attackers. Another bandit leaped onto the side wall and pushed off into a somersault, landing on one of the guards.

A brawl erupted.

"We've got to get out of here," Hana hissed. She dragged Chuck toward the door of her workshop, halfway down the alley and away from the fight.

Chuck resisted. "This must be the test. I can help them fight. I've gone to kung fu classes. I'm turning on the physical boost."

"But you don't know which side to fight for," Hana said. "Let's get safe."

She fumbled at the latch and pushed her way into her workshop.

Chuck hustled in behind her, and Hana shoved the door closed and threw the latch. She rushed to a window and pushed the wax paper shade aside to monitor the fight. At least they were safe in here.

She spotted a flash of white and gray in the melee. It was Tomás.

He tried to dodge his way through the fight, pushing at both sides and ducking the blows.

"What is he doing here?" Hana asked.

"It doesn't look like he knows what he's doing. I'm going to help him." Chuck slipped out. "Tomás, I'm coming!"

Hana had to do something. She should turn on a boost. Which one? Physical was obvious. She could help Chuck rescue Tomás. Or AI. She could outsmart the brawlers.

No time to think.

She opened her menu and clicked on the first boost that caught her attention.

13

Sensory.

The world exploded with multicolors and sounds. The *CRACK-WHAP* of the fighting sticks outside. The *THWIP* of the wax paper shades crinkling under her fingers. The dust motes sparkling as they danced in the sunlight's shaft.

What a bèndàn—fool—she was! Hana hadn't meant to pick the sensory boost. How would she help Tomás by *feeling* things?

Outside, Chuck barreled her way into the fighting.

Taking a deep breath, Hana opened the door and stepped into the brawl.

One of the bandits pelted the guards with oranges. The tangy citrus of the broken fruit assaulted Hana's nose. Yells, grunts, and thuds filled her head like an echo chamber.

Chuck traded jabs and kicks with a leather-clad guard.

Tomás was caught in a pocket between two sets of brawlers. He was cut off from the exit of the alley and couldn't reach Hana or Chuck. His eyes flashed in anger.

Even in all the noise, Hana's extrasensory hearing picked up his mutter: "I'm coming."

She scooped up an orange. Its pocked rind felt like soft plastic.

Two women thrust and jabbed their sticks at each other, feet dancing forward and back.

Tomás's face flashed in and out of view as the women dodged and weaved. The next time the women moved out of the way, he was gone.

Hana stretched on her tiptoes to catch a glimpse of him.

White and gray on the ground.

"Chuck, help me get to Tomás!" Hana hurled the orange at the guy Chuck was fighting. It hit the guy's head with a satisfying *thunk*.

The guy swung around with an outraged shout, and Chuck shoved him into another fighting pair. While the brawlers were focused on each other, she rushed over to join Hana. The two sidled their way to Tomás, who lay sprawled on the ground. He had fallen. Or fainted. Or something.

Chuck scooped him up by the arms and Hana picked up his feet. Physically boosted, Chuck had no problem muscling her way past a struggling pair while Hana ran to keep up with her, jostling Tomás's legs.

They shouldered their way back into the workshop. Hana slammed the door shut and they fell into a pile on the ground.

"Nice time to take a nap," Chuck said.

Hana and Chuck hovered over Tomás, who sat up and looked groggily at them, his eyes swirling like molten chocolate. The water-powered mechanical fan cooling her workshop *click-clacked*. Hana shook her head and swiped off the sensory boost.

He scowled. "What happened?"

"That's what we want to know," Chuck said.

"Why did you follow us?" Hana asked. "You could've gotten hurt."

Tomás grimaced and rubbed his brow. "I decided to check out the market. When I saw the group follow you into the alley, I came to help you."

"And then we had to help *you*. What happened out there?" Hana said.

He blinked. "I . . . er . . . tried to turn on physical and my head felt like it was about to explode. That was the last thing I remember." Tomás pushed himself up to his feet. "I'm okay now." An unsteady smile.

Chuck patted him on the shoulder. "That's my thing, saving people." She peered out the window. "It's quiet now. Hana, what boost did you turn on?"

Hana felt her face warm. She didn't want to admit she'd chosen the worst boost. A message flashed across her field of vision:

Magpie, Wind Walker, and Peasant4762, you have
completed the first in-game challenge. You will receive
your scores when you exit the game. You have twenty
minutes to explore before you are due back to class.

"I wonder how we did." Tomás still seemed dazed.

"I'm sure we did amazing," Chuck said. "We got out of
that fight unharmed, and Hana and I were practically
heroic."

Hana was grateful the announcement distracted Chuck
from her question about the boosts. "Since we have some
time, let me show you around my workshop."

Chuck picked up a bird automaton. "Did you make
these?"

Hana nodded.

"How did you learn to do this? They're amazing."

Hana hesitated. Most people didn't get her love for the
bots, but Chuck seemed curious. "I make them on the
outside. My grandma taught me. Then it became a thing
my dad and I did together."

"Very cool!" Chuck wound up the automaton and set
it walking along the counter. She shifted abruptly. "Wait
a minute. You make real bots on the outside and virtual
ones in here?" She laughed. "You could do anything or be
anyone in *Way of the Warlords* and you choose to do the
exact same thing."

Hana laughed ruefully. "I guess I'm boring."

Tomás looked up from examining the automatons on the shelves. "It sounds like you're consistent."

Hana wasn't sure if that was a compliment or an insult. It annoyed her that she couldn't read Tomás.

The chimes above the door tinkled.

Hana jumped. She did have a few regular customers who would come by the workshop, but she wasn't expecting anyone.

A tall and wiry boy entered. He was about fifteen or sixteen. His straight black hair covered half his face, and he kept his head low. Hana didn't recognize him from any previous game sessions. Strangely, no avatar handle showed up. Something about his interface was off. His actions lagged by a few microseconds. He raised his head and met her gaze. "Hullo, Hana. Remember me?"

Hana stared.

Ice-blue eyes. A knowing smirk. Exactly like Ink, from the junkyard.

He sauntered over and leaned one hand on the worktable, a crab tattoo on his wrist. It *was* Ink. Instead of a large spiky-white-haired girl, he was a thin black-haired guy, but the chaotic energy was the same.

"What are you doing here? How did you get in the game without a profile?"

Ink rolled his eyes. "You're a bag of questions." He added in a mocking tone, "Nice avatar."

Hana bristled, eyes narrowing.

Chuck closed in, a scowl on her face. "Is there trouble here?" Her avatar—Wind Walker—looked down on Ink and outweighed him by a good twenty or thirty pounds of muscle. On the outside, it would've been the reverse, with Ink outmatching Chuck in age, bulk, and meanness. Something inside Hana thrilled at Chuck's protectiveness.

Upon seeing Chuck's armor, Ink's expression changed. He raised his left fist and covered it with his right hand and dipped his head slightly. "No trouble, Wind Walker. Greetings."

Chuck broke into a grin and returned the warrior greeting. "You know wushu too? Where'd you learn?"

"Nowhere you would've heard of."

Before Hana could say anything, Ink shot her a warning glance. He rotated his head, as if stretching his neck, and cracked it. The entire scene went off-kilter. A low hum of white noise permeated the room.

"What did you do?" Hana demanded.

"We can talk now," Ink said. "I turned on a disrupter. Stops the game minders from hearing what we're saying. They'll see the visuals, but the soundtrack's been"—Ink flicked his wrist—"muted. So act like you're happy to see a customer." He nodded to the others. "And don't stand there looking like idiots."

Tomás fiddled with a sundial, hovering close by. Chuck shuffled over, throwing Ink a look halfway between suspicion and curiosity.

"I'm here with a message and to offer a trade," Ink said, "but we have to put on a show. Now hand me one of those things. You gotta pretend you're selling me something."

Hana blinked, her mind in a whirl. She had done her best to put Ink and Wayman's talk of conspiracy out of her mind, but now here was Ink intruding in her Start-Up world. She picked up a paper-and-wire cricket bot and showed Ink how the legs moved. She had no idea game play could be manipulated like this. Layers within layers. "What do you mean, a trade?" Her mind flashed to the watch.

Ink peered at the cricket with great interest. "Remember the bird Tish took from you with the e-scroll in it? She won't give it back."

Hana wound the spring mechanism and set the cricket on the table. "What's it got to do with me? It sounds like your problem."

Ink picked up the cricket and peered at the underside. "You're already involved. Here's the thing." He handed over a couple of brass coins. "Tish decided she likes the bird, but she doesn't know there's a scroll in it. If you make her a new bot, she'll return the other one to Wayman and everyone's happy. What do you say?"

Hana considered Ink for a good long time. Ink returned her stare, holding her gaze. "How did you get in here?" She nestled the cricket in a small box lined with straw.

"I've got my ways. When Wayman needs things online,

I'm the one to help him." Ink took the box and held out his palm with a smile, like a happy customer sealing a deal.

Ink's hand seemed to taunt her. It felt like Ink was sucking her back into something she didn't want to be a part of. After a long moment, Hana offered her hand, remembering the charade they were playing for the monitors. His palm felt surprisingly warm.

He winked at her startled look. "And the message." He leaned in, his smile not reaching his eyes. "Wayman wants to know if you've thought about his offer to train in qigong."

Wayman and Ink wanted an awful lot from her, so she had some leverage. And she wanted something too. "Give me my watch back, and I'll think about both the trade and the offer."

Ink snorted. "You and that watch. Don't think too long, Little Bird."

"How do I get in touch with you? Do you have a comm?" Hana bared her teeth in an imitation of a smile.

"No comms. I stay off the radar. Come to the junkyard in two days with a new bird. When I leave this game, the disrupter will stop working," Ink said. "Don't start yammering about me until you're offline. Dǒng ma?"

The chime tinkled as he left.

Hana didn't dǒng, or understand, any of it. Until she met Ink, she'd never questioned the benefits of getting meshed or the honor of being a Start-Up. Just a few minutes ago, she'd been thrilled to be a part of her first official Start-Up test. But the fact that Ink was able to hack *Way of the Warlords* while Start-Up students were being tested was unnerving, and Ink's earlier warning, *Not everything's what it seems,* chipped away at her certainties.

"You sure run an interesting shop, Hana," Chuck said with a bug-eyed stare.

Tomás kept a poker face. He glanced to the upper left, his eyes tracking back and forth.

The timer flashed a five-minute warning to end their session. Hana hurried them out of the workshop. "It's time to go back."

14

*H*ana stepped out of her VR pod, swaying slightly. Her mind spun. The brawl. Her brain fart picking sensory as her boost. Ink's strange interruption.

All around, kids jabbered about their in-game experiences.

"Wow, that was amazing!" the tiny girl, Christa, said.

"When I amped up physical, I flew so fast, fighting Warlord Shu's minions," one of the twins said. According to Hana's glasses, their name was Asa Turner.

"Yeah, and when I added AI, I could see so many more moves ahead." Their twin, Ben, threw an air punch.

Chuck and Tomás came out of their pods. Chuck shot a curious look at Hana, and Tomás rubbed his head cautiously.

Mr. Zoble quieted the class. "We've ranked each of you based on how you reacted to the challenge."

A translucent scoreboard hovered in front of Hana, a list of several hundred names. Though she'd gone into the game with her thirty classmates, Hana now realized the whole school of three hundred students had taken part in the test. Her name glowed midway down the list, a score of 50 percent, with a note:

> Points deducted for picking a suboptimal boost at
> critical juncture.

Her face grew hot. She had helped save Tomás. Why should she be penalized for how she did it?

"Time for an outdoor break," Mr. Zoble said. "Every day you will go outside for thirty minutes with your glasses and suits powered down. Research confirms you need a small period of being completely offline each day."

They lined up at the door.

"We also take nutrition very seriously. Your brain uses a lot of calories during the VR process." Mr. Zoble held up a juice carton. "This will maximize your performance and replenish any deficiencies."

"Are you all right?" her teacher asked as Hana approached him.

"Yeah." She tried to wipe off her worried expression.

Mr. Zoble handed her a drink.

She stepped outside to a blacktop with climbing structures and ball courts and open fields beyond. Hana breathed in deeply. Leaves and debris blew down from bluffs past the fields. The front of the school looked like any street, but the back—other than the billboard screens set to mimic bricks—was wild and free. It was the one part of the school that didn't feel buttoned-down. Hana liked it already.

Kids from other classrooms joined them outside, until the whole school spread out over the courts, blacktop, and surrounding fields.

Chuck bounded over. "That was wild! I can't believe we got caught in a street fight."

Tomás joined them and the three headed toward the fields.

"Spill, girl," Chuck said. "Who was that creepy guy in your workshop? You some kind of spy?"

Hana looked around the open space. "Is it safe to talk here?"

Tomás scanned the area. "It's fine."

"How would you know?"

He shrugged. Hana was beginning to think that was his trademark move. "I don't see any spyware around, so I assume we're good," he said.

Their suits and glasses were turned off, and they were far from the exterior screen walls, so Hana agreed. "Okay." She didn't know where to begin or how much to tell them, but inside the game, Tomás had tried to save her, and Chuck had tried to save him, and that made her think that maybe she could trust them—at least, with some of the story. A knot loosened inside.

"I've met that guy before. She's a girl offline. Her name

is Ink," Hana began. "On Enmesh Day, I ran into her at the junkyard. We got caught in a corporate sweep and I ended up with an e-scroll she might have stolen from one of the Corporations. I tried to return it the next day, but then another kid stole it from me. Now Ink wants me to make a bot for that kid to get it back."

"Wait, what?" Chuck gripped Hana's arm. "It sounds like you *are* a spy. What's on the scroll?"

Hana kicked at loose pebbles. "A code of some kind."

"One of the Corporations is after it?" Tomás asked.

"I guess." Hana didn't tell them about Wayman or the Ghost Crab Nation or the DNA codes, or that Wayman had named I Ching and Nile and mentioned Start-Up too. Talking about a possible Corporate conspiracy would make it seem real. And while she wanted to trust Chuck completely, she wasn't sure about Tomás yet.

"So will you make the bot?" Chuck said, jogging backward.

"Maybe." Hana took a sip of the juice. A blast of flavor, with a bit of sweet and a hint of tang, shot through her mouth. "Oh, wow." She stared at the box. "Have you tried this?"

The other two took sips. Tomás's eyes lit up.

Chuck threw her head back and closed her eyes. "So delish." She read the label. "It says fruit punch, but I've never had anything like this before. I hereby call it the Miraculously Delicious Drink, or MDD."

Hana inspected the carton, with its Start-Up logo. "It's a whole lot better than what we used to get in my old school. Anyway," she said, returning to the earlier topic, "making a bot would make Ink go away." Reaching the edge of the courts, Hana tossed her empty juice box into a composter, and they walked out to the field. The rest of the students stayed close to the building.

A stiff breeze caused stray leaves to swirl around them.

"What's up with Ink showing up in the game?" Chuck cricked her neck like Ink had done. "Remember that freaky head move?"

Tomás's eyes narrowed. "Yeah, I've never seen that before."

"I thought you didn't play *Way of the Warlords*," Hana said.

Tomás took a long sip from his drink. "I mean, I haven't seen that online before—where someone hacks your space while you're in it."

"A lot of the kids from the Bottoms aren't meshed into the official systems," Hana said. "Maybe their tech can do things ours can't."

"How do you know that?" Tomás asked.

"Ink told me."

Tomás shot her a questioning look.

Chuck's face clouded. "I think Ink's sketchy. It's probably not a good idea to get involved with her. I definitely wouldn't want to—especially since I don't want any distractions from Start-Up. I need to do well for my parents." She frowned.

Hana noticed this was the second time Chuck's mood plummeted when mentioning her parents, but Chuck could be right. It would be easier to focus only on Start-Up.

Chuck picked up a small rock and pitched it hard toward the trees. She grinned. "Can you beat that?"

"Oh yeah." Hana picked up a stone and hurled it as far as she could. It landed almost in the same spot.

"We're twins!" Chuck said. "What's your rank in the game?"

Hana frowned. "Fifty percent. How about you?"

"Oh." Chuck seemed embarrassed. "I got seventy-five percent. I don't see why you got a lower score. We both did the same in the fight."

"I know, but they said I chose a 'suboptimal boost.'" She cringed again thinking about that choice.

"How about you, Tomás?" Chuck asked.

Tomás picked up a rock and tossed it a few feet with an underhand lob. "Forty-five percent. Probably cuz I passed out."

"Are you okay?" Hana asked. "Did your tech break down?"

"I'm fine." He frowned. "There's nothing wrong with my tech." He picked up another pebble, tossed it high into the air, and caught it. "You know when your junkyard friend showed up at the workshop, I tried to look Ink up on the multiweb."

"And?" Chuck asked.

With a flourish and an impish grin, Tomás opened his palm, now empty of the pebble. "And nothing. Ink's a ghost."

Hana smiled despite herself at his pebble trick. "How's that possible?"

"Exactly," Tomás said. "Who has no online footprint?"

Hana thought about Tomás's dad, with his info blacked out. "Maybe if you live in the Bottoms, it's not that weird," Hana said. "But how would you even try to look Ink up? In the game, all I can see is someone's username."

Tomás looked away. "I'm good at computers. You'd be surprised how easy it is to hack an avatar and figure out someone's real ID."

"You don't play computer games, but you hack them?" Hana said.

"Forget it." Tomás's brief bout of friendliness disappeared. He picked up his pace to widen the space between them.

Hana said to his back, "What does your dad do again?"

He stiffened, then turned with a dead-eyed stare. "It's none of your business."

"It's called being friendly," Hana shot back. "You might want to try it sometime."

He grimaced. "No thanks."

She immediately felt a little bad. His dad was obviously a sore subject, and she knew about problematic parents.

"Look." Chuck pointed to a large insect flying toward them from the trees. Its body glinted in the morning light.

About three feet before it reached them, a spark flashed. With a zap, it fell to the ground, as if running into an invisible wall.

Hana rushed to where it'd fallen. She crouched down and spotted a small, charred metal object. She picked it up and held it out for Chuck and Tomás to see.

"Whoa," Chuck said. "It's a cyber bee."

"You can tell from this twisted bit?" Hana said.

"They're robots from Dowsanto," Chuck said. "They're all over the news. First the natural bees died out. Then enmeshed Bees went on strike and stopped pollinating, so Dowsanto now uses these robots."

"They're programmed to do what Dowsanto wants?"

"Yeah," Chuck said. "They're little flying computers with syringes that look and act like bees, flitting from flower to flower to collect and spread pollen. I wonder what happened to it."

Hana tucked the little guy into a pocket.

Tomás moved around like a mime, feeling for whatever stopped the bee. A few feet away, he knelt. "Here's another one." He picked up another burnt cyber bee.

"What's up with these?" Chuck asked.

Hana gazed at the air in front of them. "Maybe something stops the bees from coming close to the school."

"An invisible force field? Cool." Chuck swept her arms around.

Tomás looked at the school building. "I'm heading back. They'll call us soon." He slipped his hand into his pocket and strode away.

When he was out of earshot, Hana asked Chuck, "Don't you think he's sort of strange?"

"Tomás?" Chuck said. "I like him. He's different, which makes him interesting."

"I don't know. There's something squirrelly about him." They continued to walk along the field, heads down, looking for more bees.

Hana couldn't help but notice that there seemed to be a lot of strange events happening around Start-Up: the new timeline for getting meshed, Ink showing up in the game, and now these bees. She remembered Wayman's comment about changes to Start-Up, and his warnings, and a heavy feeling crept over her.

"Chuck, do you ever worry about getting meshed?" Hana asked.

"Here's another." Chuck darted forward to pick it up. "No way. I can't wait. When I'm meshed, I'll be able to level up in games, fight battles, and save people all the time." She turned serious. "And to be honest . . . my parents are fighting a lot, about everything. I have to stay in

Start-Up and get meshed early, or they'll have one more thing to argue over."

"I'm sorry." Hana put her hand on Chuck's arm. "But it's not up to you to keep your parents happy, right?"

"It feels like it is, though," Chuck said. "When I got into Start-Up, that was the happiest they'd been in so long. As long as I do well and make them proud, they'll stay together."

"I hear you," Hana said. But she didn't really understand. Her problem was getting Ma's attention, and it sounded like Chuck's parents really cared about Chuck if they had fights about her. "I want to get meshed too," Hana said, "but this weekend I found out my grandma is against it, and she can't tell me why. I also found out my grandpa was an AntiTech. I wish my dad were still alive because he'd help me think about all of it." Hana wished she could mention Wayman's warnings too, but Chuck had been freaked out just hearing about Ink.

Chuck placed a bee in Hana's palm. "So sorry about your dad."

"Thanks."

With a grin, Chuck pulled her over to the springy blacktop. "I know what'll cheer you up. If we're going to be friends," she said, "I need to show you some of my fighting moves." Chuck bounced around on her feet and jabbed the air with her fists.

If we're going to be friends was the best thing Hana had

heard all day. Chuck was like a giant planet pulling her in with a huge and irresistible force. It was strange and completely awesome.

It was almost enough to make her forget about her terrible test score, junkyard scavengers, and broken cyber bees.

15

That night, her family had a rare sit-down dinner. Popo had cooked Hana's favorites—garlic soy sauce chicken with mung bean noodles, steamed pork with rice flour, and stir-fried bok choy. They also had leftover dumplings from the party, panfried to crispy perfection. It was almost like old times, when Ba was alive and they ate together every night.

"How was your day, Lin?" Ma picked up dumplings with her chopsticks and plopped them on their plates, while Popo, Lin, and Hana served themselves the other dishes.

"I'm exhausted." Lin's eyes were bloodshot, and her leg jittered under the table.

"Your nerves are overstimulated," Ma said. "It'll take a while for your body to get used to the new normal."

Lin had a few days off before starting her internship at I Ching, so she spent all her free time at the City Center game parlors with Cassie.

"Remember, you can reduce your inputs and give yourself a break," Ma said. "Downtime is as important as uptime."

Hana snorted at that, coming from Ma, the Queen of No Nanosecond Left Behind. Ma was probably doing research in her head as she spoke.

"Hana, how did you like Start-Up?" Ma asked.

Hana frowned. "It's the first day and I'm already falling behind. I don't want to end up in the bottom half of the class."

Ma cut her a sharp look. "You need to put in an effort."

"I am!" Hana stopped, hating to hear herself whine. The details of her day—the marketplace brawl, Ink's interruption of the game, and the zapped bees—tumbled around her mind.

"Have you met any new friends?" Ma asked.

Hana broke into a grin. "I met this great girl. Her name is Chuck. She's funny and kind of hyper, but in a good way."

"Where do her parents work?"

"They both work at Nile."

Ma put down her chopsticks and her lips pressed into a thin line. "Nile is a problematic Corporation."

Hana bristled. I Ching and Nile were the two main corporate rivals, but it didn't excuse Ma's judgmental attitude. I Ching controlled most of the enmesh platforms, tech, and sciences, while Nile made and sold almost everything, from food to military supplies. Each always tried to encroach on the other, while also fighting off other companies, like Pear or Plex. From Hana's perspective, the companies didn't seem all that different.

"They control too much of the economy," Ma said, glancing at Lin, probably shooting her a mental message asking for backup.

"They've concentrated their power too much," Lin chimed in, answering Ma's call.

Hana sighed and stared at her chicken. Lin always sided with Ma. "What does that have to do with Chuck or her parents?"

"You're right," Ma said, though her expression was hard to read, almost like she was in some kind of pain.

"And what about I Ching?" Wayman's warnings came to mind. "No Corporation is perfect."

"Of course not," Ma said smoothly, "but think about guiding principles. I Ching is the premier source of scientific and industrial innovations. We have a different philosophy than Nile, which is materialistic and militaristic."

Hana had to change the subject before she blew up. "Lin, what are you and Cassie playing these days?"

"We're in War College. It's an add-on to *Way of the Warlords* that unlocks when you get meshed," Lin said. "We're doing a unit on deception. You know, Sun Tzu's famous quote . . ."

Ma jumped in and the two said in unison, "'All warfare is based on deception.'"

Hana let her chopsticks fall to the plate. When Ba was alive, Ma and Lin never excluded her like this. Or at least she hadn't noticed it because Ba had been on her side.

"In War College, we run through famous deception campaigns. Cassie and I are building the Trojan horse," Lin said. "You'd love it. It's like making a giant automaton."

Hana looked up, intrigued.

"I'll show you our blueprints," Lin said, "and you can give me tips."

"I'd like that," Hana said, grateful for Lin's crumb of kindness.

Popo looked up from her dumpling and said, "Sun Tzu also said the supreme art of war is to subdue the enemy without fighting."

Ma set down her chopsticks. "Good one, Mom."

Popo took a sip of tea.

"Girls," Ma said, "I'm on a big project for the next few weeks. After tonight, you won't see me around as much." Hana snorted inwardly. She hadn't seen much of Ma for a long time, so she probably wouldn't even notice if Ma was gone more.

Popo set the cup down with a clatter, splashing the tea. "I need to talk to Anwei."

Ma leaped from her chair to steady Popo. "Mom, you know Dad is . . . not around."

Popo looked at Ma, eyes glinting. "Oh, right, Sophia. I got confused."

"Let me walk you to your room so you can lie down." Ma guided Popo away, her face creased with worry.

Popo glanced back at Hana and her lips twitched in a small smile.

Hana and Lin finished their dinner in silence. Hana had been wrong. This was nothing like when Ba had been around, and Popo was the worst Hana had seen in a while. She really needed to be in the top half to stay in Start-Up. Her family was fraying, and getting meshed would be the key to putting it back together—to getting along with Lin, to connecting with Ma, and maybe to finally finding a way to help Popo.

16

You can try as hard as you can,
and sometimes it's not enough.

—H. H. June 10, 2053

Hana went to school the next day with mixed feelings. She was eager to see Chuck again, but she wasn't so sure about Tomás. He was kind of ornery, though she liked the idea of having one and a half friends more than one friend. After the past year of being so lonely, she was greedy for friendship.

She was also eager to improve her score, but she was unsettled by the odd things that had happened yesterday—the disorganized start, Ink showing up in the game, and the zapped bees. Maybe she *should* keep an eye open for Ink and Wayman. Or even just for herself.

In the locker room, she found Chuck on a bench, suited up but with her head in her hands. Hana scooted next to her. "Are you okay?"

Chuck lifted her head, her face pale. "I don't feel great." She stood and swayed.

Hana scrambled up to catch her by the elbow. "Do you want me to take you to the infirmary?"

"I'm fine." Chuck pulled away.

"I bet you can ask Mr. Zoble to sit out today's challenge," Hana said.

"I can't." Chuck grimaced. "I need to be in the top half of the class. Once I'm in the VR, I'm sure it'll be fine."

Hana hoped Chuck wasn't getting sick. "All right, let's go."

When they reached the classroom, Hana and Chuck found some empty VR pods near the back, near Tomás.

"Good morning," Mr. Zoble said. "Today you will be tested on how well you use the physical boost in three-on-three competitions. Your training session is brought to you by Nile, the world's leading provider of military equipment and technology." He grimaced slightly when giving Nile's spiel.

At the mention of Nile, surround screens appeared in their field of vision with Nile promo vids. Physically amped soldiers crashed through a tropical jungle, footage from the Amazonian War. A woman sat in a pod chair in an empty room. She appeared to be meditating, but the screen wall behind her showed the drone destruction she rained down using her neural connections.

"Go ahead and pick your teams of three," Mr. Zoble said. "If you don't have a partner, choose the random match."

Hana and Chuck shared easy smiles. *Wow.* This was so simple, with none of the worry from her old school when teachers asked her to pick a partner.

Who'll be our third? Chuck messaged through her glasses.

Hana's eyes slid to Tomás. Maybe she should give him another chance. *How about him?*

Chuck looked at her curiously. *I thought you said he was strange.*

Hana shrugged. *Like you said, he's different.*

Chuck arched an eyebrow and grinned. "We're tagging you into our team," she said.

Tomás blinked. "Okay."

"Class," Mr. Zoble said. "Get into your pods, and I'll explain the rules on the other side."

Hana got into a pod next to Chuck. Tomás caught her eyeing him and she glanced away. He intrigued her, but she had more pressing things to focus on. The important thing was to win this challenge and bring her score up.

⸻

The clearing in *Way of the Warlords* was hot and sunny today. Hana's friends materialized next to her in their sixteen-year-old game selves. A warm breeze blew hair into her face.

Mr. Zoble strode across the field in his old-style court

robes. "Your team will be pitted against another team of three. You will test your ability to use the physical boosts. Remember, what you will experience is a simulation of getting boosted with chemicals, making you feel faster or stronger. Your challenge today will be a capture-the-flag contest where the team that brings back the flag first will automatically be in the top half of the scores."

With a flourish, Mr. Zoble swiped up floating screens with different scenes—the Artisan Village, markets, and more. Flipping through them like a stack of cards, he picked a scene and pointed at groups of students. As he paired the groups, they faded away and the chosen screen blinked out with them.

When it was Hana, Chuck, and Tomás's turn, Mr. Zoble pointed at a scene with falling snow. He chose the twins, Asa and Ben, and Christa to be their opponents. Christa looked the same as she did on the outside, and Asa and Ben were in their purple superhero outfits.

With a dizzying wrench, the screen zoomed forward, engulfing them.

Hana, Chuck, and Tomás stood on a path on the side of a mountain. An icy wind stung Hana's face. Fat, heavy snowflakes fell briskly, weighing down branches of the towering pines lining a steep slope. It was hushed all around.

Hana now wore a fur cloak. Chuck's unruly blue braids peeked out of a cap with furry earflaps. Tomás's winter coat was as tattered as his previous peasant outfit.

"You really don't try, do you?" Hana stifled a smile. "You could change the default skins, you know."

Tomás tugged at his jacket. "What's wrong with this? It's very hip."

Hana snorted.

Chuck galloped around the crunchy snow. "I feel great!" She came to a stop, her face flushed and breath misting. "What now? Where's the other team?"

Tomás scanned the horizon.

Hana followed his gaze. Below them sprawled a mountain village, like a town out of a fairy tale with snow-covered houses surrounding a central square. At their back, the mountain sloped up, meeting a sheer rock face that loomed like a wild craggy building.

Flashing words scrolled across their view:

Welcome to the physical challenge. Your goal is to make it up to the summit before your opponents and capture the flag.

What are you waiting for? GO.

"Well then, let's go," Hana said. "Don't forget to turn on physical."

With their physical boosts on, she and her friends practically flew up the switchback path. Their boots crunched in a quick clip up the slope.

"I love it," Chuck said. When they reached the base of the rock wall, Chuck launched herself at it, scrambling up the sheer wall like a skittering spider.

Hana followed. But even with physical toggled to the max, she couldn't keep up with Chuck. She had to pay attention to the finger- and toeholds, and her arms began to tire and shake. Amping up physical was supposed to make it easy.

Hana jiggled her head. Something was wrong with her boost.

Tomás lagged behind. "Is your physical working?" she called down.

He grunted and picked up his pace. Slightly.

Hana leaned her head against the rock. It took most of Hana's energy to cling to the wall. Why wasn't her physical boost working, and why wasn't Tomás trying harder?

A clanging interrupted her thoughts.

About thirty yards away, their rivals, Asa, Ben, and Christa, stormed up the side of the mountain. Using ropes and anchors, they climbed and pulled their way up the sheer rock face like a well-oiled machine. Or a family of intrepid goats.

She swallowed a groan. With her mechanically inclined mind, she should've thought of ropes and pulleys.

Determined to beat them, Hana surged with a brief burst of energy. She lunged from fingerhold to fingerhold and her toes scrabbled to grip the slick cliffside.

She clung flat to the rock wall. If they fell in the game, they wouldn't actually die. They'd get kicked out and lose. She closed her eyes. They couldn't lose. She needed to be in the top half of the class.

Chuck called down from above. "Come on. Tomás, you too."

Tomás caught up. In a furious burst, he pushed past Hana. He wedged his left foot into a crevice near her waist. He pushed off and reached to grab a crack above her head.

He missed.

"Unngh!" Tomás lost his footing and slid by Hana.

Without thinking, she shot out her arm and grabbed his wrist as he hurtled by.

He closed his hand around her wrist. A sharp pain shot through her shoulder as his full weight dragged at her. Her other limbs death-gripped the cliffside as Tomás struggled to hold on to the rock with his legs and other arm. It took everything she had to anchor them both, her muscles screaming.

Until Tomás's wild motions rocked her and wrenched her away. They slip-slid their way down the sheer rock face.

And slammed painfully into a narrow ledge. She tried to grip the rock, but her numb fingers slipped, and she was falling again.

She tumbled over the edge.

This time it was Tomás who grabbed her by the wrist. Another sharp pain on the same shoulder.

She dangled and slammed against the rock face, her legs pinwheeling. All she could see of Tomás was his arm, muscles straining as he held on, and dark hair flapping in the wind.

"Don't let go," he grunted.

"I won't if you don't," she said through gritted teeth. She found a small outcropping with her free hand and dug a toe into a tiny crack, which stopped her flailing.

With a yell, Tomás heaved and pulled her back to the ledge. Dust and rocks raked her face and body.

Hana landed next to Tomás.

They panted and stared at each other with wild eyes, her heart jackhammering. Tomás edged away into a crouch and sat against the cliff, breathing heavily.

Chuck began to crab-crawl her way down. "Are you okay?" she yelled.

Hana slid next to Tomás and slumped against the cliff, the rock solid at her back. She took a shaky breath and called, "Yeah. Be up in a minute."

The snow died down. Now that a patch of sky peeked through and the cloud cover had thinned out, the view was stunning—jagged snow-covered mountains as far as she could see, with the tiny village in the distance. She glanced up. The other team had paused to see if they were okay, so she waved to them. Her breath, now calmer, swirled in the freezing air.

Tomás gave her a small smile. "Thanks for saving me. Again."

She snorted. "Anytime. Thanks for saving me too."

He nudged her and jutted his chin to the valley below. "Next time we're here, let's go to the village. I bet there's a card house."

"What's your game, poker?"

"Pai gow."

She cut him a glance. Interesting. Everyone learned to play poker as a kid, but pai gow was much less common. Chuck was right. Tomás was turning out to be an interesting puzzle.

"What are you doing?" Chuck landed next to them. "We're in a race and you're chatting about pai gow?"

"We're fine. Thanks for asking," Tomás said.

Chuck scowled. "I can see you're fine now." She jabbed Hana. "Don't ever do that to me again. Aren't you the ones who need to get higher scores?"

Hana pushed herself to her feet. The other team was back to its billy goat–climbing ways, about a third of the way up the remaining distance to the top. "We can still catch up. Let's win this challenge." She reached up to climb but yelped at the sharp pain in her shoulder.

"What happened?" Chuck said. "Don't you have physical on? It's supposed to give you fast healing."

"I don't know why it's not working. I'm not sure I can make it back up."

Tomás's brows furrowed. He looked up, curved his finger and thumb to his mouth, and let out a piercing whistle. "Yo!" he called to the twins and Christa. "Do you have some rope?"

Their opponents huddled, and Asa unclipped a coil of rope. "Knock yourself out," Asa said.

Chuck caught the rope as it hurtled down.

"We'll rig a harness, and between the two of us and your good arm, we should be able to make it," Tomás said.

Chuck looked at him curiously. "You know how to make knots?"

Tomás nodded and gazed into the distance, as if trying to remember the knots. He created a harness, which he and Chuck helped Hana into.

Hana kept up as best she could. Now it seemed Tomás could amp up physical after all, but Hana's still wasn't working. The three pulled and climbed their way up the cliff, making good time, not too far behind their opponents.

They reached the top to see Ben pocket a rainbow-colored flag and wink out of the game.

Chuck dropped her head into her hands.

"I'm sorry." Hana couldn't help feeling their defeat was her fault, even though it wasn't her fault that her physical boost wonked out.

"Yeah, me too." Chuck strode to the pile of flat rocks where the flag once perched and slapped the stone with more force than needed.

A silhouette of a bird with three legs circled high above them.

The scene around them dissolved.

17

Hana stepped out of the pod gingerly, her shoulder throbbing. Unlike yesterday, when kids gave each other high fives and celebrated their wins, today the students moved slowly. Two rows in front of her, the twins slumped against their pods like limp pasta, with barely enough energy to celebrate their victory.

Tomás stepped out of his pod and rotated his shoulders experimentally. Chuck stumbled out of hers.

Hana made her way over.

"What went wrong with your boost?" Chuck leaned heavily against her pod.

"I don't know," Hana said. "It was okay at first, but then I couldn't turn up the power."

Chuck frowned. "That's not right."

"Congrats to the winning teams," Mr. Zoble said. "Your rankings will show up on the roster. This is a cumulative average that takes into account your past scores. Don't forget to pick up your juice on the way out to break."

"Tǎoyàn! Look at our scores," Chuck said. Their names scrolled up:

Charlene Cohen: 63%

Hana Hsu: 48%

Tomás Ortiz: 45%

Hana's heart sank to see her score below the halfway mark. Now she would have to work harder to catch up. She moved over to Tomás. "What happened to you? Did your physical conk out too?"

His eyes darted to the ground. "It worked fine."

"But you had trouble with physical in the last game too, remember?"

"Yes. I mean, no. I was fine in the last game. And my physical worked fine here."

Hana studied Tomás, but he wouldn't meet her eyes. Back at the workshop, he'd said his physical messed up, so either he was lying then or he was lying now. But if his boosts were working, he wouldn't have done as poorly as she had.

"What does it matter, anyway?" he muttered.

"It matters because I need to be meshed early and be a Start-Up." She didn't know how to explain it to him. Since Ba died, her family felt broken. Lin had drifted away, and Ma was never around. The holes in Popo's memory were growing. Being part of the Start-Up elite would fix all that, because she would belong with Ma and Lin. "Never mind."

They went to the door where Mr. Zoble handed out

the juice boxes for their break. Chuck grabbed hers and guzzled it before she even left the room. Tomás took his and strode out with the box tucked in a cupped hand.

"Here you go," Mr. Zoble said. "This will restore your energy."

Hana recalled the amazing rush that came out of this box. "What's in this?"

"Electrolytes, glucose, that sort of thing. Go on. Get some fresh air."

Hana took the drink, then paused. "My tech didn't work in the game. I couldn't turn up my physical settings."

Mr. Zoble's nostrils flared. "There's nothing wrong with the tech. You probably didn't use the interface correctly. If you want to stay for the break, I can show you how to use it."

Hana bristled at Mr. Zoble's insinuation that it was her fault. She glanced at her friends, who'd already gone outside. She wanted to join them, but needed to make sure her tech wouldn't fail again. "Thanks, I'll stay."

When he finished handing out the drinks and the class emptied out, Hana approached him.

Mr. Zoble raised an eyebrow. "Let me see your glasses so I can do a quick diagnostic."

She handed him her glasses, which he snapped on. After a moment, he returned them. "They're working fine. I've left you a simple tutorial on how to use eye movements to choose menu items. My guess is you thought you'd activated the physical boost, but you didn't select the option."

"That's not true," Hana protested. "It was working earlier in the game. Partway through, just before Tomás and I fell, the power boost failed."

Mr. Zoble regarded her. "I'll review the recording later and take a look."

"Thanks." Hana didn't like how dismissive he was, but hopefully he'd figure out what was wrong and fix it by the next challenge. As she headed to the door, a red light flashed on one of the VR pods. Mr. Zoble hurried to it.

It was Christa. She hadn't moved from her pod. Mr. Zoble's eyes unfocused, and moments later, Ms. Malhotra rushed into the classroom and the two teachers eased Christa out of the pod.

Hana rushed over. "Is she okay?" Christa was awake but looked woozy.

Mr. Zoble glanced at her. "Sometimes students get overwhelmed by the experience. She fainted, but she'll be fine. The nurse bots at the infirmary will take care of her." He smiled. "Go on. I'll give everyone extra time for the break."

The teachers half carried, half led Christa out of the room. Shaken, Hana went outside and found Chuck leaning against the wall.

"What took you so long?" Chuck asked.

After explaining about Christa, Hana asked, "Are you

still dizzy from this morning? Were you okay coming out of the VR pod?"

Chuck lifted her empty juice carton. "I'm great now. I tell you. This is some miracle drink."

Āiyā. Hana realized she'd left her drink in the class. Oh well, she didn't need it. "Let's go see what Tomás is doing." She tugged at Chuck. "I want to talk to you both." She needed to talk to them about everything that was happening.

Chuck grinned and nudged her. "What's with you and Tomás being all friendly now?"

Hana bumped Chuck back. "Nothing. I'm trying to be more like you, péngyou to all."

They reached Tomás, who was balancing on a slackline. "Check this out," he said, strutting.

Chuck stepped on the line and pumped it up and down. "Check *this* out," she said with an evil smile.

Yelping as the strap snaked wildly, Tomás windmilled his arms and stumble-jumped off the rope.

"Sorry to interrupt." Chuck held out her hand to him. "Hana wants to talk to us."

He ignored her outstretched hand and pushed himself to his feet. In an unspoken agreement, the three walked to the field where they'd found the cyber bees yesterday. They could talk there without worrying about being listened in on by the school walls.

As they walked, the wind blew her hair into her face,

and Hana smiled. She loved the unruly outdoors.

"I have something I need to tell you both. Remember Ink from yesterday?" Hana said. "When the junkyard bullies stole the scroll from me, she took me to this old man named Wayman, who warned me about Start-Up."

"Why didn't you tell us about this Wayman yesterday?" Chuck asked.

"I'd just met you," Hana said. "I thought you'd think I was weird with my bots, and it was hard enough to explain Ink."

Chuck crumpled her drink and tossed it in a composter. "And now you know us *so* much better?"

Hana laughed. "I need someone to talk to about this. Wayman is part of a group called Ghost Crab Nation," Hana said. "The scroll that the guards were looking for has some DNA codes on it, and I Ching is after it. Somehow these codes have to do with Start-Up, and Wayman asked me to keep an eye out here for anything strange."

"Changing the schedule to enmesh some of us early is strange," Chuck said.

"An invisible force field around the school with dead cyber bees is strange," Tomás added.

Hearing Chuck and Tomás say these out loud hit Hana hard. It wasn't her imagination that things were off at Start-Up. It would be simpler to ignore these oddities and focus on raising her score, but what if part of the tech problem she'd faced also had to do with I Ching and Nile possibly interfering with Start-Up? The fact that I Ching might be involved also made her nervous. If anything nefarious was going on, she would think Ma would want to know about it.

She made up her mind. She'd tried to ignore all the abnormal things yesterday, but she couldn't keep pretending that everything was normal.

"I'm going to do it," Hana said. "Too many strange things are going on. I'll help Ink get the scroll back from that other junkyard girl and tell Wayman I'll spy for him." She turned to her two friends. "Will you come with me? We can go tomorrow after school."

"No thanks," Chuck said. "Normally I'm all up for uncovering mysteries, but I've got to stay focused on Start-Up." She frowned. "And I'm tired."

Hana looked to Tomás, who was swiveling his head, probably looking for more cyber bees. "How about you? Want to join?"

Tomás shrugged. "Sure, why not?"

Hana didn't think that was the most enthusiastic response, but at least she wouldn't have to go back to the junkyard alone. And after all, he had saved her in the game. It felt good to have someone have her back.

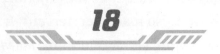

fter Start-Up, Hana hurried to the maglev stop. It was only the second day, and she was more than ready to greet the strawberry smoothie waiting for her at home. As she skipped up the escalator, puffy clouds blew overhead, casting shade and light.

At the top, Hana paused for an iris scan at the gate, which slid open. She slowed to a stop at the platform. Tomás sat at one of the benches at the far end, hunched like a human question mark. Grateful for his offer to come with her to the junkyard tomorrow, she headed over, plopped her bag down, and sat next to him. "Hey."

Looking up, he blinked. "Hey." Something was different about him, but she couldn't pinpoint it. Hana was still trying to figure out what was up with Tomás in general, since he seemed both prickly and strange, but had helped her in the game. "What do you think of Start-Up?"

"It was okay." Tomás's face darkened. "I wish . . ."

The train pulled up. They waited for the doors to hiss open. "What do you wish?" she said.

Stepping into the car, Tomás took an open seat near the door, and Hana joined him. "I wish they weren't testing us," he said. "I don't like how we're all competing to be in the top half of the class."

"Don't you want to get meshed early and get the boosts?"

He furrowed his brow. "Not really. It's not that big a deal."

"It's totally a big deal," Hana said. "I like making my bots and all, but my mom and sister are at a different level, doing things I can't."

Tomás glanced at her. "Maybe they're not."

"Not what?"

"At a different level."

"How would you know? You're not meshed."

He leaned his head against the train window.

"Are you really a hacker like Ink?" Hana asked.

Tomás glanced at her. "I don't know what kind of hacker Ink is, but yeah, I can get into systems and mess around."

Hana narrowed her eyes. "Could you hack into those cyber bees that got zapped and see what happened to them?"

He shook his head. "They're fried. If I had working ones, I might be able to hack them, but it'd be hard, because they're owned by Dowsanto, so the security's going to be way high." He shrugged. "But everything can be hacked, if you have enough time."

Their train car whooshed along the near-frictionless track, and soon, the crowded tin roofs of the Bottoms appeared. Moments later, the train hissed to a stop.

"Oi!"

"Move along!"

"You move along!"

Two guys and a girl with lopsided haircuts, tattoos, and torn clothes tumbled into the car. One of them shoved the other, laughing.

The one who'd been pushed straightened up.

Hana recoiled. It was Ink. Their eyes met.

Ink sauntered over and winked. "Bird bot girl." Ink grabbed the handhold and crowded lazily in.

Hana leaned away from Ink, squishing Tomás in the process.

He came halfway to his feet, glaring. "Leave her alone."

Ink raised a brow.

A surge of warmth flooded through Hana. No one had ever stood up for her like this before. Not that she needed his help, but Tomás didn't know that. "It's okay, I know her," Hana said.

Ink turned to Tomás. "And who are you, oh Knight in Shining Armor?"

Tomás pressed his lips together. "Who are you?"

Ink barked out a laugh. "Feisty."

"He's Tomás," Hana said. "You met him in the game. He was the peasant at the workshop." She shifted. "And this is Ink. She's the one who crashed our game, the guy in the shop with the crab tattoo."

Ink and Tomás stared at each other. Ink's eyes tracked back and forth across his face like she was trying to access his info. Tomás glared back, his eyes following Ink's. It was almost like they'd forgotten her. Something was going on between them, and she didn't understand what. One of Ink's friends, a lanky guy with greasy hair, bumped into Ink. "You done talking to these Vaps?"

Ink shoved him back. "I talk with who I want." With a slow smile, she said, "Nice to meet you, *Tomás*," as if doubting that was his name.

He narrowed his eyes.

Ink invaded Hana's personal space again. "Did you think about my message?"

Hana stiffened at Ink's pushiness. "I did. I'll bring you a bot for Tish when you give my watch back." The watch wasn't even that important anymore. Well, her bot wasn't complete without it, and she couldn't help but feel that it was the piece that might win Lin back, but with everything going on at Start-Up, it had faded into the background. She mostly wanted to show Ink she wasn't easily cowed.

Ink grinned. "See ya at the junkyard tomorrow. And bring your bodyguard." She winked at Tomás, who glowered at her.

When the doors slid open at the next stop, Hana grabbed Tomás by the elbow and pulled him to his feet. "Come on."

Tomás opened his mouth to protest but followed her

off the train. As it pulled away, Ink waggled her fingers at them from the window.

"This isn't my stop," Tomás said.

"Mine either, but I wanted to get away from Ink. Besides, we're close. You live in the Vistas, right?"

He nodded.

"I know a shortcut. This way." They'd gotten off at the stop by the edge of the junkyard. She led him to the old train tracks that would take them back to their neighborhood.

After a time trudging in silence, Hana asked, "Thanks for helping me with Ink, but what was that about back there? You don't seem to like her much."

Tomás hopped from an old railway tie to another. "She's a bully." He looked at her with his dark brown eyes. "I'm not coming with you tomorrow."

"Just because you don't like Ink?"

Tomás glanced away. "You don't need me. You handled Ink fine."

Hana pursed her lips. Something more was going on, but she didn't feel like figuring it out. She just wanted to enjoy the moment. "Race you to the big tree!" She took off in a run.

Tomás's footsteps clattered behind her.

"Whooeee!" Hana ran as hard as she could. As she reached the tree, Tomás caught up. They slapped the trunk at the same time, panting.

"I could've beat you," he said.

"So why didn't you?"

"I didn't want to make you cry." His eyes crinkled when he smiled.

"I don't cry that easy."

They walked down the path companionably until they reached the bottom of the hill of her house. When their shoulders accidentally brushed, a small shiver went up Hana's arm. She didn't know what to make of this strange boy, but he was growing on her.

"I live up there." Hana gestured up the scraggly hill.

"Nice. See you tomorrow." Tomás ducked his head and walked on.

It wasn't until Hana was halfway up the hill that she realized what had been bothering her about Tomás.

His eyes. They were dark brown on the train—not the hazel and caramel they were this morning.

But that couldn't be. All the excitement of the day must've addled her memory. She powered her way up the hill.

19

6.11.2053. *Appeals Court Approves Marriage of Biohybrid Robot to Cyborg.* In a victory for marriage equality among humanoids, the DC Court of Appeals upheld the marriage of biohybrid robot (androids enhanced with human tissue) Deckard Still to cyborg (humans augmented with cybernetic parts) Misha Goala. Ever since AI was added to androids, ethicists and politicians have fought over what makes someone human. **>>> AutoAI Updates**

The next morning, Hana stopped by her workshop and rummaged for a bot to take to the girl Tish after school to trade for the scroll. Her hands landed on the dragonfly Wayman had returned and a small thrill spread through her. She loved this little guy, but looking into its marble eyes, Hana knew its destiny was not to stay hidden in her workshop. Ba would've wanted it to continue its journey, so she placed the dragonfly in her bag to give to Tish.

The morning dragged. Instead of game time in *Way of the Warlords*, Ms. Malhotra taught them the history of the neural network and how fake information caused the Infotech War. Now that she knew her grandpa had died in the war, Hana tried to pay attention, but it was hard to connect the old vids with Ma's dad, who'd always been a nebulous figure in her life.

When she got to the junkyard after school, it was quiet. Hana picked her way through piles of waste, on the lookout for Ink. She climbed up a pile of heavy-duty coils, testing each one before shifting her weight. A giant Raven flapped away.

A whistle cut through the air—two low notes, followed by an up swoop. A shiver traveled down her spine.

Ink's head and then the rest of her appeared over the crest of the garbage mound—the familiar white-blond hair, icy eyes, and tattoos, her large frame in a tank top and baggy pants. The girl with the triangle bangs who had taken her bird bot trailed Ink with a sullen expression.

"Bird bot girl." Ink's eyes always seemed amused. "Did you bring the bot?"

Hana turned to Tish. "Do you have the bird?"

"Ya." Tish reached into her bag and held out the blue jay bot.

Hana held out the dragonfly automaton. "Trade you."

Tish's face lit up, like someone opening a present.

Ink nodded. "Nice. That's the one Wayman returned."

Hana looked away quickly, pleased Ink remembered

and then annoyed at herself for caring what Ink thought about her. "What about my watch?" she said, to cover up her confused emotions.

Ink smirked. "You and your watch." She dug her hand into her pocket and tossed it to Hana. "I didn't forget."

Hana caught it, giddy. She handed the dragonfly to Tish, who traded it for the blue jay. Hana angled away from them and worked the hidden lever in the belly. Relief flooded through her—the e-scroll was there. Tish sat on a metal scrap, examining her new dragonfly.

"Where's that other guy you were hanging with?" Hana asked Tish. She didn't want to run into that bully again if she could avoid it.

Tish scowled. "Guille hasn't been around for two days. The JingZa or some other corporate goons might have got to him."

Hana was taken aback. Tish seemed only mildly concerned about her friend. "What'll happen to him?"

Tish shrugged. "Maybe he'll be put to work, but at least he'll get fed."

Hana stared at the girl. Her parents always warned about getting on the wrong side of corporate police, whether it was the JingZa of I Ching, the SecZa of Nile, or any of the other Corporations' security forces. When people broke Corporate laws, they were detained until they paid exorbitant fees. And even though Hana's family could scrape together the money if she ever got in trouble, Ma worried most about their family's reputation and her own job at I Ching. This was the first time she saw the other side of the Corporations' security operations, where they could snatch someone off the streets and put them to work, another reminder the rules were different for people from the Bottoms.

"Or he could be mindlost in a game," Tish said. "I'm not his minder."

"Little Bird," Ink said. "You gonna hand me the bot?"

Hana put aside her questions about Guille and turned to Ink. "How did you get into our game?"

Ink raised an eyebrow. "Can't exactly reveal my secrets to a stranger."

"I want to know how it works. Can you get into all networks?"

Ink gave her a bemused expression. "Thinking of becoming a jacker hacker?"

"Is that what you are?"

"Could be." Ink picked up a piece of plastic scrap and tossed it over the coils.

Tish stood up to go.

Ink grabbed her arm and leaned in. "Tish, if you want to run with me, don't bother this girl anymore."

Tish side-eyed Hana and nodded. She climbed up the slope, checked the wind, and tossed her new bot into the air, whooping as the dragonfly fluttered over the trash pile.

"Start-Up, huh," Ink said.

"Yeah." Hana hunched her shoulders, then straightened, annoyed at herself. She didn't need to feel defensive about being a Start-Up.

"What kind of boost will ya pick when you get jacked?"

"Probably AI." If she even made it through Start-Up, Hana thought as she sat on one of the coils.

Ink put a foot on the coil and leaned in. The crab tattoo on her wrist quivered as she flexed her hand. "You gotta be careful. If you let AI think for you, before you know it, you're not in control anymore."

Hana wondered at Ink's friendliness, but she wasn't going to question it. This girl was so interesting. Different. "Did you get a boost when you got meshed?"

"Nah," Ink said. "It doesn't work that way with my jack. Besides, the fewer boosts, the more control I got."

Hana tumbled the bird bot between her hands. "Where did you get the scroll from?"

"I stole it from Nile before the Fixer could get it." She held out her hand. "Gonna hand it over?"

Hana considered this hard-edged and cunning girl. A part of her wanted to walk away, but the mysteries tantalized her: Start-Up pushing them to get enmeshed; the warnings from Popo, Wayman, and even Ink; and, above all, what the code on the scroll meant. She didn't know Wayman, but Ink was already feeling more familiar. "Will you show me what's on the scroll before we go to Wayman?"

Ink broke into a slow grin. "You're a smart one. Info always has value."

Hana returned the smile. "I want to help Wayman, but I want to know what I'm getting into first."

Ink nodded appreciatively. "Gotcha. All right, let's get out of here."

Hana's heart quickened. "Where're we going?"

"If we're to suss out the code, it's not happening here." Ink swept her octopus-covered arm over the trash heaps, brushing away a cyber bee. "The Dump, lovely as it is, ain't exactly the place to be breaking into an e-scroll."

Hana showed her wristband. "Will I be tracked?"

"Now you're thinking like one of us." Ink held out her hand. "Here, we'll give your band to Tish, who'll hang out for an hour or two." She grinned. "Pretend she's a Vap looking for treasure."

"So the GPS will show me hunting in the Dump."

"Ding, ding. Give the girl a prize."

Hana hesitated. A few days ago, Tish had been a bully who robbed her of her bot, but now she was a girl playing with her dragonfly. The people of the Bottoms were part of a world she hadn't paid attention to before. "You trust her?"

"The junk rats listen to me cuz I get them what they want."

Oh, great, Hana thought. Now she was hanging out with a gang leader. The whole situation was out of her depth, but she couldn't help it—she was curious, and more than a little worried. She wanted to find out about whatever was going on with Start-Up, and about the genetic code on the e-scroll, especially if it had to do with I Ching and, by extension, with Ma. If something bad was going on, she would want to warn Ma about it.

Hana slipped off the wristband and Tish took it. She flexed her wrists, suddenly feeling free. Three days into Start-Up and she already missed the days when she could do anything she wanted without being monitored. Normally she wouldn't care if Start-Up knew what she was up to, because she wouldn't be doing anything that would even interest them. But if Start-Up and the Corporations were involved in something sketchy and saw her changing her usual patterns, she might be questioned—and might get herself, and her family, in trouble. Whatever was going on, she knew the JingZa had been searching for the e-scroll, and she didn't want to run into them again, so it was best not to draw attention to herself. Especially not if her place in Start-Up, or her mom's reputation with I Ching, could be at risk.

"So where're we going?"

"To the heart of the Bottoms."

20

I nk led Hana through the narrow streets of the Bottoms, a maze of shacks and winding alleys built from a hodgepodge of stuff salvaged from the junkyard. A teen rattled by on a loud contraption that looked like a hovercycle, narrowly missing them.

"Watch it, boyo!" Ink yelled.

A plume of dark smoke came out of the back of the boy's ride. Now Hana recognized it as a motorcycle, old tech rarely seen outside of the Bottoms.

They sidestepped nasty puddles, kids playing poker, and old folks huddled around xiàngqí games. Stray cats stalked giant Pigeons. The smell of spicy noodle soup from street carts blended with less savory scents. They passed a fenced-in area where kids played basketball in the old way, with actual balls and hoops. The sounds of the ball bouncing and tennies running up and down the court were the rhythm, and the shouts and taunts the melody of a song Hana didn't know she needed to hear.

A grin stole across her face. This was the first time Hana had been to the Bottoms aside from the junkyard, and it was so vibrant, especially compared to the sterile Vistas.

"Here we are." Ink stopped at a brick shanty with a wavy tin roof. She pulled out an old-fashioned key and stuck it in a lock, items which Hana had only seen in Ba's antiques collection. The battered metal door swung open, and they stepped in.

Once her eyes adjusted to the dim interior, Hana let out a gasp of delight. The single small room overflowed with stuff. The walls were lined with crates and wire shelving, every surface filled with tech, screens, and junkyard finds. Crammed to one side of the room was a makeshift kitchen with a rickety table and mismatched chairs. A pile of bedding on the floor and a ratty jelly chair took up the other side. What little could be seen of the ground was covered in a threadbare puke-colored carpet.

Hana could get lost here, rooting through the odds and ends for bot parts.

Ink pushed away the remnants of a meal and moved some plasti-boxes off the table. "Let's see the scroll."

Hana took it out from the bird bot and handed it over.

After snapping it open, Ink studied the screen and zoned out, connecting wirelessly to it. "If you're gonna help, we need you on the multiweb." Ink rummaged through a crate near the jelly chair and found a mangled piece of film. "Here." She tossed it over. "The finest VR glasses of the Bottoms."

Hana unrolled and snapped the glasses to her face, flinching at the unaccustomed roughness.

"You'll need these too." Ink flipped her some earbuds and tattered haptic gloves.

Hana fingered the earbuds dubiously, blew off the dust, and put them in. She donned the gloves, and the glasses powered on. The setup was different from her Start-Up glasses, but it had a similar full-surround view with multi-web access and menu icons.

"Do all people in the Bottoms have these?"

"Nah. Most people here are jacked. I rigged this up before I got jacked."

"You don't use comms, but you're meshed—er, jacked—and you have VR gear?"

Ink sank into her torn-up jelly chair. "Comms got spider spies on them, and spies are everywhere on the multiweb. With those"—she waved to Hana's eyepiece—"and my custom implants, we can sneak in without being seen. We'll be like ghosts in the multiweb."

Hana hadn't known it was possible to be meshed and not be monitored. The more she learned about Ink and the Bottoms, the more she realized life was not as simple as she had been led to believe.

Ink closed her eyes.

Through her glasses, Ink's jumbled and messy hovel transformed. Ink was now the male avatar Hana had met in *Way of the Warlords*, black hair and all.

They stood on an empty beach, between sand dunes with waving grass and an ocean of frothy waves.

Hana sucked in a breath. The water was the familiar blue-gray of the Atlantic Ocean, but everything else was different. Though Hana lived an easy maglev ride from the beach, the shoreline wasn't safe to visit, with its half-sunken buildings, bleached-out trees, and rusted amusement parks. Ever since the collapse of the Ross Ice Shelf in Western Antarctica fifteen years ago, most seaside towns were under at least five feet of water.

In contrast, here in Ink's mind beach, gulls wheeled overhead. The sky was a rare, brilliant blue; sandpipers ran along the shore on busy feet; and seaweed lay strewn about. It was a pristine beach from at least thirty years ago. Hana wasn't meshed, but between the sweeping beach view and the sounds of the waves, she could almost imagine the salty smell of the ocean air.

"This is where I do my multiweb research," Ink said. "It's calming."

Hana's heart softened at this unexpected side of Ink. Most people had virtual spaces for multiweb research. For Hana, it was her workshop in *Way of the Warlords*. Seeing Ink's haven as a wild, windy beach from a forgotten time made her like Ink that much more.

"The Corporations can't spy on us here?"

"Nope. The algorithm of the waves keeps out the spies."

Ink sure was full of surprises, with his talk of algorithms. His strange looks and street accent were deceiving.

"Why are you a guy here and a girl out there?" Hana asked.

Ink spared her a glance. "Yin and yang. Two parts make up a whole. Sometimes I'm a boy, and sometimes I'm a girl." He shrugged. "I'm still the same person."

It made sense to Hana. Whether Ink was a girl or a guy didn't change who Ink was. "What are your pronouns?"

"I use he/him online and she/her offline, but that's for convenience." Ink smiled. "I'm not always the gender I appear, and I answer to all pronouns. No one's gonna box me in their gender constructs."

A small crab with pop-up eyes scuttled near Hana's toes into a hole in the sand, causing her to jump back and stumble. Her field of vision flickered back to Ink's place, where she found herself sprawled on Ink's bedding on the floor.

"A word of warning, Little Bird," Ink said, also back in the messy room, her eyes crinkling with amusement. "Don't go jumping around or getting too wild. You're not in a jelly chair, so what you do in the virtual happens here too. I don't wanna have to clean you off the wall."

"Thanks, I just figured that out."

Hana adjusted her glasses and the scene re-formed into the beach. She decided she was better off sitting on the sand, which would keep her safely on Ink's bedroll.

"So here's the info I copied from the scroll." Ink

opened his hands and the DNA code floated in a midair hologram. "My multiweb search found two matches." Ink swiped the air in front of him and the code animated into a 3D model of double helix genes, which transformed into an animated fungus embedding itself into an ant's brain. "This part of the DNA is . . ." The word "Ophiocordyceps" hovered in the air.

"Ofio . . . core . . . di . . . seps." Hana sounded it out. She remembered the article about it on her kitchen screen wall.

"The other part of the code . . ." Ink gestured again, and a snippet of DNA code spun into an animated parasite that burrowed itself into a cat's brain. The words "Toxoplasma gondii" floated between them.

"Toxo . . . plas . . . ma," Hana read, "gone . . . dee."

"So here's what's wacked," Ink said. "There's not much online beyond basic biology and a few corporate press releases." He swiped up a list of articles.

Hana tapped one open and skimmed it. "I Ching accuses Nile of stealing the zombie ant fungus they're researching," she said. "Ew. Listen to this."

The zombie ant fungus (*Ophiocordyceps*) is a parasite that infects host ants. It hijacks the ant's central nervous system to control its muscles while leaving the brain aware but helpless. The ants become "the walking dead."

Ink snorted. "So I Ching's researching a fungus that could turn things into zombies. Nothing sinister there."

Hana pressed her lips together. There had to be a reasonable explanation why Ma's company would study this. "Here's an article about the other thing, *Toxoplasma gondii*."

> *Toxoplasma gondii* is a parasite that rewires mice's brains, making them unafraid of cats. The mice get eaten by cats, allowing the parasite to find its way back into cats and multiply.

She wrinkled her nose. "Why would this DNA be on the scroll?"

"Let me see." Ink pulled the article closer. "Nile accuses I Ching of stealing its research on how the parasite affects mood stabilizer brain chemicals." He strode through the translucent articles, shattering them into thousands of floating pixels before they re-formed. "Sounds like the usual—Corporations spying and stealing from each other.

"You can't trust the news," he continued. "It's a spinnery thing. Facts and lies spun together like a giant spiderweb." As he spoke, Ink gathered the articles and teased them apart in the air, turning the words into slices of light and lines, and weaving them into an intricate airborne web.

"Whoa." Hana couldn't help grinning. "How'd you do that?"

Ink pushed the shimmery web away. "I don't share trade secrets. The point is, info is elastic. Whoever controls the info controls the minds."

"So why isn't that group you're in, Ghost Crab Nation, more visible?" Hana asked. "I've never heard of it before last week. If you're fighting against the dangers of enmesh tech, shouldn't you be more public?"

Ink gave her a sideways smile. "The secret's in our name. Like ghost crabs, we hide away."

Hana wasn't sure about that philosophy. "I think you should show your face. If you want to change minds, do it in a big and splashy way, like that hacker group Bezorio—they're always taking over the news with their memes." She recalled the hungry yellow circle chomping the news bytes.

Ink sniffed. "Groups like Bezorio claim the limelight, but don't be fooled, we've got our claws everywhere. Changing minds goes deeper than memes, and it's better not to be on the radar." He gave Hana a friendly tap on her shoulder. "I'll let you know when I go big and splashy. You got what you needed here?"

Hana hadn't. Knowing what the DNA was didn't help her. She didn't know how it was connected with Start-Up, or why the research was so important that I Ching or Nile would be after it.

She blew out a slow breath. It was time to go to Wayman to offer her help and find more answers. "Can you take me to Wayman?"

Ink studied her for a long moment. "Let me show you something first." He crouched down and put his hand next to a hole in the sand. A small ghost crab scurried out and onto his palm. "This is an access pass. I'm gonna embed it in your *Warlords* account." He swiped open a window to show Hana's login credentials for the game.

"That's private," Hana protested.

Ink smirked. "Sweet summer child, if you haven't figured it out yet, nothing's private online." He tapped the ghost crab, and it scurried into her in-game treasure purse. "But this here crab key is the closest you'll get. It'll bring you back to my beach, and you can use it if you need to get onweb unmonitored—but only once."

Hana's eyes widened. It felt like a big deal to have Ink trust her with the key to his beach mindscape. "Why are you doing this for me?"

"It's not for you," Ink said. "If you're gonna help us, you need some tools." With a half smile from him, the scene dissolved back into Ink's cramped room. Hana peeled off her glasses.

Ink had the same half smile on her face as she pushed herself out of the jelly chair. "Well, whatcha waiting for? Let's go."

21

*H*ana followed Ink back through the crooked streets of the Bottoms, winding their way around street vendors and stray dogs.

"I've been meaning to ask," Hana said, thinking about the winking crab during the kraken simulation, "did you hack into my sister's Challenge on Enmesh Day?"

Ink gave Hana a sideways glance, lips quirking in a small smile. "I don't know what you're talking about."

They came to another shack. At the door, Ink whistled, two low notes and a high one. After a moment, the door cracked to reveal Wayman's wrinkly eyes. He opened the door more. "Come in."

His house was larger than Ink's. Mismatched couches sat on one side of the room, and a kitchen area and table filled the other. A hodgepodge of pseudo-wood and metal shelves with dead-tree books lined the walls, interrupted by an archway leading to a hallway. Seeing the books calmed the flutters in Hana's stomach. They reminded her of her dad's study, and anyone who loved old books had to be somewhat trustworthy.

Wayman waved to the couches. "Sit. I'll bring you some tea."

Hana settled into a couch while Wayman puttered in the kitchen. Ink propped herself at the table and leaned back until her chair wobbled against the counter, eyes losing focus as she sank into some neural rabbit hole.

"What did you think of Start-Up?" Wayman brought over a tray with cups and tea. "Did you see anything unusual?"

"I don't know what's normal," Hana said, "but it seems disorganized. Half the kids didn't have their entrance nano pills, and my tech glitched in my recent challenge."

Wayman's brows knitted together. "How did they explain that?"

"My teacher didn't explain it, and then we were interrupted when one of the girls in my class fainted." Hana took a sip and felt a welcome warmth spread through her. It was the same chrysanthemum tea he'd given her in the woods, and it was delicious. Whether from the heat or the mix of herbs, she felt herself relaxing.

Wayman sat at a shabby brown armchair and steepled his fingers under his chin. "Do you have the code?"

Hana handed him the scroll. "It contains the DNA codes from two types of organisms."

Wayman gave her an appraising look.

"Ink helped figure it out." Hana told Wayman about the

zombie ant fungus and the cat brain parasite. "Why does I Ching want these genetic codes?"

Wayman set down his teacup. "We don't know the full story yet. I sent Ink to nip the e-scroll from Nile before I Ching could get to it, but there's still more info we need."

"By 'we,' you mean the Ghost Crab Nation?" Hana asked.

"Yes."

"How big are you? Ink said you were everywhere."

"We're a loose movement of groups around the country and the world," Wayman said. "We work in decentralized cells, so each group doesn't know what the others are doing."

That sounded super shady. "What's your purpose?"

"We want to change the status quo. Some factions fight for political change, others economic and social. The common theme is we don't trust the Corporations and their closed information ecosystem, which you know as the multiweb."

"What do you mean, closed? The multiweb has all the knowledge in the world," Hana said.

Ink leaned in. "What you think is the multiweb is a small slice of what's out there. It's what the Corporations feed you, especially for people who are jacked."

"The neural mesh works both ways," Wayman added. "You think you're just shopping or watching a show, but not only are the algorithms learning all your opinions and activities, they're also predicting and molding your future thoughts. The Ghost Crab Nation disrupts this by bringing new information to people."

"But we gotta be subtle," Ink said.

Hana sat back. "Do you have leaders?"

Wayman took a sip of his tea. "We do, but only the top-level people know each other. We're very well-funded. You don't learn this in school, but after Pear lost the Infotech War, its billionaire founder, Olivia Strong, went underground and vowed to continue fighting I Ching secretively."

Hana felt like a tiny cog in a large machine. Turning to Ink, she said, "How did you get involved? Is everybody in the Bottoms part of the Ghost Crab Nation?"

"Nah, just some of us who came across Wayman while hustling for scraps." In a rare show of emotion, Ink's voice wavered. "When your parents get snatched to the factory farms and you're left to fend for yourself at twelve, finding an adult who doesn't take advantage of you makes you sorta loyal to them." She shrugged. "I happened to have a knack for coding, so the Ghost Crab Nation found me useful."

Hana struggled to contain her shock and sadness. Ink's life—and all the scavenger kids'—was so different from her own. Even though seeing the shanties from the trains made her uncomfortable, she never thought deeply about what their lives were like. Now that she had a glimpse of Ink's story, and remembering how that boy Guille might have been taken by the JingZa, Start-Up felt less shiny. The idea that people like Ink were fighting against corporate brainwashing, and the whole system it supported, appealed to Hana, but now she worried that Ma and Lin were trapped in I Ching's world. "So you want me to help you spy at Start-Up school, because you think that the changes there are connected to this code from I Ching."

"Correct," Wayman said. "But only if you feel safe."

"My mom works at I Ching. I can ask her about it. Maybe she can help us from the inside."

Wayman's head snapped up. "Don't talk to your mom."

Hana frowned. "Why not?"

He pressed his lips into a thin line, as if debating what to say. "You don't want to worry her."

Hana snorted inwardly. Ma would only worry if she paid attention. Besides, why did Wayman care if Ma worried?

"Tell you what," Wayman said. "Keep your eyes open and come by after school, and I'll teach you qigong."

"How will that help?"

"It will help you keep your mind clear. Getting enmeshed has its dangers, and this is a better way to enhance your mind," Wayman said. "'Qi' means 'energy' or 'life force,' and 'gong' means 'work.' Qigong involves meditation and deep breathing to increase your qi and keep it flowing, which will make you stronger and healthier."

"I know people have learned qigong from *Way of the Warlords*."

Ink made a *pfft* sound.

"What?" Hana said.

"Nothing," Ink said. "I'm sure someone could learn a lot of qigong from a game."

"There are many paths to the river," Wayman said. "Why don't we start your first lesson right now?"

Hana looked around. There didn't seem to be enough space to do any moves.

"We'll start with a breathing lesson," Wayman said. "Qigong is about moving your qi around your body through deep breathing. Sit straight but comfortably, and I'll show you how to breathe."

Hana arranged herself cautiously. She already knew how to breathe, but she figured she'd be polite.

"Close your eyes. Breathe in through your nose to a slow count of three," Wayman said. "Imagine the air inflating your belly like a balloon. Exhale slowly through your mouth for a longer count."

Hana followed his instructions. As he counted "in, two, three" and "out, two, three, four," she felt a tension leave her.

She could get used to this.

But her thoughts darted and veered like hummingbirds. From what she'd read about the zombie ant fungus and the cat brain parasite, their effects on animals were serious. The zombie ant fungus took over the ant's brain and made it a puppet. The cat parasite made mice put themselves in danger. What were I Ching and Nile doing with these, and how was it related to Start-Up?

Now she wondered if Ma might know about what I Ching was up to. Hana didn't want to think that she could be involved in anything bad. But disturbing memories of Ma floated up. When she asked Hana if she'd seen anything unusual at the junkyard. The mysterious man on Enmesh Day.

What if Ma was a part of this?

Hana opened her eyes, leaped to her feet, and grabbed her bag. "I need to go." That was enough breathing—she needed to act. Even though Wayman didn't want her to, she had to ask Ma about the research to find out what she knew.

22

::::: **HSU FAMILY NETWORK** :::::

NEWS:

6.11.2053. *Smart Animals Overtaking Smaller Relatives.* Ever since animals became meshed as early test subjects, the enmeshed Animals have evolved to be larger and smarter. Scavenger species like Squirrels, Pigeons, Coywolves, and Ravens have thrived in urban areas. **>>> AutoAI Updates**

MESSAGES:

JUNE 11, 5:00 P.M.

HANA: Ma, I need to talk with you. Call me?

JUNE 11, 5:23 P.M.

MA: Hi, sweetie, sorry can't chat. Be home late, at eleven. Will try to catch you in the morning. How was school today?

::::: **HSU FAMILY NETWORK** :::::

NEWS:

6.12.2053. *Permafrost Releases New Round of Pathogens.* The melting of the permafrost, the layer of frozen soil that once covered 25 percent of North America, released previously eradicated anthrax and smallpox viruses. **>>> I Ching News Service**

MESSAGES:

JUNE 12, 7:23 A.M.

MA: Good morning, honey. Had to leave early for work. Will try to make it home by dinner, but no guarantees. Have a great day!

JUNE 12, 7:27 A.M.

HANA: I have some questions about I Ching. When are you coming home?

JUNE 12, 8:36 P.M.

MA: Can it wait until the weekend? Sorry missed dinner. Swamped. Promise we'll talk.

JUNE 12, 8:43 P.M.

HANA: Lin, didn't you start your internship at I Ching today? Did you see Ma? What's she been up to that's made her so busy?

JUNE 12, 8:44 P.M.

LIN: Yeah, the internship's great. Ma was holed up in meetings all day. You know I'm sitting on the bed next to you, right?

A pillow thwapped Hana on the head. Lin sat on her bed, rolling her eyes. "We can talk in person, you know."

"You sure? Sometimes it's easier to get your attention online." Hana hugged the pillow. "What's up with Ma? She's come home late and left early every day this week."

"She's working on the usual, you know, genetic research to save the world," Lin said. "What's up?" Lin had perfected an infuriating combination of boredom and condescension the past year, but something else also flickered in her eyes.

Hana grasped at that elusive thing. The Lin who used to spend hours with her had to be in there somewhere. She took a wavering breath. "Something's going on," Hana began, not sure how much to share. "When I was at the junkyard the other day, I met someone who warned me about Start-Up."

Lin's expression flitted from puzzlement to concern. "Who's this person, and why are you hanging out with a stranger at the Dump?"

"Ink's cool," Hana said, "and she's not a stranger anymore."

"Why would a junkyard kid care about Start-Up?" Lin asked.

"It's not just Start-Up," Hana said. "Apparently I Ching and Nile are interested in a fungus that turns ants into zombies and a cat parasite that mind-controls mice."

"So? I know that fungus—it's *Ophiocordyceps*," Lin said. "Ma's lab is studying it."

Hana's heart pattered. So Ma could be involved and

might know why the fungus DNA was on the e-scroll and why I Ching chased Ink for it. "What's the lab doing with it?"

"Because the parasite takes over an ant's brain and makes it move against its will, Ma's lab is studying it to learn how central nervous systems work," Lin said. "You know, so they can help paralyzed people. I don't know what that has to do with your junkyard friend or Start-Up."

That sounded legit, but why would I Ching have been after the e-scroll that contained snippets of the DNA? She could tell Lin wasn't interested in hearing about a possible conspiracy, so she tried a different tack. "Do you remember what happened when you were fighting the kraken on Enmesh Day?" Hana said. "We never talked about how I could message you, even though private channels were supposed to be locked down."

"There's nothing to talk about," Lin said. "It must've been a glitch."

"Why would there be a glitch with tech that's so established?"

Lin glanced at her. "It's not unusual. Enmesh tech isn't perfect. Why are you asking these questions?"

"Something seems off about Start-Up," Hana said. "I mean, aside from the changing rules. There are more glitches—I had trouble with my physical boost. I went to Mr. Zoble, and he told me everything's fine with my boosts."

"And is it?"

"I don't know. We haven't had another challenge to test them."

"Listen, let me give you some advice," Lin said. "You want to get through Start-Up and get a good internship? Keep your head down and do your best, and don't go chasing fireflies."

Hana suppressed a sigh. Lin glided through life on the tracks laid out for her, but Hana was noticing the rest of the world didn't have it so easy. Finding out what was happening under the surface seemed important. Maybe even more important than making it into the top half of her class and getting a good internship.

"I've got to get back to my game. Cassie's waiting." Lin sank against her pillow, her eyes losing focus. The pigeon bot Hana had given her lay on the nightstand, where she'd tossed it on Enmesh Day. Hana thought of the watch she'd finally gotten back from Ink, but she hadn't had a chance to finish the bot yet.

Hana sighed. So much for sister bonding. She'd hoped to confide in Lin, but Lin's unquestioning support of Start-Up and its tech had made it difficult to tell her the whole story. And if Lin wasn't going to help her, Hana would have to find another way to get answers.

She opened her calendar. In a couple of weeks, their class was scheduled to go on a field trip to I Ching. That might be the best chance for Hana to get to the bottom of everything. A plan began to form in her mind. She'd visit Ma's lab and snoop around to find out what exactly Ma knew about what I Ching was doing with Start-Up, and if there was a connection with her research and the e-scroll. If she had a chance, she'd ask Ma directly. She just had to wait until then.

In the meantime, she'd go back to Wayman for qigong training. Between Ink's and Wayman's warnings and the troubling events at Start-Up, Hana worried about the idea of getting meshed, but she still didn't want to be left behind. Getting meshed would bring her closer to Ma and Lin. Without it, she'd always be on the outside, unable to keep up with the two of them. So despite her growing concern, she decided that she'd do her best to be in the top half of her class by the end of the summer. Maybe qigong would give her the edge she needed to improve her Start-Up score.

23

*Breathe in through your nose
and out through your mouth.*

—H. H. June 23, 2053

The next couple of weeks settled into a pattern. Ma continued to work long hours, and in their few dinners together, it was never the right time to ask about the scroll, so Hana resigned herself to waiting until the I Ching field trip. Hana told Chuck and Tomás about her visit with Wayman and kept her eyes open at Start-Up, but nothing unusual stood out.

At school, with no new challenges, they practiced their skills in *Way of the Warlords*. Chuck was always tired, but inside the game, she was full of energy. When Chuck roped Hana into a raid to rescue a prince, they amped up physical and took off in flying leaps through the tops of the bamboo forest. With sensory on, the wind flowed over her skin like silk and the clacking of the bamboo stalks echoed in her bones. They snuck up on the soldiers guarding the compound, patient, until they weren't. Hana loved copying Chuck's kung fu moves, chopping, kicking, and shouting their way through the guards and the wooden doors. When they got to the prince lounging on a lacquered bench, he complained they'd taken too long to get there, his tea having gotten cold. They left him where he lay, un-rescued, taking his shih tzu instead.

Without new tests, Hana's score stayed at 48 percent. Her boosts seemed to work, but not consistently or always at full strength. She went back to Mr. Zoble, and he gave her a new pair of glasses, but it didn't seem to make a difference.

Chuck, Hana, and Tomás spent their lunches together, dissecting their in-game raids and discussing the merits of each boost. While Chuck still loved the energy drink, Hana began to skip it. She noticed that it had started to leave a strange aftertaste.

After Start-Up most days, she went back to Wayman for qigong lessons, figuring that clearing her mind would help her increase her score next time they had a challenge. For almost two weeks, he'd taught her to breathe slowly and deeply and asked her to empty her mind of thoughts. They began and ended each session with his delicious tea.

Today, Hana sat cross-legged on the flat rock by the stream with her eyes closed, a cup of chrysanthemum tea and Chuck by her side.

"When do we get to the good part?" Chuck stage-whispered.

Hana opened one eye. Chuck shifted uncomfortably.

"We're supposed to be breathing, not talking," Hana said in a low voice. She'd convinced Chuck to join her after school for a qigong session with Wayman and Ink. When Hana showed up with Chuck, Ink had looked at her quizzically.

Chuck placed a hand over her fist and gave a brief bow. "It's me, Wind Walker."

Ink grinned and bowed back. "You're bittier than the last time I saw you in the game."

Just like that, Ink and Chuck had bonded, pretty much the opposite of Ink and Tomás's first meeting.

Ink sat across from them, back straight, eyes closed. Without her tough junkyard demeanor, her face relaxed and gave off the vibe of a tattooed white-haired monk. Wayman stood by the stream, his face slack and eyes unfocused, arms floating up and down like seaweed.

Hana sighed. She'd pictured learning cool martial arts moves, like shooting bolts of energy from her hands, but according to Wayman, qigong was about breathing and controlling one's internal energy.

A breeze ruffled her hair, bringing a fresh scent of moss. Something buzzed and landed on her knee. A bee. Hana reached out a finger to pet it.

"I don't think you're supposed to be playing with bugs," Ink said.

Hana wrinkled her nose at her.

Ink smirked and returned to her pose.

"It's probably a meshed Bee." Chuck scooted over and placed her hand next to Hana's knee.

"How do you know?"

"Natural bees are ultrarare since the great die-off, and this one's larger," Chuck said as the Bee headbutted her outstretched finger.

"The little dude likes you," Hana said.

"Must be my magnetic qi." Chuck fluttered her fingers at the Bee. "If I had my glasses, I could talk to this Bee."

"Really? I thought translator apps for Bees were corporate trade secrets."

Chuck smiled. "One of the perks of having Yatagarasu as a friend in *Warlords* is it comes with animal translator apps." The apps were crude, but they let people communicate with Animals to some extent. The Bee crawled onto Chuck's palm and wiggled its butt.

At Hana's giggle, Wayman cleared his throat.

Hana sighed. "How much longer do I have to meditate before I get to the good stuff?" Hana wanted to learn some fighting moves or more concrete lessons.

"Be patient," Wayman said. "You won't master qigong in a few days or even a few months. It takes years."

"Years?" Hana scrambled to her feet. "I need to get good at qigong now so I can do better in my Start-Up challenges."

"Qigong isn't a cut-and-dried process that follows a schedule," Wayman said. "I'm offering you a different way to be in the world. Instead of fighting for a goal, qigong is about quieting your mind and being in the moment."

"I want a way to help save my grandma," Hana said. "If I'm meshed, I can do that, and also help save the world, according to my mom."

A strained look came over Wayman's face. "Maybe you should save yourself first." He sounded like Popo, saying things that only almost made sense.

"Will qigong help me at all in Start-Up?" Hana asked. She didn't have time for these riddles—she needed to know if she was wasting her time.

"What I've taught you so far, breathing to direct your energy, will calm your mind and heartbeat, which should help you in your challenges. Next time you face a difficult situation, put your breathing to the test."

Hana sighed. She'd been expecting to learn special moves to use in Start-Up that would improve her score, not just breathing techniques. Wayman's advice sounded vague, but she supposed she could try it. She took a sip of the soothing tea.

Chuck pushed herself to her feet and stumbled.

"Whoa." Hana caught her. "You okay?"

"Yeah." Chuck frowned and sat back down. "A bit dizzy."

"Why don't we call it a day?" Wayman checked his old-timey watch. "I've got a call to make." Quick as a crow, he gathered the cups and tea and ghosted down the path back to the Bottoms.

Ink sprang to her feet. "All right, kiddos. Let me show you how it's really done."

"How what's done?" Hana asked.

Instead of answering, Ink held out her hand to Chuck, who hesitated a moment before grabbing it. Ink hoisted Chuck to her feet and nodded toward the stream.

The water snaked through a narrow stretch and around a tumble of rocks. Stepping nimbly from rock to rock, Ink made her way across the stream.

Hana and Chuck exchanged glances. It was hard to resist Ink's momentum. Hana followed and Chuck brought up the rear, navigating the rocks. Once they reached the other side of the stream, they plunged farther into the woods.

"Where are we going?" Hana said.

Ink smiled and continued walking. Hana kicked at a pebble. She should've known by now not to expect an answer.

As they tramped through the woods, Hana asked, "What's the deal with Yatagarasu?"

Chuck's face, haggard with fatigue, lit up. "Yatagarasu is a Japanese myth, a three-legged crow who lives in the sun. The Chinese version is called Sunwuzu."

"Does it mean anything?"

"For the Chinese, the three-legged crow helped move the sun across the sky. For the Japanese, it was a sign of heavenly intervention."

"So when it shows up in *Way of the Warlords*, you're chosen to be special?" Hana asked.

"I'm not sure about that," Chuck said. "It's just a good friend. Yatagarasu is always there for me when I need it."

Hana smiled at the thought. Her bird bots were like that for her.

The trees thinned out and the ground became spongy as they came to the edge of a partially flooded cypress swamp. Their boots squelched along a spit of land until they reached a rusty fence covered by vines and shrubbery.

"Come on." Ink grinned and clambered over the fence, past the faded PRIVATE PROPERTY: NO TRESPASSING sign.

Hana hesitated. It never occurred to her to ignore signs like this, but Ink's energy was magnetic. She grabbed the fence and climbed. Chuck smiled grimly and pulled herself up, pausing halfway, panting.

"Will you make it?" Hana asked.

"Yeah . . . sure."

At the top of the fence, Hana broke into a delighted

grin. On the other side was an abandoned amusement park—a Ferris wheel creaking in the wind, a merry-go-round with faded wild animals, and broken-down game and ticket booths, all surrounded by overgrown bushes and patches of murky water.

Hopping off the fence, Hana let out a whoop and reached up to help Chuck down.

Ink loped over to a metallic structure with a dozen long swings hanging from spindly arms. "Take one of the chairs and run." She grabbed one, hooking her arms through and leaning her body onto the chair.

Hana and Chuck spread out and copied her. It wasn't very comfortable, but Hana soon forgot the clunky chair under her arms. They walked and the swing chairs creaked. Faster and faster, they ran in a circle, their feet kicking up dirt. They ran until the chairs swung into the air and their momentum had them flying, feet splayed out.

Round and round, up and down, they flew, hair streaming, feet flying.

Hana laughed and Chuck yelped.

"Now let go!" Ink said.

Hana flung herself from the flying chair and barely managed to keep her footing as she stumble-ran in the dirt. Chuck tumbled off and ended on her back nearby. Hana dropped down by her in a heap.

Ink jogged up to them. "When was the last time y'all played like a kid and forgot everything? Forgot about school and teachers and what you're supposed to do?"

Hana smiled. "I can't remember."

"Me neither." Chuck spread out her arms and closed her eyes.

Ink swept her arm, encompassing the vines, swings, and merry-go-round, and dipped into a half bow, half curtsy. "Well, here you go."

"And then it's back to reality," Hana murmured.

"We'll think about reality tomorrow," Chuck said.

"I'd rather stay here all the tomorrows."

"You can." Ink tapped her head. "They're all in here."

Hana let out a contented breath, leaning against Chuck. Somehow Ink made more sense than Wayman had.

24

There are secret layers under the secret layers.

—H. H. June 25, 2053

Two days later, Hana and Chuck jostled their way onto the hoverbus for their field trip to I Ching in City Center. Finally, Hana could start figuring out what Ma knew about I Ching's interest in Start-Up. Her plan was to visit Ma at her lab and snoop around, and if she had the chance, ask questions. She hoped Ma had a decent explanation—or even better, knew nothing about all of this. The possibility Ma could be involved made her gut twist. She took a seat behind Tomás, and Chuck slumped down beside her. They buckled in as the hoverbus levitated and put on speed, leaving the school behind.

"I need your help today," Hana said.

Chuck leaned her head against Hana's shoulder. "I'm so tired of being tired. What's up?"

"Remember I told you how Ink and I figured out the e-scroll had the DNA of the zombie fungus and the cat parasite?"

"Yeah," Chuck said.

Tomás turned around. "You're friends with Ink now?"

"She's awesome," Chuck said.

Tomás scowled. "You're friends with her too?"

"Why don't you like her?" Hana asked.

"I don't trust her."

"Well, she's really smart." Hana smiled. "I like her—a lot."

"What do the parasites have to do with Start-Up?" Chuck leaned back and rubbed her forehead.

"That's what I need to find out. My mom works at a lab in I Ching, and we can go visit and ask her about it."

"Why haven't you asked your mom before now?" Tomás asked.

Hana frowned. Of course he *had* to remind her that Ma had been ignoring her for the past two weeks. "I've tried, but she's been busy." Out the window, the crowded hill neighborhoods and the surrounding corporate junkyards and shanties scrolled by below. "I can't wait till I can drive a hovercar," Hana said.

"I can wait," Chuck said. "Most of it is autopilot anyway. There's not much driving besides setting the coordinates."

"Still, it's something to look forward to," Hana said. Even though hovercraft piloted themselves, people got licenses at sixteen to learn how to operate them and to be human backup in case of emergencies. She glanced at Tomás. "You on Team Can't Wait to Drive, or Team Rather Be a Passenger?"

Tomás rolled his eyes and looked out his window, not answering her question.

Hana sat back, trying not to let his snub bother her. Just as she was starting to feel like they were really friends, after they'd been spending time together, he seemed to close himself off again.

As they approached the rooftop landing pad of the glass-and-metalloid building soaring out from City Center, Mr. Zoble announced, "Welcome to I Ching." The students got off and funneled into glass elevators heading down to the lobby one hundred floors below. The elevators hugged the inside of the circular building lined with a spiral walkway and a central atrium laced with floating hydroponic plants.

On their way down, the glass walls blinked with I Ching ads. A hologram appeared of Chair Mayling Chen in a shimmery robe that swirled around her ankles. "Welcome to I Ching, the world's most powerful Corporation. Once the largest search engine and commerce platform in China, we are now known for our expertise in science and industry, entertainment, and communication.

"We are one of the Big Five, but we are the biggest and best. Pear invented enmesh tech, but we took it to the next level by bringing the multiweb to your brains and inventing the boosts for our leaders. This technology spread rapidly throughout the world. Maskbook's surveillance tech keeps us safe, Plex houses the databases, and Nile provides our infrastructure, but without I Ching, none of us could use any of it with a mere thought.

"You will find our trademarked VisReal glasses at the visitor kiosk, which will give you a fully interactive tour of our facilities. Don't worry about getting lost, because your location will be logged at all times, and you will only have access to public spaces." Chair Chen evaporated into a thousand sparkling pixels, leaving behind a whirling logo, the old trigrams of Heaven, Earth, and Water.

At the lobby of the soaring atrium, surrounded by synth-trees and a waterfall fountain, Mr. Zoble said, "Meet at the cafeteria on the thirty-second floor at noon."

Hana, Chuck, and Tomás each picked up a pair of glasses.

"Where to?" Chuck said, leaning heavily against Hana.

"To my mom's lab. Are you going to be okay?"

"I just need a minute to catch my breath."

"I'm going to look around," Tomás said. "I'll find you later with the geotags."

Hana had been to Ma's lab before but double-checked the directory. She and Chuck got back onto an elevator to the fifty-fourth floor. They exited onto the spiral ramp, the curved walls lined with promo feeds and doors with narrow windows revealing labs inside. When they reached a door with an info screen, DR. SOPHIA HSU, COMPTROLLER, BIOTECH AND NEUROSCIENCES, Hana peered inside.

Ma stood with some scientists and lab workers. Hana knocked and stepped in.

Ma's eyes widened, and she broke into a smile. "Hana, what a nice surprise."

Hana sighed. She'd told Ma they'd be coming today, but of course Ma hadn't paid enough attention to remember. Ma turned to Chuck. "And this is?"

"Hi, Mrs. Hsu." Chuck presented her palm in the polite way. "I'm Charlene. Please call me Chuck."

"Nice to meet you," Ma said. "I'd show you around, but it's not a good time. My assistant Julien can help you." She gestured to a corner, and then turned back to the scientists around her. Although Hana was disappointed Ma was busy again, at least they could poke around the lab.

In the corner of the lab where Ma had pointed, a hologuy in his twenties sat twirling a laser pen in front of a machine—a centrifuge, Hana's glasses informed her. People who worked from home could send their holograms, which glowed slightly at their edges, to work. Their home offices were tied into corporate servers, and they could control the lab equipment remotely through their neural connection to the multiweb. Hana's glasses told her he was Julien Dubois, Enmesh Class of 2045, a grad student in genetic engineering.

"Hi," Hana said. "My mom, Sophia Hsu, said you could tell us about what you're working on."

Julien pasted on a wan smile. He manipulated the

deskscreen to pull up a holomodel. "We're isolating and working with the gene sequence of a fungus, *Ophiocordyceps*." He repeated what Hana already knew about the zombie ant fungus.

She wished she knew more about how genetic manipulation worked. Just because Ma worked on the same fungus that was on the scroll didn't mean they were connected. "What are you doing with it?"

"In broad terms, the fungus teaches us how the nervous system works so we can apply it to things that benefit people, like reversing paralysis," Julien explained.

That was what Lin had told her. Hana glanced over at her mom across the room, who was deep in some mental conversation. Then Ma scowled and rushed out of the lab.

Hana gripped Chuck's arm. "Something's up with my mom. Let's follow her."

Chuck sagged a bit. "Okay."

Hana thanked Julien for the information and hustled out, with Chuck close behind. Outside the lab, at intervals along the spiral walkway, glass elevators moved up and down. Ma got into an elevator off to the right, and it headed down.

"Can you keep up?" Hana run-walked down the ramp, tracking the descending elevator. Chuck nodded and followed. The elevator came to a stop two floors below them and Ma walked briskly to a nondescript gray door, looked both ways, and entered the room. Hana and

Chuck circled down the ramp, around and down, until they came to the door. Chuck leaned against it, gasping for breath. A message scrolled up Hana's glasses:

Welcome to the analog workout room. All wireless connections, including neural net ones, are turned off while in this room. Visitors, your eyewear will be deactivated upon entry.

Hana and Chuck glanced at each other. Hana pushed open the door and peered inside. No sign of Ma. It was a large open gym with windows facing the cityscape below, hovercars zipping by at dizzying angles. Spread around the gym were old-fashioned single-purpose exercise machines, weights, and open mats. People ran around the indoor track and sparred on the mats. Rows of lockers lined the inside walls, with banks of lockers and shelves forming protected cubby areas.

Hana dragged Chuck behind one of the cubby areas and whispered, "It looks like we can talk here without being overheard since this room's offline."

Chuck sank onto a bench. "Why are we whispering?"

"We're hiding. I don't want my mom to see us." Although Hana's original plan had been to talk to Ma, after seeing her rush out of the lab with that grim look and act all secretive ducking into the offline gym, Hana decided to lie low and see what her mom was up to before approaching her.

"Look, fencing stuff." Chuck pulled out a white jacket from a shelf holding sports equipment and handed it over to Hana. "Let's put them on so we can move around without being identified."

"Smart," Hana said. "You could be a spy."

They found the underarm protectors, gloves, masks, and a rack with some foils. Hana and Chuck fumbled their way into the gear. Once they had the masks on, their faces were completely covered from view.

"Let's do this for real, so we don't look suspicious," Chuck said.

"I don't know anything about fencing," Hana said as they made their way to the mats in the middle of the room, past others practicing martial arts.

"I don't either, but I think we start by yelling, 'En garde!' and we jab each other like this." Chuck shuffled back and forth and poked the foil at Hana.

"En garde!" Hana craned her neck, looking for Ma.

"You're on." Chuck thrust her foil back, and they whacked their weapons at each other randomly while Hana scanned the room.

Chuck doubled over, breathing heavily. Hana held out a hand to steady Chuck, then stilled. Over Chuck's hunched form, she spotted a familiar figure near a cubby area.

It was Ma.

Hana gestured Chuck to sidle over.

Ma was completely focused on a man who approached her. Instead of the usual palm-to-palm greeting, the two gripped their hands together in an old-fashioned handshake Hana had only ever seen in a vid.

Her breath caught.

It was the same man that Ma had met at Lin's Enmesh Day Ceremony. The two bent their heads together and spoke urgently. They looked furtive, reinforcing Hana's suspicion that the gym was a place people went when they had something to hide. As they approached, the man took her mom by the elbow and directed her out of their line of sight behind the cubbies.

This way, Hana gestured. They shuffled to the cubby area, around the corner from where her mother and the man stood. They couldn't see them but could hear.

"Pedro," Ma said. "Do you have the *Ophiocordyceps* and *Toxoplasma* data?" Hana sucked in her breath at those names.

"I wasn't able to get those, but I have something else."

"What is it?"

"This drive has some . . ." Their voices faded as they moved away from the lockers and came back into view near the gym exit.

The man handed Ma something small, which she put

in her lab coat pocket, then he guided Ma to the door with a hand on her back, and the two left.

Hana yanked her mask off and leaned heavily against a locker.

"What was that about?" Chuck whispered. "They were talking about the fungus and the parasite, weren't they?"

Hana trembled. "It sounds like it. I don't know why my mom is involved."

"I swear, Hana, you're the most interesting person I know."

Before she could answer, Tomás appeared, staring at the door that Ma and the man had gone through, his face pale.

"Where did you come from, and what're you looking at?" Hana asked.

Tomás shook his head, as if waking from a daze. "I followed you in. I saw . . . my dad. Those two who left . . . The man was my dad."

Hana blinked hard. She was still processing the conversation they'd overheard. Now this. "That was your dad? He was with my mom."

It was Tomás's turn to gape. "What?"

Chuck scanned the busy gym and herded them to a nearby exercise mat. "Let's talk here."

They sat down.

"What's your dad doing here meeting my mom?" Hana demanded.

"It seems pretty obvious, doesn't it?" Tomás practically spat, giving her a death stare.

Hana frowned. She had seen his dad with Ma on Enmesh Day and thought they'd looked too chummy for her taste, but that wasn't what this was about.

"What does your dad do, anyway?" Hana asked.

Tomás frowned. "He's not part of any one Corporation. He says he's a 'fixer'—of problems, I guess."

Fixer. That's the word Wayman had used in the forest, when he explained that Ink had stolen the e-scroll from Nile before "the Fixer" could get it to I Ching. It was all coming horribly together—the strands connecting the Ghost Crab Nation to the mysterious e-scroll and Start-Up also reeled in both Ma and Tomás's dad.

"Remember I told you about the stolen code from the junkyard? I think your dad was supposed to get it to my mom, but Ink got to it before he did, and now he just gave her something else." Hana told Tomás the little she and Chuck had overheard.

As she spoke, Tomás blinked rapidly.

"Why would your dad involve my mom in his schemes?" Hana said.

"Why do you think it's my dad's fault? Your mom was there too," Tomás muttered. He gave her a look halfway between bitter and hurt.

Hana's lips pressed into a thin line. "Don't snap at me. I'm not my mom."

"And I'm not my dad."

"Fine."

"Fine."

"Um," Chuck said. "Let's talk about what we should do next."

"We?" Hana and Tomás said at the same time.

Chuck held out her arms. "We, as in the three amigos. Péngyous."

Hana glanced at Tomás, who refused to meet her eyes. Right now, it didn't feel like the three amigos. More like two amigos and one sort-of enemigo.

Hana's insides felt like they were scraped hollow. She didn't know which possibility was worse, Ma betraying Ba's memory, or Ma somehow involved with the stolen scroll. It appeared that not only did Ma know about it, but she might also be in deep. Hana pushed herself up. "We need to go back to the lab and find my mom."

Tomás shook his head. "I'm not going."

"We could run into your dad," Chuck said.

Tomás glowered. "Exactly." He pushed himself from the mat and stalked away.

Chuck checked the time on her comm. "It's too late. We need to meet the rest of the class," she said.

Hana clenched her fists in frustration. She ripped off the fencing gear and shoved it back on the shelf. She couldn't stand the thought that Ma might be part of a conspiracy, and she was no closer to any answers.

25

For once, Ma was home for dinner. Popo wasn't up to cooking, so they ate takeout Vietnamese. Hana slurped her pho ga, trying mightily to only think about the tangy soup. After they'd eaten in silence for some time, Ma said, "It was nice to see you at I Ching today. What did you think?"

Hana lifted her head from her bowl. Unbelievable. Ma acted like everything was normal. She glared at her mother. "Let's play a game."

Ma put down her chopsticks.

"It's called What Would You Do."

"Okay . . ."

"What would you do if you found out someone at school was doing something wrong? Would you report it to the headmaster, or would you try to deal with it yourself?"

"Are you in trouble at school?" Ma said sharply. "Is it your new friend, Chuck?"

"What do you have against Chuck?" Hana asked.

"I'd report it to the headmaster," Lin said. "Let your teachers deal with it. It's probably not even your concern."

"If something's not right, go to an adult you can trust,"

Ma said. "I hope that would be me, but you can always go to Primo Zed. He's practically family and I trust him implicitly. In fact, we've been working on several projects together."

Hana's stomach dropped. She hadn't really been planning on going to the headmaster, but if Primo Zed was involved with whatever was going on, there was truly no one to turn to. If only Ba were still alive . . . but he wasn't.

Popo wiped her mouth and said, "A stone dropped into the ocean makes no waves."

Lin rolled her eyes.

"What does that mean?" Hana asked.

"Not everything has to be connected," Popo said.

Ma shook her head. "Mom, your obscure Chinese proverbs aren't helpful when no one can understand them." She pushed away from the table. "Excuse me. I'm heading upstairs before I go back to the lab. I've had a tough day."

She'd had a tough day? If they compared notes, Hana was pretty sure she would win the worse-day competition. Ma might be in cahoots with a fixer, whatever that was, and involved in a shady corporate plot.

Popo reached over and patted Hana's hand. "Give your ma a break. It's hard to live in a chaotic world when you're a linear person."

Hana squeezed Popo's hand. Even when she didn't understand Popo, sometimes Popo's words hinted at hidden possibilities and bigger truths.

After dinner, Hana headed to the study, where Ma usually hung her lab coat, hoping it might still hold that mysterious object she'd seen Ma pocket at the gym.

Ma hadn't redecorated the study, so it was the one part of their house besides Hana's workshop that still felt like Ba. One wall was lined with bookshelves of dead-tree books and knickknacks, and the small room was dominated by a scuffed wooden desk. The screen wall rotated through post-postmodern art, the only nod to Ma's tastes.

Sure enough, Ma's lab coat was draped over the desk chair. Hana hurried over and fished around in the side pocket.

Nothing.

Of course Ma wouldn't leave it lying around in the lab coat. Could it be back at the lab? Hana studied the office. Her gaze landed on Ba's emperor's box puzzle on the desk. She'd been so proud when she'd figured out the solution a couple of years ago. He always kept little treats in it, and she loved twisting the wooden panels to find them.

Hana shook the box and heard the rattling of small objects. She quickly worked the puzzle and opened the box.

Yes—a small black item. Hana recognized it as a flick drive. Nowadays, data transfers took place wirelessly between enmeshed brains or through comms, but Hana used to play with old drives like this that Ba kept in his desk. This must be the item that Tomás's dad had given Ma at the gym today.

Also tucked in the box was a silk jewelry pouch. Hana snapped open the padded flap, and her breath caught at the sight of Ba's wedding band and Ma's diamond ring. She felt the pull of a vortex of pain and darkness. But she didn't have time for this. Hands trembling, she shoved the pouch back into the box.

Hana pocketed the data drive and opened the bottom left drawer of Ba's desk to look for another drive to replace it so Ma wouldn't notice it was gone. *Everyone needs a junk drawer*, Ba used to say. In it was a jumble of old tech, light pens, scrolls, and, *yes*, several flick drives.

Hana snatched one and popped it into the puzzle box and reassembled it. On impulse, she picked up a couple of other drives and stuck them in her other pocket.

"Are you okay?"

Hana jolted at Ma's voice, hoping she didn't look as guilty as she felt.

Ma leaned against the doorway, tired lines etched on her face.

Hana sat back in the chair and frowned. She wasn't okay, because Ma might be involved in something shady. But she couldn't come out and say that, so she said instead, "No, I'm not okay. They're meshing half the kids at the end of the summer and if I'm not in that group, I'm going to get kicked out of Start-Up. But I'm stuck in the bottom half, at forty-eight percent."

Ma came over and rested against Ba's desk.

Hana swiveled her chair, easing the drawer closed with her foot.

"If there's one thing I know," Ma said, "you can do anything you put your mind to."

Hana let the chair settle to a stop.

"I'm not as good as your dad in cheering you up, but things will be fine. I promise. I know I haven't been around that much—I have a lot happening at work. When you get enmeshed, you'll understand." Ma gave her shoulder a side hug.

Hana wanted to believe Ma. She wanted Ma to hold her and tell her everything would be okay, but she had questions. "I saw you with a strange man at the gym at your work today. Who is he?"

Ma's brows twitched. "He's a friend."

"Are you seeing him?" Hana almost didn't want to know the answer to this question.

"No, nothing like that," Ma said, flustered. "His name is Pedro, and we're . . . acquaintances. We share information about research."

"Does he work at I Ching?" Hana knew he didn't but wanted to hear what Ma had to say.

"Not exactly."

Hana narrowed her eyes. "What kind of research?"

"It's complicated, but essentially, we're trying to improve the neural lace and brain interface when people get enmeshed."

"But why are you working with someone from a different company?" Hana said.

Ma gave her a curious look. "Hana, don't worry about how I do my job. You need to focus on doing the best you can at Start-Up."

Hana stared at her mom, wondering if they would ever be on the same wavelength. Whatever was on the flick drive burning a hole in her pocket would probably have better answers than Ma's evasive ones.

"I'm going to my room." Hana had to stop herself from hurrying out of the study. She had to figure out how to read the flick drive and return it before Ma noticed it was missing.

———

Hana found Lin on her bed, immersed in the multiweb. Lin gave her the usual annoyed look. "What do you want?"

The familiar sinking feeling returned at Lin's cutting tone. Hana hadn't been able to interest Lin in her questions before, so she didn't plan to ask her about the flick drive she'd swiped from Ma. Instead, she showed Lin one of the other drives she'd taken from the office. If Lin could help her, she'd know how to access the one Ma had hidden. "Look what I found in Ba's desk. Do you know how to read this?"

Lin rolled her eyes. "You really know how to interrupt. Cassie and I are working on our Trojan horse."

"Please, it's important."

"All right." Lin took it. "This doesn't have anything to do with your junkyard friend, does it?"

"No, I found this drive at the bottom of Ba's desk drawer."

After a few moments of neural net surfing, Lin reported back. "I can read this through my neural mesh, but I need to upload software. Hold on." After a moment, she smiled. "Got it." Her eyes unfocused as the info uploaded wirelessly to her brain. "These are old vid files. I'll need another app to play them."

"Is that safe?"

"Sure. Antivirus software comes with the mesh implant. Let me get the app."

While they waited, Hana said, "What do you think about what Popo said at dinner?"

Lin's brow furrowed. "You mean her nonsense about stones in the ocean?"

Hana sighed. If only they could talk like they used to, back when Lin didn't dismiss her questions. "It seems she's trying to tell us something."

"You can't pay too much attention to Popo."

Hana rolled back to face Lin. "When you got meshed, did you worry about losing a part of yourself?"

"No. When you get meshed, you're adding to yourself. Like, now I have AI, and it's great." Lin's tone was emphatic, but she didn't sound all that great. She sat up, eyes glazing over. "The vids are playable now."

Hana scooted close, as if she could see through Lin's neural net. "What are they of?"

Lin yelped in delight. "They're vids of us when we were little. Hana, you've got to see them. I'm sending you a link. Do you have more of these?"

Hana handed over the other one she'd taken from the desk. "Here's one, and there are more in Ba's bottom desk drawer."

"What a trip. I can't believe you were actually cute once." Lin's eyes blanked out and watered.

Hana made a face, but her heart jumped. This was the Lin she remembered. "When you play the vids, there's a record of it, right?"

"Of course. Everything you do onweb is recorded."

Āiyā. There went the easy way to view Ma's flick drive. Hana reviewed her options. She could take the drive to Ink, who probably had tech to read it without alerting corporate authorities, but Hana couldn't wait until tomorrow. She had to read the drive before Ma noticed it was missing.

She thought of Tomás. He was a hacker, so he had the

skills. Plus, he lived close by, though he had stormed off today at I Ching and probably wouldn't want to help her.

She pushed herself off the bed. She had no choice. "I'm heading out to my workshop."

Lin murmured something indistinct, her attention already turned back to their old home videos.

26

Hana hurried to her workshop. The trees lit up, but she didn't worry about Ma paying attention, since she came out here often enough and Ma was about to head back to the lab. She waved on the workshop lights, which cast a soft glow over the cozy space, and called Tomás on her comm. Saying anything to him about zombie ant fungi or cat parasites would flag corporate monitors, so she had to be crafty.

Tomás appeared as a hologram on the just second buzz. His hair was mussed, like he'd woken from a nap. "What's up?"

"Can you come over? I have something to show you."

A long pause. "What?"

"Um. Remember you wanted to see some of the bots I make?" She stared laser beams at him, willing him to understand she was talking in code.

"No."

Ugh. He was so dense. "It's something I think you'd be very interested in." She gave him a long, pointed look.

An even longer pause. *C'mon, Tomás.*

"Okay," he finally said.

"Meet me at the tracks behind my house." The back part of her yard was not monitored, so she could sneak down the hill.

Fifteen minutes later, Tomás appeared like a ghost out of the dusk shadows by the old railroad track. "You got something to show me?"

"Up there." She led him back up the hill into her workshop.

Upon entering, Tomás's eyes widened, and he broke into a grin. "This is like your shop in *Way of the Warlords*."

Hana's face warmed. Letting him see the tumble of parts and bots felt like sharing the inside of her brain with him. Everything about this place—the jumble of her creations—embodied who she was.

Maybe he felt something too, because Tomás was quiet and the prickliness he'd shown earlier was gone. "What's up?" he said.

She showed him the flick drive. "This is what your dad gave my mom this morning. Can you read it without triggering the monitors? Everything in our house is networked."

Tomás stepped back. "I told you I didn't want anything to do with this."

"You don't want to know if your dad is involved with something weird or dangerous?"

Tomás's face screwed into a pained expression. "He

has a lot of secret projects, but that doesn't mean they're harmful. I respect his privacy."

Hana stared at him. Tomás himself had a lot of secrets. What if he knew what his dad was up to? "Even if it might affect us, or Chuck, or the other kids at Start-Up?"

He paced back and forth in the crowded space between shelves and the workbench. "People don't understand my dad. He's brilliant, and he has reasons for whatever he's doing." Emotions flitted across his face—anger, frustration, and finally, a decision. "Let me see that."

He took the flick drive from her, their fingers briefly touching. A spark of static electricity buzzed, startling them both. He turned it over a few times, blinking. "I can help, but we need to go back to my house. I have some tech that can copy this."

"Is your dad home?"

"No."

"Don't you have the same problem that anything we do onweb is recorded?"

Tomás gave her a sly smile. "Who said we're going onweb?"

Hana followed Tomás to his house. The Vistas, like most enclaves, was built on top of former landfills. Hana lived in the section for I Ching executives, so their houses had actual space between them. Tomás led her through some alleys until they came to his street, with townhomes jammed together.

Inside his home, everything was super old-looking, with dark wooden beams and floors. The living space was the width of a single room and went back to the end of the unit. Unlike her house, there were no screen walls anywhere. She hadn't pegged Tomás's dad for an AntiTech type.

"Come on." Tomás loped up the narrow stairs to the second floor.

Hana followed him to his room with an unmade bed, clothes strewn around, and a desk pod in a corner. She wrinkled her nose at the musty smell of old socks.

Tomás sat down on a jelly chair. "Let's see what you have."

Hana handed him the data drive.

"I have something that can copy it." He scooted under his desk and pawed through a box, coming up with a small cylindrical object.

"What's that?"

"A universal e-scroll."

"A what?"

"It's like a regular e-scroll, but it can copy data from any digital format from the last twenty-five years. It's completely offline."

"I've never heard of such a thing."

"My dad uses them for his job, so he can work without Corporations spying on him."

"Why did he give you one?" Maybe she shouldn't

have asked Tomás to help. He might side with his father when he found out whatever was on the drive.

"He didn't. My dad doesn't know I have it."

Hana smiled. They had this in common—swiping things from their parents.

He placed the flick drive next to the scroll, which glowed briefly. "All done." Tomás unsnapped the scroll and handed it to her. "There are vid files, but they're encrypted. I can't work on them in the house, because my dad can see everything tied into the home server."

"At least we have this copy, and I can return the flick drive to my mom." Hana hoped it wasn't too late already. "Tomorrow I can take it to Ink."

Tomás shot her a look. "Ink, huh."

"You should get to know her. She's got deep thoughts about info and data. You'd have a lot to talk about."

Tomás fiddled with the e-scroll, avoiding her gaze.

"Thanks for helping." On impulse, Hana held out her hand to match palms.

Instead of the usual palm-to-palm goodbye, Tomás took her hand and closed his fingers around it, and she closed hers in response. Like their parents, they shared an old-fashioned handshake. She wondered why people didn't do this anymore. It was so solid and warm.

Their eyes met and, for the first time, Tomás's smile lit up his face. A warmth filled Hana's heart, and she tightened her grip on his hand.

A chime announced someone's entrance downstairs, and they sprang apart. A wary look came over Tomás's face. "My dad's home."

"What do we do?"

"It's okay," Tomás said, though he didn't sound so sure. "I'll walk you out."

Hana followed Tomás as he hurried down the steps. "Dad!"

"Mijo." His face transformed with a delighted smile as he and Tomás hugged each other.

Hana's stomach twisted into a pretzel. Ma never looked so happy seeing her.

Tomás's dad looked up at Hana on the stairs. "Hello." His greeting held an unvoiced question.

"This is Hana, a friend from Start-Up."

His dad's eyes darted to Tomás. "Nice to meet you, Hana. I'm Pedro." Pedro's eyes crinkled like Tomás's did when he smiled. "Tomás has never brought a friend home before." He gave his son an affectionate shoulder rub, which Tomás ducked away from.

Hana cleared her throat. "We're doing a class project together. About, er, cities disappearing around flooded river deltas."

"That's a serious problem." Pedro's face turned grim. "I've been learning about environmental issues from a new colleague." His face softened when he mentioned the colleague and Hana's stomach sank. He was probably thinking about Ma and their work together.

Hana hurried to the door. "I've got to go. See you tomorrow, Tomás. Nice to meet you, Mr. Ortiz."

Tomás held up a hand in goodbye. As she closed the door, her last glimpse was of Pedro with his arm around Tomás, their heads bent together. A pang went through her. She couldn't remember the last time Ma showed her that kind of affection.

27

6.26.2053. *One of the Last Human Reporters Publishes Memoir.* Eighty-four-year-old journalist John Winsome published a memoir about growing up in the pre-digital age and witnessing the rise of AI-created and -curated news, crowdsourced info, and big data. Nowadays, few humans are involved in the creation and dissemination of news, as AI-powered corporate bots scrape info and decide what to share. **>>> AI News Network**

*H*ana and her classmates gathered in the VR room, waiting for the morning briefing. She couldn't help thinking about the universal e-scroll with the vid files in her bag that she planned to take to Ink after school. She desperately hoped whatever was on the scroll would clear her mom instead of making things worse.

She looked for Chuck and Tomás and found them huddled by one of the VR pods, laughing. Her stomach flopped. She was glad her two friends got along so well, but she couldn't help feeling left out.

"Hey," she said.

"Hey." Chuck looked terrible, with dark circles under her eyes and her skin a sickly yellow.

"You okay?"

Chuck shrugged. "My mom thinks I'm coming down with a summer cold. At least I know I'll feel great in the game."

Hana said to Tomás, "Thanks again for helping out last night."

Chuck gave her a side-eye. "Last night? What did I miss?"

Hana was about to answer when Tomás looked around and said, "Not here."

After last night, Tomás's paranoia didn't surprise her. His dad was a "fixer," and he had all that tech in his house designed for secrets.

"I'll tell you later," Hana said to Chuck.

Chuck looked at her dubiously.

Hana sighed. Things may have improved with Tomás, but now Chuck was upset. It seemed like Hana wasn't the only one who sometimes felt left out.

"Students," Ms. Malhotra announced, "it's time for the next contest to help decide who gets enmeshed at the end of the summer. Today we will test your use of the AI boost. You will be teamed with the same team you had in the physical challenge *and* your rival team from that day."

Hana glanced at the three they'd faced in the mountain-climbing physical challenge. Christa leaned against a VR pod, a forlorn look on her face. The twins, Asa and Ben, smiled at her, and Ben raised his hand in a half wave. They looked almost as terrible as Chuck. Whatever summer bug she had must be going around the whole school.

"This contest is sponsored by Plex, the leader in info and search technology." Floating ads with Plex's WE KNOW WHAT YOU WANT TO KNOW BEFORE YOU KNOW IT slogan swirled around their heads, reminding Hana of how Ink had talked about the spiderweb of data, strands of info sticking to their brains.

Ms. Malhotra explained, "Each group will solve a puzzle, and you will be timed. The faster you finish, the higher you'll score."

Hana sidled up to Chuck. "Looks like we're teammates again."

Chuck fiddled with her equipment, not answering.

"I can explain about last night."

"That's not . . . I don't care about that," Chuck said.

"Then what's wrong?"

"I hope your tech works today." Chuck frowned. "You and Tomás are dragging down my scores, and I really need to stay in Start-Up to keep my parents happy."

"You don't have that much influence on your parents," Hana said. She couldn't make her mom pay attention to her, so how Chuck thought she could save her parents' marriage was beyond her.

Chuck flinched as if slapped.

Hana brought a hand to her mouth. "I'm sorry, I didn't mean it to come out that way."

"Forget it. Let's get ready for the test," Chuck muttered.

Hana winced. This friendship thing was harder than it looked. She would have to smooth things over with Chuck after the challenge. And the thing was, she did share Chuck's worry about another glitch.

When the teacher came by her VR pod, Hana said, "In the last challenge, my physical boost didn't work, and since then, sometimes it works and sometimes it doesn't. Did Mr. Zoble check on my tech?"

Ms. Malhotra's eyes unfocused. "He left a memo. It says, 'Checked Hsu's tech interface and all is fine.'" She smiled at Hana. "Looks like you won't have any more problems."

"Thanks." At least that was resolved. She turned on the simulation to start the AI challenge.

They materialized in a stone courtyard in an old Chinese compound in their *Way of the Warlords* avatars. The low structures surrounding the courtyard were made of wide gray bricks with wooden beams, wood-latticed windows, and elaborate tiled roofs. Ms. Malhotra paced next to an apricot tree blossoming with white and pink flowers.

Tomás, still in his peasant outfit, looked warily at

their teacher. Chuck, the blue-haired armor-clad warrior, danced from side to side and jabbed the air, as if trying to punch a hole through it.

"You're not kidding when you said you feel better in here," Hana said.

Chuck cracked her neck and looked straight ahead, not replying.

Hana sighed. She'd have to make it up to Chuck and do her best in the challenges. Even though she was more and more wary about Start-Up, she wanted to stay in the program. She was still worried about being left behind by Lin and Ma if she didn't get meshed soon, and she'd have a better chance of uncovering what was going on from inside the program.

Their former rivals also gathered in the courtyard. Asa and Ben knocked into each other like overgrown puppies in superhero outfits, while Christa stood by, a worried expression on her face. Like Chuck, they seemed to have gotten their energy back.

"When I leave, you will enter the house and solve a puzzle," Ms. Malhotra said. "Don't forget to turn on your AI boosts." Their teacher faded away, leaving the six of them.

"Let's go." Hana hurried through an open doorway, followed by Chuck, Tomás, and their new teammates. Once they were inside, the door fused into the wall, trapping them in a closed room.

The latticed windows filtered light on a man in an elaborate silk robe waving a fan. Behind him, three scholars sat at polished desks. Each wore a different-colored embroidered robe—black, red, and white—and each faced a scroll with an ink brush.

"Welcome," the man said. "These scholars are either liars or truth-tellers. Your task is to tell me what type of person each one is, based on the clues they will give you. If you are correct, you are free to leave the room. You will be timed and compared to the other teams facing the same riddle." The old man faded to 50 percent opacity.

Hana and her classmates exchanged looks. This was an intellectual puzzle, and she could use her AI. She relaxed.

The scholar in the red robe tacked a scroll up on the wall. It said *All of us are liars.*

The second scholar in white painted a mountain scene.

The third scholar in black hung her scroll. *Exactly one of us tells the truth.*

Hana toggled her settings to turn on her AI, but nothing happened. A familiar dread welled up. "My AI is not working." She couldn't believe her boost had failed again, especially after Mr. Zoble assured her everything was okay. "Can you use yours?"

Chuck nodded. "I can."

Tomás blinked quickly. "It's a logic problem. We don't need AI. We can figure it out by thinking through it."

Hana tried to fiddle with her AI again, but it was no

use. Her heart thumped and her palms grew clammy. She thought of Wayman's breathing lessons and took a deep breath, trying to calm herself. Her heart didn't cooperate—it beat faster. Wayman had said qigong would help her in a stressful challenge, but it didn't seem like it was working.

Chuck paced the room. She rounded on Hana. "Why does your tech always fail, Hana? What is wrong with you?"

Tomás put a hand on Chuck's arm. "It's not her fault."

"Oh, sure. Now you two are buddies, doing things without me," Chuck snapped. "I thought we were friends."

Tomás shot Hana a pleading look. Asa, Ben, and Christa shifted uncomfortably.

Hana had no idea what she could say to Chuck that would make her feel better. "We *are* friends," she said. "And I need you now. You have AI. What does it say to do?"

Chuck gave her a flat stare, then let out a heavy sigh. "Fine. My AI says to think about each clue methodically."

"I agree," Christa said. Asa and Ben nodded in agreement.

Hana wondered why her tech was the only one that failed yet again.

Chuck looked up, grim-faced. "Okay, let's think this through. So clue number one: Ms. Red's sign says, 'All of us are liars.' If that statement is true, that would mean each of them is a liar."

Hana pushed aside her worries and thought about what Chuck said. "But that would mean Ms. Red is a liar who told the truth, which can't be right. So her statement, 'All of us are liars,' is a lie."

"Which means," Christa interjected slowly, "Ms. Red is a liar, so her statement is false, which means at least one of the other two is a truth-teller."

Hana's head hurt, but they were making progress. "Okay. Ms. White over here is painting mountains. That doesn't help us at all."

"I'd like to paint mountains," Chuck said.

"That doesn't help either," Tomás said.

"Mr. Smarty Pants, what's your great idea?" Chuck retorted.

Hana felt like she was caught in a vise, with their team falling apart. The twins looked at them.

"Are y'all always like this?" Asa asked.

"Like what?" Tomás and Chuck asked at the same time.

"Like siblings." Asa looked at Ben. "I mean, *we're* like this all the time because we're twins and can't get out of each other's faces."

Hana took a deep breath. "We can do it. Let's focus. I believe in us."

Chuck gave her a surprised look.

Tomás shot her a smile.

"So we know Ms. Red lied when she said all of them are liars," Hana said.

"And Ms. Black says, 'Exactly one of us tells the truth,'" Chuck said. "We need to think about this logically—figure out what it means if her statement is true, and what it means if it's a lie, and then see which situation matches up with what we already know." Hana liked this side of Chuck, focused and smart.

"So if we suppose Ms. Black is a liar, then by process of elimination, we know Ms. White the artist must be a truth-teller, since we figured out earlier there is at least one truth-teller," Tomás said, working it out. "But then Ms. Black's statement that exactly one of them is a truth-teller would be correct, but as a liar, she can't tell the truth."

"In other words, it's impossible for Ms. Black to be a liar," Chuck said.

"So Ms. Black must be a truth-teller." Hana smiled.

"And since her statement that only one of them can tell the truth is true, and she's the truth-teller, then Ms. White must be a liar even if she hasn't said a word," Ben concluded. He turned to the faded-out man with the fan. "We know the answer."

"Ms. Red and Ms. White are liars, and Ms. Black is a truth-teller," Christa said.

The three scholars winked out and the man in the robe reanimated. "Very good." He checked an ornate timepiece. "You have half an hour left. Enjoy the rest of the game." The man dissolved, this time for good.

The twins high-fived each other.

"We did it!" Asa pumped their fist.

Hana and Tomás exchanged grins, and Chuck and Christa gave each other a quick hug. Hana looked over at Chuck, who flashed a small smile. It was not the hug she wanted from Chuck, but it would do for now.

"Are y'all hanging around? Let's explore this dusty town," Asa said.

Chuck, the twins, and Christa practically bounced out of their skins, while Tomás peered at one of the hanging scrolls. Hana couldn't help but notice the extreme difference between how Chuck and the others acted before the game, and how they acted now, inside the game. As Hana stared at them, the coin purse in the margin of her vision pulsed.

Ink's digital crab key.

Ink had said it would open a secret portal back to her mind beach, where they couldn't be monitored. They had some time, and this would be the ideal opportunity to talk to Chuck and Tomás about everything privately, in a place where nobody could spy on them. She also wanted to investigate her recurring tech failures, and maybe figure out what was going on with Chuck and the others. She wanted Chuck and Tomás to join her but didn't know Asa, Ben, or Christa well enough to trust them with something like this.

"Y'all go ahead," Hana said. "Chuck and Tomás, I want to show you something."

"See ya," Ben said, and he and the others blinked away.

"What's going on?" Chuck asked.

Hana tapped the coin purse, and the ghost crab skittered onto her palm. "This is a key. Tap on it, and we'll go to a historical beach."

Tomás gave her a long look. "I guess I'm up for a beach trip," he said cautiously. He tapped the crab and blinked out.

"Whoa." Chuck gave her a wary look. "Always something new and secret with you." She shrugged and touched the crab.

As she winked out, Hana tapped the ghost crab too.

28

Hana materialized in the windswept and deserted beach Ink had brought her to before. The sky was the brilliant blue from historical vids, fine spray tipped the waves, and the dune grasses swayed.

Chuck looked around cautiously. "What is this place? I've never been here before in *Warlords*."

"It's not part of the game," Hana said. "This is Ink's private mindspace."

Tomás crouched down, running sand through his fingers, his head tilted as if listening to something. Blinking rapidly, he said, "This place is amazing. It's like a hacker pocket, but better."

"Hacker pocket?" Hana asked.

"A safe space you carve out when you're hacking into another system, but this one's got off-the-charts security," he said.

Hana wondered how Tomás could see all that from sifting the sand. "We have half an hour," she said. "I brought you here so we could talk about the strange things that have been going on."

Chuck walked to a sand dune and ran her arm through

the grass. "What were you two up to last night?"

"That's what I want to talk about," Hana said. "Remember when Tomás's dad gave my mom something at the I Ching gym? I took it and it turned out to be an old flick drive, and Tomás made a copy last night." She explained how it contained an encrypted video they couldn't watch without alerting authorities.

Chuck scowled. "You didn't call me."

"Tomás is the one who can hack into things, and I didn't want to bother you," Hana said.

"Friends bother each other. That's what we're for," Chuck said.

Hana's insides squeezed together. "I'm sorry."

"I was so tired last night, I probably wouldn't have helped anyway," Chuck said glumly, "but it would've been nice to have been asked."

"I know that now," Hana said. "I promise I won't leave you out anymore. Also, isn't it strange you're so tired and sick outside of the game but feel great inside?"

Chuck wrinkled her brow. "It's just a bad cold. You and Tomás are both fine outside but didn't do well in the first two challenges."

"Let's think about one thing at a time," Tomás said. "Hana, with your glitchy boosts, what have you done differently than everyone else since we've been at Start-Up?"

"Nothing." Hana had wanted to be meshed to be close with her family and help her grandma, so she'd tried to improve her score by going to the woods . . . Oh, right. That was different. "I've been learning qigong from Wayman," she said slowly.

"What's that got to do with anything?" Chuck asked.

Hana thought about her qigong sessions, sitting on the rock and clearing her mind. With each session, she drank . . . the chrysanthemum tea.

"I've been drinking this funny tea every time I see him." A feeling of unease prickled. "Maybe that messed with my brain in the game and affected how I did." Every time she drank the tea, it relaxed her. Maybe it slowed her reflexes or made her less responsive in the game.

Chuck's brows furrowed. "Do you think the energy drink we have at school has something to do with how we feel?"

"Maybe it helps cover up the really bad effects," Hana said. "I haven't been drinking it lately."

Chuck frowned. "What about you, Tomás? You don't do well in the games, and you've been drinking the MDD and not Wayman's tea. You're messing up our theories."

Tomás swirled the sand with his toe. "I have no idea."

The grains of sand lifted and blew away in ghostly sparkles. Again, Hana wondered about Tomás. His tech and hacking abilities. His so-so performance in the games. Yet, despite his secrets, he had let down his guard last night and they had bonded.

And then there was Chuck, the twins, Christa, and

others. Outside the game, the dark circles under their eyes made them look like the undead. In here, they were full of energy and seemed completely fine.

She scanned her menu. As a place to research, there had to be access to the multiweb. Hana clicked on a crab icon, and a giant animated paper clip with googly eyes appeared.

"It looks like you're trying to search the deep multiweb. Do you need any help?" it asked in a chirpy voice.

"What's the deep multiweb?" Hana said. "And yes, we could use help."

"The deep multiweb is the part of the web that's not indexed for search," the paper clip said. "It's—"

"Not for noobs." The air shimmered, and black-haired Ink appeared. He eyed the three of them and gave Hana a bemused look. "You brought your friends to my secret beach." Hana's face must've shown her sudden apprehension because he grinned. "It's okay."

Ink reached over to Chuck, and they exchanged a palm greeting. Tomás nodded but seemed to make a point of avoiding eye contact. Ink crossed his arms. "What can *I* help you with?"

"We're trying to figure out why some of my friends feel sick outside but fine inside the games," Hana said. "It might be connected to the drinks Start-Up gives us."

Ink plucked a strand of data from the air and began

weaving. "I'll dig into Start-Up servers." He built a web of data, a glittery snowflake made of sand. "Here's something." A list holo-hovered before them.

Y$0UFFU, NYOU+1QY 16.5.41 KJ1

W1Y0S, CU0 16.8.41 KJ1

W1KEV$A, 0YDUU0 10.1.41 KJ1/FKB

WK1U0 WRY$NULU 5.7.41 KJ1/FKB

MYA0Y$V, W1$Q+FY 1.12.41 KJ1/FKB

+MAF1U, WA0F1QY 16.5.41 FKB

FE$0U$, Y+Y 22.6.41 KJ1/FKB

FE$0U$, XU0 22.6.41 KJ1

ZVY0U0, XK$Q+ 3.2.41 FKB

It went on for more than a hundred lines. "Great, another undecipherable code," Hana said.

"It shouldn't be hard to run a decoder script on it," Tomás said.

Ink glanced over and nodded appreciatively. "You're right." He studied the characters for a moment. "It's a simple reverse plus shifted code with some upside-down 1980s calculator thrown in." Ink wove his fingers through the list, and it became readable.

Arnette, Lakeshia 16.5.41 oph

Chang, Wen 16.8.41 oph

Choudry, Naveen 10.1.41 oph/tox

Cohen, Charlene 2.11.41 oph/tox

Maynard, Christa 1.12.41 oph/tox

Smythe, Cynthia 16.5.41 tox

Turner, Asa 22.6.41 oph

Turner, Ben 22.6.41 oph/tox

Zdanek, Boris 3.2.41 tox

Hana's eyes grew wide.

"My name is there!" Chuck said.

"And others from Start-Up," Hana added. "Oph and tox must be short for the *Ophiocordyceps* and *Toxoplasma gondii*."

"Why am I on the list?" Chuck demanded.

Hana felt a growing dread. "I think they're doing something to you with the parasite and fungus," she said slowly. "Chuck, remember the first day you got the nano pill that was supposedly a medtech update you missed? So did Christa, Asa, Ben, and the others who were pulled out of class, and they're on this list too."

"What do the zombie ant fungus and the cat parasite have to do with the pills?" Chuck said.

"The fungus takes over an ant's physical actions, turns it into a zombie," Ink mused. "The cat parasite lowers the fear response. Maybe I Ching is using some kind of gene therapy based on these DNA snippets."

"They're turning me into a *zombie*?" Chuck said.

"They wouldn't do that," Hana said.

"Why did only some of us get the pill?" Chuck asked.

Tomás scrunched his brows together. "It's a science experiment—half of us are the control and half are the experiment."

"I don't believe it," Chuck said. "I want out of here. This is all too much."

Hana bit her lip. "We need to give Wayman this information. He can help sort this out. Plus, we can show him the files from the flick drive I took from my mom."

Chuck shook her head.

The timer counted down to five minutes remaining.

Even though her mind whirled from the new revelation, she had one more thing she needed to do. "Ink, could you check the Start-Up records to see if there's anything about the failing boosts?"

Ink nodded. "Let me show you how it's done. See these files tagged with your name? Pluck them like a string." Ink pulled at a file, and a shimmering line of data streamed out and opened in midair.

Hana let out a surprised laugh. She found more files with her name, plus some of Chuck's files. She pinched at them and drew the strands into two piles, weaving them into separate floating snowflakes. Her web had several broken links, while Chuck's glowed, intact.

Hana touched her finger to one of the broken links, and a report opened.

> Subject Hsu's VR pod breathalyzer shows reduced intake of Start-Up serum drink and increase of unauthorized vitamins and compounds, contributing to suboptimal linkage.

"What does that mean?" Hana said.

"You're not drinking enough of whatever they're giving ya and too much of something else," Ink said.

Hana gasped. "There *is* something about the MDD drink and Wayman's tea," she said. And maybe having drunk the tea was why the MDD drink tasted strange.

The timer chimed.

"We've got to go. Ink, let Wayman know I want to see him."

Ink raised a brow. "Will do." He plucked the ghost crab from Hana's hand and the mind beach melted away.

29

*H*ana stepped out of her VR pod, mind spinning at the implications of what they'd uncovered. Half of the students were being drugged somehow with altered DNA, and their abilities in the game were affected by the MDD drink. Plus, the chrysanthemum tea interfered with her boosts. Chuck emerged with a groggy expression and could barely hold herself up, leaning against her pod. Christa, Asa, and Ben didn't look much better.

Others emerged from their VR pods, some in good shape and others like Chuck, Christa, and the twins. Hana guessed they were the half of the class that had received the nano pills the first day. She glanced at the scoreboard and saw her score was blanked out. Quickly scrolling through the other students' scores, she noticed the same with Chuck and Tomás, but Christa, Asa, and Ben had all scored well above 50 percent.

Mr. Zoble and Ms. Malhotra strode over, his lanky frame and her short muscular one making them look like a bad comedy duo.

Hana straightened. She had to act like everything was okay. "How did we do? We got the answer quickly."

"You did, but that's not what we need to talk to you about," Mr. Zoble said. "The three of you did something strange at the end."

Chuck's eyes widened and she glared at Hana.

Hana had no idea what the teachers had seen, but she trusted Ink's security. The teachers must've seen something different from what they had experienced.

"Come with me." Ms. Malhotra guided them out of the classroom. Chuck lagged, her feet dragging.

Hana slowed and put her arm around Chuck. "You okay?" she whispered.

Chuck pulled away. "I can't get in trouble now," she hissed.

"You won't. They can't make us tell them anything," Hana whispered.

They reached a small viewing room, and the kids sat in the theater-style chairs. "I'll replay your simulation, and you'll tell us what's going on," Ms. Malhotra said in a clipped voice.

The wall split into three screens displaying their experience in *Way of the Warlords*. Their eyepieces had recorded everything, including whatever scrolled up in their field of vision. Hana squirmed. She knew they were constantly monitored during the game but hadn't realized the extent.

Ms. Malhotra fast-forwarded the replay. "Explain this, at the end of your session."

There was no evidence of them at Ink's mind beach, not even the moment they activated the ghost crab key. Instead, the three screens showed the group jogging through a vast, empty field of swaying grass, with the sound off.

Tomás's gaze blanked out, and he said nothing. Hana clamped her mouth shut, trying to puzzle this out. It must have been a cover story that got triggered when they went to Ink's beach, but as far as she could tell, it was pretty weak. She'd have words with Ink about this.

Hana tried to come up with something that made sense. "There's not much to explain." Her heart picked up its pace, probably recorded on her wristband and suit. Even though Wayman's breathing lessons hadn't helped her in the challenge, she tried again. She inhaled slowly through her nose and out through her mouth to settle her heartbeat, but it didn't work now either. "We were just having fun," she said in a strangled voice.

Ms. Malhotra's face didn't budge. "There should've been sound, and that field is not part of the game. We will investigate, and until it is resolved, you will have your scores frozen at your current standing."

Chuck paled. Tomás jolted forward.

Before this challenge, Hana's score had been stuck at 48 percent, in the failing half of the class. She pushed to her feet. "That's not fair. We did well in the challenge, even though the AI boost glitched again for me. Something is wrong with the tech."

Ms. Malhotra's face darkened. "Our systems are fine—the tech is quality-checked every morning. You are on probation. Any more irregularities, and we will remove you from Start-Up."

Hana seethed as they walked back to class. At this point she was very wary about getting meshed, especially after everything they'd learned about what Start-Up was doing to her classmates, but she didn't want to get kicked out of the program either. They were on the verge of figuring out what was happening with the students, and staying in Start-Up was the best way to find more info.

As soon as they were on break outside and away from the listening walls, Hana strode with Chuck and Tomás to the windy fields.

"I can't believe we might get booted out of Start-Up," Hana said.

Tomás kicked at a clump of weeds.

Chuck looked at her juice box and frowned. "I really want to drink this. It's the only thing that makes me feel better."

"But we just found out it may be affecting your mind," Hana said.

Chuck opened the box. "I don't care." She chugged it and within moments, she sighed. "So. Much. Better." She glared at Hana. "What was that about on the beach? What did you drag us into?"

Hana gripped her friend's hand. "This is bigger and more serious than we thought. We need to go to Wayman and the Ghost Crab Nation for help. He can look at the scroll to see what's on the encrypted video."

Chuck shook her head. "I don't know. I feel fine inside the games. I'm sure I'll feel fine once I'm meshed too. I just need to keep going."

Hana stared. Chuck seemed to be in denial that she was part of a science experiment.

"I'll go with you," Tomás said.

Hana felt a surge of gratitude and some suspicion. "Why?"

"My dad is involved too."

A brief lump formed in her chest as she remembered how close Tomás and his dad were last night. Hana nodded gratefully.

"We can go this weekend." Hana turned to Chuck. "Join us?"

"I don't think so." Chuck folded up the empty juice box as if it were the most important task in the world. "I'm going to ask to switch to another team for the challenges."

"What?" It was a gut punch. "Please don't do that. We'll figure out what's happening."

Chuck's face screwed up. "I have to be in the early group of meshed kids, and then I'll be all better. You have Tomás, so you don't need me."

Hana pressed her lips together. "What's wrong with you? You don't care that you're being experimented on?"

Chuck blinked back angry tears. "Why do you care? You're like I Ching royalty with your mom practically in charge. My parents . . ." She paused. "Never mind, you'll never understand." She looked away. "I'm going back inside."

Hana's heart sank as Chuck walked away, stray leaves swirling around her feet.

A touch on her arm. Hana turned. Tomás held out a small piece of metal, his eyes soft. "Another fried cyber bee." He placed the mangled robot in her hand.

Hana clenched her fingers around the dull and lifeless bot. She was on the verge of being kicked out of Start-Up and losing a friend in Chuck, but she needed to hold on, both to find answers to the conspiracy and to save her friend.

30

After school, Hana and Tomás walked to the train tracks. Hana was still gutted by what Chuck had said at break. Hana had said all the wrong things and had only succeeded in pushing Chuck away. "I wish Chuck would come with us when we give Wayman the scroll with the vids on it," she said.

"Why do we need Chuck?" Tomás asked.

"She's the one suffering from whatever they did to her. They gave her something that could be changing her brain, and Wayman has a network of spies and scientists, so maybe they can help her."

"She doesn't want to have anything to do with us," Tomás said. "You heard how she wants to change teams."

"I need to convince her we can help her feel better." If only Hana could get through to her, Chuck would have to come around.

Then it came to her. She would go to Chuck and have a heart-to-heart and bring a peace offering. She would make Chuck a bot to show her how much she cared, and this time, she wouldn't mess up like she did with Lin's bot.

When she got home, she cut through the kitchen on

her way to the workshop. Popo sat at the table watching her telenovela while snapping the ends off green beans and singing along with the theme song: "Fuimos por la gloria pero quedamos por la magia . . ." *We went for the glory but stayed for the magic.*

"Hi, Popo."

Popo smiled. "Hello, Hana."

Hana's smile widened. It was a good memory day. "Wanna join me at the workshop to make a bot?"

Popo waved her show off and pushed herself to her feet. "I'd love to. We can pick up where we left off."

"Um, sure." The last time they'd been to the workshop together was at least a year ago. She helped Popo put away the beans, and they walked across the patchy yard.

Inside the workshop, dust motes danced in the shaft of light. Popo's eyes lit up and her face relaxed. Hana pushed aside clutter to clear a space on the worktable. They settled into their old spots, Hana on one side of the worktable and Popo at the end. Hana set to sorting through a box of scrap parts. "I'll make a crab bot." Crabs and their antics reminded her of Chuck.

"I love crabs." Popo picked out aluminum scraps and bent them into curved shapes, her fingers holding their own memories. "When I used to live at the beach, my favorite time was dusk in the summers." Popo's eyes softened with memories. "The ghost crabs would come out, skittering at our feet."

Hana looked up sharply. "Ghost crabs?"

"You know, those sand crabs with pop-up eyes." Popo pressed her fingers into the soft metal.

"Have you heard of the Ghost Crab Nation?"

Popo's eyes flickered briefly. "Is that some kind of band?" Popo made small, neat holes in the metal, tapping with a mini-hammer and awl.

"No, not a band." Hana fit together two comm shells to form the crab's body. "When you warned me, was it about Start-Up and getting meshed?"

Popo blinked twice. "I'm making an armadillo." Popo lined up two of the metal plates and threaded a wire through the holes. "These plates will form the protective shell. Did you know only two species of South American armadillos can roll themselves into a ball if they're threatened?" She twisted the wires off with small pliers. "Nature has developed so many ways to protect itself."

A surge of warmth flooded through Hana. Even though talking to Popo could feel like two ships passing in the night, at least she was out there bobbing on the ocean, a warm and steady presence.

A buzzing sound droned briefly, reminding her of the fried cyber bees. She dug one out of a box and showed it to Popo. "Look what I found at school."

Popo peered at it through her glasses. "A robotic insect mindlessly following computer code. The problem with electronics is they're susceptible to disruptions. That's why I taught you to make automatons. You can always rely on the laws of physics." She handed it back to Hana.

Hana set the bee aside. "Is that why you didn't become an engineer?"

"Biology and genetics were always my first love." Popo twisted more wire into the armor plates. "And I met my second love, your grandfather, at my graduate school lab. Between the two of us, there wasn't much question what your ma would end up doing."

Hana sometimes forgot Popo had been a scientific whiz, studying at MIT and Stanford before they were bought out by the Corporations. It was hard to think of her as anything other than her funny, dumpling-cooking, telenovela-watching grandma who sometimes forgot her name. She hated that she only got glimpses of this other side of Popo.

As Hana held the crab bot, an even better idea for Chuck's gift came to mind. She put aside the half-built crab and gathered the parts she would need for her new automaton. She tried one more time. "Why didn't you get meshed?"

Popo looked up. "Privacy."

"What do you mean?" Hana asked, thrilled Popo was clear-minded.

"When you get meshed," Popo explained, "the Corporations track all your actions—what you buy, the shows you watch, who you're talking to. Your entire life is on the multiweb, and the Corporations use all that information to sell you more things and to shape your thoughts."

Hana thought it interesting how she echoed what Ink and Wayman had said.

"But it goes even deeper than that," Popo continued. "In the eighteenth century, the philosopher Jeremy Bentham invented a prison system called the panopticon, where one central guard tower could look into a circle of open prison cells. The guard could watch the prisoners at any time, but the prisoners could never tell if they were being watched."

"What does that have to do with getting meshed?" Maybe Popo's mind had wandered again.

"When you're meshed, you're in a kind of prison, always under watch. It's important to live some part of your life not tracked, recorded, or stored—a private pocket where you can try things and do things for no one but yourself."

"Like we're doing now," Hana said.

Popo smiled. "Exactly. There's also the precautionary principle."

"The what?"

"It's fancy science-speak for 'better safe than sorry,'" Popo said. "I did my doctoral thesis on the effects of electromagnetic radiation on the meshed brain. For me, the risks of getting enmeshed outweighed their benefits, because we didn't have enough information about its long-term safety."

"If it was so dangerous, why didn't you stop Ma from getting meshed?" Hana asked.

"I also believe in informed consent. I shared all my results with her." Popo laced her fingers together. "Your mother was headstrong, and she believed the benefits outweighed the risks. I had to respect that."

"Do you ever wish you'd gotten jacked, so you could remember things better and keep working?"

A wistful smile crossed Popo's face. "Sometimes. Not to remember better, but to understand your ma better."

"That's why I want to get meshed too, but it seems dangerous now."

"It's always been dangerous."

Her grandma attached the legs of her armadillo and reached out to squeeze Hana's arm. Hana finished her new bot too—a three-legged crow. Yatagarasu's friendly washer eyes shone in the light. She hoped it would be enough to win Chuck back.

Then she knew what she had to do. Hana opened a drawer and took out the watch she'd gotten from Ink. She felt a brief pang giving it to Chuck instead of Lin, but Ba would've approved. She clipped off the worn straps, laid some glue on the back, and gently pressed the watch to the crow bot's breast. Pulling a scrap of antique paper from her stash, Hana chewed on a pencil and scribbled a note:

Did you know crows work together to get food and protect their families? You're part of my family now.

—H. H. June 26, 2053

She rolled up the note and stuck it in the crow's underbelly. "You want to put a note in yours?"

"No thanks." Popo tapped her temple. "I keep my thoughts up here. It's safer."

Hana sighed. It was moments like this when she could see the benefit of getting meshed—Popo would have a place to store her memories somewhere other than her failing brain.

Popo rolled the armadillo along the worktable. "For you, Meimei." It curled into a tight metallic ball and came to a rattling stop at Hana's hands.

Hana cupped the ball of armadillo and held it close to her chest. "Thank you, Popo."

6.28.2053. *I Ching Ethics Board Approves Chimera Experiments.* I Ching approved experiments in human-animal chimeras, where animals like pigs and mice are injected with human genes and develop human organs and cells. The panel rejected concerns that implanting human organs developed in animals could introduce foreign retroviruses. **>>> Crowdsource News Network**

The next day was Friday, and Chuck didn't show up to school. On Saturday, Hana could barely contain her impatience on the train ride to Chuck's neighborhood. Treelawn was like the Vistas, crowded townhomes built on former landfills. Following her comm's directions, she hurried through the narrow streets.

At Chuck's doorstep, she called her on the comm. It took several tries before Chuck picked up. "Hey." Chuck's hologram hovered.

"Are you feeling okay? You weren't at school," Hana said.

"I was tired, so my parents said I could stay home."

"I need to talk to you. Can I come over?"

Chuck looked uncertain. "What do you want to talk about?"

"I'll explain in person," Hana said. "Actually, I'm here."

"Here?"

"Downstairs."

Chuck's hologram swiped the call off. Hana gazed at the door, wondering if this had been a waste of time and effort.

After several long moments, Chuck opened the door.

Before she lost her nerve, Hana launched into her plea. "Tomás and I are going to Wayman's to show him the scroll. I really need you to come too."

Chuck looked at her dubiously. "It didn't seem like you and Tomás needed me the other night."

"I'm sorry. I couldn't trust the comms, so I had to see him in person. I'm also sorry we got in trouble at school, but don't you see something's wrong at Start-Up?"

"Trouble seems to follow you, Hana."

"Whatever is happening is happening to all of us."

Chuck sat down on her stoop, which Hana took as a promising sign.

Hana sat down beside Chuck's slumped figure, and it hit her. Giving her an automaton wasn't going to fix things between them. Like Wayman said, she needed to be in the moment and pay attention. In this case, it meant listening to her friend. "What's really going on? It's not because of the glitches in the game, is it?"

Chuck glanced over and sighed. "It's my parents. I hate that they are always fighting," Chuck continued. "I keep thinking if I felt better and did well at Start-Up, that'd make them happy."

Hana took a breath. "I'm sorry I haven't been listening to you when you worried about your parents. I have to remember that what you're going through in your family isn't the same as what's going on with my mom." Hana stuffed her hand into her bag and offered up the Yatagarasu bot. "I have a gift for you."

Chuck's eyes widened. She took the bot and ran her finger across the watch face.

"Open it. There's a latch under its belly."

Chuck picked at the hatch, found the rolled-up note, and read it. "What's this for?"

Hana gulped. She'd never explained to Chuck how her bots worked. "It's something I used to do with my dad. We would write down our feelings, put them in our bird bots, and fly them out to the world or give them to someone we care about."

Chuck looked up and gave a small smile. "Thank you."

"I think the best way for you to feel better is for us to figure out what's happening at Start-Up. You can't do well and make your parents happy if you're so sick."

After a long pause, Chuck said, "You're right, and I don't want to wait around. I need to help. I'm in."

"You'll come with Tomás and me to show Wayman the scroll?"

Chuck smiled. "What are we waiting for?"

As they hugged, Hana grinned so hard her lips hurt.

31

6.29.2053. *Animal Translations a Hoax?* Though people can communicate crudely with enmeshed Animals via neural nets, scientist debunked purported translations of Animal social media networks. The latest translation making the rounds: "Chairman Meow screeched: There is no truth to the so-called parasite *Toxoplasma gondii*. We Cats need no stinking parasite to MIND-CONTROL HUMANS. The *Toxoplasma* conspiracy is one big LIE!" **>>> via Cat Memes Converter™**

*T*he next day, Hana, Chuck, and Tomás made their way to the junkyard, to an area filled with old plastic bins and coolers.

"I thought we were going to Wayman's," Chuck said.

"We have to leave our wristbands here," Hana said, "so we don't get tracked to his house." Ever since they were put on probation, she worried how much Start-Up, I Ching, or Nile tracked their activities. Today was the first time she'd come back to the junkyard since then.

A flippety sound came over the crest of a trash pile, followed by a gliding dragonfly bot.

"Tish," Hana said.

The girl jostled her way down. "Oi. Who are they?"

"They're my friends from Start-Up. Can you take our wristbands?"

Tish pushed her bangs from her face. "Nope. I don't want to end up like Guille."

"What happened to him?" Hana asked.

"He never came back. The JingZa must've picked him up," Tish said. "He don't have anyone to pay his way out, so he's stuck working off his fine."

"That's awful." Hana didn't know what Guille had done, but it didn't seem fair that he was stuck in a Corporate sweatshop, working for them until he made enough money to get free. His disappearance made her even more nervous about hanging around at the junkyard. They needed to get to Wayman's quickly.

"Sure is." Tish picked up the dragonfly bot and hustled away.

"They can take people?" Chuck said. "Like, kidnap them? That's terrible. Maybe we shouldn't be here either."

"We shouldn't," Hana said, "which is why we need to get out of here."

She found a small cooler and opened the dirt-encrusted top. "Let's leave our wristbands here." As she led her friends toward the Bottoms, Hana gave the cooler a parting glance. Once they got to Wayman's, they'd get the help they needed.

Wayman peered over his cup of tea. "What's the occasion for this honor?"

Hana, Chuck, and Tomás sat on his couches, each holding their own cup of chrysanthemum tea. None of them took a sip. When Hana had shown up with her friends, Wayman had taken it in stride, as if strangers showed up at his doorstep all the time.

Hana handed over the universal scroll. "This is a copy of a flick drive that I got from my mom, who got it from Tomás's dad. It's got encrypted vids that could be about the DNA snippet."

"Who's your father?" Wayman asked as he unsnapped the scroll.

"He works on his own, not with any Corporation," Tomás said.

Wayman looked up. "A freelancer."

"We thought Ink could help. We need a safe way to decode it," Hana said.

"You're right, Ink's the one," Wayman said. "You know me and tech."

"Did you ever wish you were meshed?"

"No. I didn't need to, because many of the Ghost Crab Nation are meshed, like Ink." Wayman got up. "Let's go to the stream. I want to show you something."

On their way out, Wayman opened a tin box on a rickety

table and picked out an old Chinese coin. On the streets of the Bottoms, Chuck and Tomás walked ahead, and Hana stayed with Wayman. They went down a street lined with stands selling fruits, herbs, and other wares. At one of the stalls, Wayman dropped the coin into a small blue-and-white vase, and a teenage girl blanked out as her eyes lost focus. "As you said, I'm not meshed, so this is how I get messages to Ink. Different coins for different meeting places," he explained.

They passed a stall with dried herbs hanging from a beam and jars with pickled vegetables and other un-recognizable things. At another stand piled high with comms, scrolls, and data drives, a boy played xiàngqí with a miniature holopig.

Wayman stopped at a stand stacked with cages holding dogs, cats, bunnies, snakes, and more. A wiry man with leathery skin and slicked-back hair barked, "Get yer pets, jacked or not."

Wayman stopped. "Two rabbits, one meshed and one not."

Hana and Chuck exchanged worried looks. Hana's stomach twisted as the man packed two bunnies in separate cages and bagged some lettuce. She and Chuck each took a cage.

"Which one's the meshed one?" Hana asked Wayman. He didn't answer.

The buildings thinned out, and they took the path Hana

had grown accustomed to, through the forested area, the tangle of underbrush and woods, and into the clearing by the stream where they practiced qigong.

"You asked why I never wanted to be enmeshed?" Wayman arranged the cages on the ground. "I wasn't against tech growing up. I played games and was online as much as anyone, but when the tech for getting enmeshed was developed, I realized it would be a much more dangerous step."

He took one of the bunnies out of its cage and handed it to Chuck, who nuzzled the surprisingly calm bunny.

"You may think qigong is a quaint way to meditate, but using qi underlies many ancient martial arts. Hold the bunny up, please."

Chuck did so.

Hana's mouth went dry. She didn't know what was about to happen, but she didn't like it.

"My grandmother taught me a rare and secret martial art called diǎnxué, which has been called the killing touch," Wayman said.

Hana started. "Are you going to kill it?"

"No. I know how qi flows in a body and pressure points, so I can direct my qi at precisely the right point and temporarily disable an opponent. I learned this from my grandmother, who learned it in China in the 1940s. It's a skill passed only to family members. Let me show you."

Wayman held his pointer and middle finger together and touched the base of the bunny's neck. It went limp like a plasma doll.

Chuck gasped.

"Go ahead and put the bunny back. It'll be fine in a moment." Chuck returned the bunny gently to its cage. Within moments, the bunny twitched, sat up, and munched on a lettuce leaf. "Now watch this." He scooped up the other bunny and offered it to Tomás to hold.

Tomás backed away. "No thanks."

He offered the bunny to Hana, who hesitated, then took it. Cradling the bunny, she tried to think soothing thoughts. It began to squirm, making it a struggle to keep a grip on it.

Wayman did his two-finger thing again. This bunny stiffened and went limp.

"Will it be all right?" The poor thing felt heavier now that it was dead weight.

"Yes," he said. "But it will take longer for it to regain consciousness. Can you guess which bunny is the meshed one?"

Hana cradled the floppy creature. "This one?"

"Yes."

She laid it gently in its cage. "Why the difference?"

"It turns out a person's or animal's qi is not to be toyed with," Wayman explained. "Adding a neural lace to your brain disrupts the flow of the qi and makes you more susceptible to threats like diǎnxué and overstimulates your brain. More generally, subjecting your brain to electromagnetic radiation can result in cancers, yet it's the basis of the wireless interface of being enmeshed."

Hana shuddered.

"That's why I don't get enmeshed," Wayman said. "If you want to master qigong, it's not compatible."

Tomás had backed away after the demo with the second bunny, his face a greenish tinge.

Chuck went to him. "Are you okay?"

He nodded, but his shallow panting made it clear that was a lie.

Hana saw Wayman with new eyes. All that breathing was fine, but this killing touch—or temporary disabling touch—was the stuff of wushu movies.

"That was so cool," Chuck said.

"If you're done standing around making bunnies faint," interrupted a new voice, "what did you need me for?"

Ink leaned against a tree. Hana had been so transfixed with the bunny demo, she hadn't heard her arrive.

"Ah, Ink." Wayman waved her over.

Ink glanced at Tomás and smirked. He gave her a wary look.

"That's Tomás," Wayman said.

"We're old friends." Ink winked at Tomás, who refused to meet her eyes.

"Can you decode this?" Wayman handed Ink the scroll

with the vid files Hana had gotten from Ma's flick drive.

Ink sat down on the flat rock, and the others gathered around. "Huh." She zoned out. After a moment, Ink smiled triumphantly and returned the scroll to Wayman. "Voilà."

Wayman snapped open the scroll to its fixed-screen position and tapped it to hit play. "Let's take a look." A small holographic vid sprang up from the thin screen.

A man Hana didn't recognize was giving a presentation. "These are the mice trials that show the practical application of the combination of *Ophiocordyceps* and *Toxoplasma gondii.*"

Two identical mazes were set up side by side. In one maze, four mice meandered through the corridors. One managed to find the food in the center, while the three others ran into walls that zapped them, causing them to scurry away. "This maze," the man said, "is our control. These unaltered mice are trained to find food using the usual positive and negative stimuli." Hana winced as a mouse squeaked at another wrong turn.

"In the other maze," the man said, "we gave the mice a special serum that contains elements of both the *Ophiocordyceps* and the *Toxoplasma gondii.* Then we enmeshed them to the multiweb. Take a look."

The four Mice wandered into the second maze. At first, they acted like the other ones. Some got zapped. But when one of the Mice found the food in the center, it froze and so did the others. Within moments, the other three Mice darted along the path taken by the first Mouse and joined it at the food. The one in the center had told the others through its brain waves how to find the food.

"It gets better." The man scooped up three of the Mice and replaced them with different ones. "I'm adding three other enmeshed Mice that have been given the serum and that have never run this maze." When he dropped those Mice in, the original one scampered over to them. The four Mice huddled together, then all scurried to the food, following the path of the original Mouse.

"As you can see, we've developed the perfect baseline mental state for our Super Brain Network project. We've lowered their defenses and fear responses, made them more susceptible, and when they're enmeshed, they are able to think and communicate as one organism."

A voice off-screen asked, "How safe is this process?"

"Very safe," the man answered. "We're ready for human trials."

The vid cut out.

Chuck's face was drained of color. "Do you think the pill they gave me, Christa, the twins, and others is this parasite and fungus mix? And they're trying to control our brains?"

Hana tightened her grip on Chuck's hand. "Maybe."

"We're the human trials," Chuck said.

Wayman snapped the scroll shut. "You kids should

go home now. My team can take it from here. I have a lab where we've been working on the problem." His gaze landed on Chuck. "Except you. If I can get a sample of your blood, we can find out exactly what they're doing, and I can work on a way to reverse the effects."

Hana bristled. Wayman was trying to pawn her off again. She took Chuck aside and whispered, "We're not leaving it all up to Wayman. I promise. We'll keep working to find out what's happening and fix it."

Chuck gave her a fierce hug.

The sounds of rustling leaves and cracking branches interrupted them.

A man and a woman in corporate security suits stood with their weapons at their side. The JingZa had found them.

32

"Identify yourselves!" the woman said. "Hold your hands where we can see them."

Hana's chest tightened. Her sight narrowed into tunnel vision and her heart hammered. The woman and the man next to her were typical Corporate security, boosted for strength and clad in exoskeleton armor suits. The woman's red curly hair poked out of her helmet.

They pointed their millimeter wave guns casually to the ground, as if reminding them they could stun anyone if they felt like it. Hana gulped. How had the JingZa tracked them? Now they would be taken in by security and held until their fines were paid. If Ma didn't have enough money, Hana would be trapped in the sweatshops like that kid Guille, and her mother would probably lose her job too.

Hana let the scroll she was holding drop to her feet, covering it with her boot as she held up her hands.

Tomás, Chuck, and Wayman raised their arms too.

Somehow, in the commotion, Ink had slipped away. Hana tried not to look in the direction she'd last seen her.

"What an interesting assortment of folks." The woman spoke as if chewing gum. "Let's ID them."

She was small, like Ms. Malhotra, and equally ripped. The woman walked over to Chuck and looked into her eyes to scan her iris.

When she approached Tomás to get his info, he partially stifled a sneeze. The woman wrinkled her nose in disgust. She tapped the side of her head. "Brenner," she snapped to the man, who had his hair tied in a thick braid down his back. "ID this kid, my software isn't working."

The man came over and scanned Tomás's eyes.

The woman moved onto Hana. Her gray-blue eyes flashed as they captured Hana's iris pattern.

The woman approached Wayman, who stood calmly before her.

Hana wished he would break out his killing touch and save them from I Ching's facilities or sweatshops. Hana could imagine it—a quick jab here and there, and *whomp, whomp,* two security officers down, in the space of a few heartbeats.

The woman scanned him and frowned. "An unregistered and unmeshed male subject. We're taking you into custody."

"It's not illegal to picnic in the forest," Wayman said. "We have a right to be told why we are being taken in."

She said impassively, "When Start-Up students are

placed on probation, we enhance tracking of their wrist-bands."

Hana clenched her jaw. She was right to have been worried.

The woman removed wristbands from a side pocket and dangled them. "Imagine our surprise when we found these over by the Dump. Evading geotagging is a Class One Corporate violation."

Hana didn't know what a Class One Corporate viola-tion was, but it sounded bad. She didn't want to get taken into custody by the JingZa and disappear.

The woman glared at Wayman. "Plus, insufficient data and/or failure to identify a citizen requires further inves-tigation." She waved her gun at them. "Let's go."

Hana's mouth went dry, and her legs felt like limp noodles. She had to keep it together and hide the scroll under her boot. "Excuse me, may we let the bunnies go free?"

The woman sneered at the bunnies munching on let-tuce leaves and rolled her eyes. "Be quick about it."

When Hana bent down to the cage, she palmed the scroll she'd been stepping on and tucked it into one of her boots. She opened the cage and shooed the bunny out. Chuck let the other one go. Hana envied them as they scampered away.

They had no choice but to follow the officers out of the

clearing. At least Ink had gotten away. Hana had never been in this kind of trouble before. Chuck walked with a slump, and Tomás trudged along, rubbing his temple.

The woman, who introduced herself as Officer Boyd, herded them onto a hovercruiser. It was a typical police flyer, with a driver's seat up front and bench seats along the sides in the open back.

They piled in. Tomás and Wayman sat on one bench, and Chuck and Hana faced them on the other. As the cruiser took off on autopilot, Officer Boyd swiveled the driver's seat to survey the group. The other officer sat next to Hana.

"Where are we going?" Hana tried to tamp down her rising panic but couldn't stop her voice from quivering.

Officer Boyd gave her a disdainful look. "The I Ching detention facilities."

Officer Braided Hair clamped the Start-Up wristbands back on them. He waved a small penlight over the bands, and the polymer melded into a seamless whole.

Officer Boyd cast them a bored look. "Your parents will be notified of your detention."

Hana's stomach sank into a black hole of despair. If Ma was involved, she'd rescue them, but then Hana would have to confront the reality that Ma was part of the conspiracy. If Ma didn't know, then Ma would be in deep trouble. Chuck gripped Hana's arm hard. Tomás, sitting across from them, on the other hand, seemed oddly calm, like he was zoned out.

The interior lights flickered, and a high-pitched warning chime rang out. The hovercruiser jolted one way and careened hard the other. Chuck and Hana spilled to the floor, landing at Tomás's and Wayman's feet.

Chuck yelped.

Hana stumbled as she tried to right herself. The cruiser continued its out-of-control ride, jostling them wildly. "What's going on?" Hana yelled, her stomach in her throat. Autopilots rarely malfunctioned.

Officer Boyd had almost fallen off the seat but pulled herself back up to take over the autopilot. Her fingers flew across the dashboard, a blur of tapping to regain control.

While the cruiser rocked up and down, Wayman moved with incredible speed.

He jabbed his fingers into the neck of Officer Braided Hair.

The diănxué move.

The man fell back in a slump.

As the flyer bucked, Officer Boyd tapped frantically on the dashboard, unaware her partner was down. The ride smoothed out, and Wayman lunged to the officer and repeated the diănxué move on her.

Jab. She slumped to the side.

The cruiser lurched and went haywire as soon as Officer Boyd stopped driving it. They zoomed to the ground below. The forest flew up at them.

"We're going to die!" Chuck yelled.

"I don't want to die!" Hana said. Her insides jostled around. She pulled herself back to her seat, and her knuckles paled from her death grip on the seat cushion.

"We're not going to die," Tomás muttered. He clawed his way to the driver's seat. "I got this." He stepped over Officer Boyd and sat down. His fingers danced across the console.

Wayman helped them back to their seats. Hana clung to the cushion until her muscles ached.

A moment before the cruiser crash-landed in the forest, it righted itself and pulled up. They rocked in a sickening way but leveled out. After skimming the treetops, Tomás slowed the cruiser and brought them through an opening in the canopy and landed the cruiser in a small clearing.

With a *thud* and a *hiss*, the cruiser settled down to stunned silence in the cabin.

33

Hana stared dully at Tomás.

He knew how to fly a cruiser. Cruisers didn't even unlock for people until they were sixteen, and he didn't have any glasses on, so he couldn't have hacked it. Hana added this to her mental list of the many unexplained things about Tomás she'd have to think about when she wasn't recovering from almost crash-landing.

Wayman leaned over the officers' slumped figures. "Help me tie them up." He took out a small knife and sawed at the hem of his shirt and tore a strip off.

Hana swallowed hard. Up until now, she hadn't done anything too illegal. Hiding her wristband was something she might've talked her way out of, but helping Wayman tie up an officer was much more serious. But she could be accused of taking part in knocking the officers out. And what I Ching and her mom might be doing was also serious.

Hands shaking, she held Officer Boyd's wrists in place while Wayman wound the strip in a figure eight and finished it with a complicated knot. Then Wayman tied up the other officer.

Tomás sat at the driver's seat, staring at the console.

Wayman moved. "We need to leave. Others are sure to come soon." He jumped lightly out of the open hatch.

With a parting look at the officers, Hana hopped out. She helped Chuck off the cruiser, and Tomás followed.

A high canopy of trees towered above. Hana didn't know where they were, except she could see City Center to the south. "This way." Wayman led them through an opening in the trees. They broke into a run.

Chuck stumbled, and Tomás caught her. They followed Wayman, their feet crashing through the underbrush.

Ten minutes later, they panted at the edge of the woods next to a road. "We need to lie low for the next few days," Wayman said. "Come back to my lab, which is under my home. I can work on an antidote, and you'll be offline for a few days. I have no tech in my home that can track us, and the Bottoms is free of corporate spyware." He pointed down the road. "There's a maglev station that way."

Hana frowned. Wayman had disabled two guards with his wild diǎnxué move. Even though she'd been learning qigong from him for the past couple of weeks, what kind of person was he really? She wasn't sure she could trust him.

But she couldn't go home either. I Ching would surely track them with the wristbands. At the very least, they had to get away from here. Hana's heart sped up. She didn't want to get caught again. They were now on I Ching's radar, but if she could get to the Bottoms, she'd be out of reach of their monitoring.

"What do you think?" Chuck said.

"We have to do something," Hana said. "Start-Up gave you something in that pill that's making you, and half the class, sick." Hana added under her breath, "I need to talk to my mom. We should go to Ink's place. She can hide us, and her tech can help." She felt safer with Ink than with Wayman, and they'd still be out of I Ching's reach.

Chuck nodded. "I'll help Wayman with my blood so he can make an antidote."

Tomás remained quiet, frowning.

Hana held her wrist out. "We need to get these off so they can't track us."

Wayman studied each of them. "Are you sure you want to do this?" He flicked open a blade.

Hana paused. Once he cut off her wristband, there was no going back. Ma and Start-Up would know she was involved with the Ghost Crab Nation. They'd look for her. She wouldn't be able to go back home until she figured out how to fix everything.

Deep breath. "Yes." She held out her wrist and let Wayman cut the wristband off with a quick flick. He did the same for Chuck and Tomás.

It was done.

"Aren't we going to get caught on the trains? How will we get past the iris scans?" Chuck said.

Wayman dug into his pockets and pulled out a small case. "Put on these contact lenses. They'll distract the iris scans with fake IDs. I'll make my way back to the Bottoms separately so we don't attract attention." He handed a thin film with colored orbs to each of them.

Chuck leaned heavily on Tomás now.

"We need to go," he said in a low voice.

Hana nodded and they took off.

The three ran down the path toward the elevated tracks and train stop ahead. Chuck lagged behind, but Tomás and Hana helped her along. They took the steps two at a time to reach the platform, both helping Chuck up the stairs.

The hovering sign told them the next train was forty-five seconds away. I Ching might be after them already. Ditching their wristbands had probably raised an alarm, and the police cruiser crash could've notified the Corporation. Luckily, the platform was crowded.

Hana glanced down to the road below the elevated platform. She gasped.

In the distance, Officer Boyd and her sidekick zoomed toward them on their extra-powered legs. They must've gotten loose with their strength boosts.

"They got free!" she yelled. The three pushed their way to the front of the platform.

Thirty seconds until the train came.

The officers gained quickly, speeding up and covering about a third of the way to the station.

The floor lights blinked. A soft chime announced the incoming train.

Fifteen seconds.

The officers were two-thirds of the way there.

Hana and her friends were about to be caught.

34

*T*he train pulled in and hissed to a stop.

The officers reached the bottom of the platform.

The three hustled and pushed their way through the crowded car.

The officers bounded up the stairs.

Close, doors. Close. Hana had never willed anything more fiercely.

The doors dinged shut as the officers reached the train. Hana ducked behind a large man, catching a glimpse of Officer Boyd as they pulled away.

They snaked their way to the front of the car and huddled around a handhold.

"So we're going to Ink's place?" Chuck asked, panting.

Hana's heart didn't seem to know to stop drumming. "Yes. The Bottoms is not monitored, and she has tech that can help us."

"She disappeared when the JingZa showed up," Tomás grumbled. "Kinda convenient. How do you know you can trust her?"

Hana frowned. Ink and Tomás seemed to dislike each other for no good reason. What did each know about the other? Hana narrowed her eyes. "What's going on with you? How did you know how to fly the cruiser, and what do you have against Ink?"

Tomás scowled. "It doesn't matter. I'm not going with you."

"How come?" Chuck asked.

Tomás shifted and looked away. "My dad has a safe house where I can keep hidden from the JingZa."

"But what if your dad is involved with the plot, like my mom might be?" Hana said.

A pained look flitted across his eyes. "You worry about your mom, and I'll worry about my dad." He pushed his way through one of the doors and moved to the next train car.

As he disappeared into the crowded car, a pang shot through Hana. She thought they had gotten over being prickly with each other, but now he'd abandoned them while they were on the run, and she was no longer sure of his loyalties. She'd thought they were on the same side, but his unexplained skills and secrets worried her.

The train glided into the junkyard stop.

"Let's go." She and Chuck pushed their way out and hurried to get to Ink's place. Even though the Bottoms was a wild space not monitored by the Corporations, the sooner they got off the streets, the better.

Under gathering gray clouds, Hana and Chuck stood outside Ink's shack and its padlocked door. After all this, Ink wasn't around. Maybe Tomás was right, and she'd gone into hiding. Hana grabbed the lock and tugged, but no luck. She raised her fist to knock.

A noise roared beside them, and Ink brought an old motorcycle to a halt, grinning. "Hey, kiddos. What's up?"

Hana wanted to rush over and hug Ink but stopped herself. "You're safe!"

"Looks like you did all right too." Ink swung herself off her ride and wheeled it to the side of her shack, pushing it out of sight among some bushes.

"Wayman did all right," Chuck said. "You should have seen him take out the I Ching guards."

"I can imagine." Ink unlocked the door and shoved it open. They stepped into the cramped, jumbled space, and Ink cleared stuff off the kitchen chairs. "What's up?"

Inside, a great weight lifted from her. Ink's jacker hacker lair was safe from prying Corporate monitors. Hana explained how they'd escaped from the JingZa. "And now we need to stay off the radar." Her eyes pleaded with Ink's icy ones. "Can we stay here?"

Ink considered her for a moment. "Not much room, but sure. You and Chuck can sleep there." She pointed to her mattress. "I'll take the jelly chair. You have to lie low, though."

Hana sagged with relief. "Thank you."

"Yeah, whatever. Not sure how I ended up being a baby-sitter."

Hana sank down into one of the chairs and pulled out her comm. Then she remembered it could be tracked. "Can I borrow your glasses again?"

Ink handed her the jury-rigged glasses and earbuds she'd used earlier, and Hana dialed Lin. After a moment, Lin's holo appeared.

"Where are you?" Lin demanded. "Ma's going ballistic."

Hana gulped. Ma must've been notified about her being caught, and probably the escape too. Hana needed her sister's help. "Can we meet somewhere to talk?"

"You need to come home," Lin said.

"I can't." Hana had to stay off the maglev trains and away from plugged-in places, and she couldn't risk bringing Lin to Ink's place, but there was one place she could meet Lin and still stay offline. "Can you meet me at the historical mall?" Hana said. "I have something important to tell you."

Lin grimaced. "I can meet you at the Waldenbooks in half an hour, but you better have a good explanation."

"I will, I promise." Logging out, Hana turned to Ink. "Can I ask another favor?"

Ink looked up from the jelly chair.

"I need to get to the historical mall, but I can't risk the maglev train again." Even though she had the contacts to change her irises, the stations and trains all had cameras. "Can you take me on your motorcycle?"

Ink gave her a bemused smile. "This is your idea of lying low? Fine." She rummaged through a box and came up with an old helmet, tossing it to Hana. "Put this on."

"Chuck, will you be all right?" Hana asked.

Chuck had lain down and now stirred. "Yeah, I'm going to take a nap."

Five minutes later, Hana sat behind Ink on the motorcycle, her arms clamped around Ink's waist and her helmet snug on her head, though Ink seemed not to care about protecting her own head. Bumping along the rutted streets was unsettling, a far cry from the smooth rides of hovercars and maglev trains.

Ink ignored any speed limits or even the suggestions of roads as they zoomed in and out of the crowded streets, leaning dangerously with every turn. The roads were rough, neglected ever since maglev trains and hovercraft became widespread. Riding through the Bottoms reminded Hana once again how out of touch she was.

At the mall, Ink said, "I'll wait for you out here."

"You don't want to come in?"

"Nah, I don't like being in that fake space."

Hana hurried into the mall and rode the escalator up to the Waldenbooks.

Lin looked up from browsing the magazine rack. "Hana, what did you do?"

"It's hard to explain."

"Try."

Hana steered her sister out of the store, and they walked along the upper level. It was time to let Lin know about what she'd learned. "Remember when I told you about the girl I met at the junkyard?"

"Yes," Lin said slowly.

Hana explained how she also met Wayman and discovered the Start-Up students were given pills with the modified DNA and saw the tests showing the effects on the Mice. At Lin's increasingly worried expression, Hana left out the part about the cruiser chase and the security guards. "And now Start-Up is meshing some of the students by the end of the summer. It all feels connected, and Ma seems to be involved."

Lin frowned. "Are you sure about this?"

"Too many things have been weird at Start-Up. Wayman thinks it's all connected."

"Why are you paying attention to an old man you met in the woods? I'm sure there's an explanation. Come home and let's talk to Ma together."

Hana rubbed the empty spot where her wristband had been. "I can't go home now. I'm staying with my friend Ink, and I'm okay, I promise. But I do want to talk to Ma. Do you know her schedule tomorrow?"

"Yes," Lin said. "She'll be at the lab, but said she's busy at ten o'clock."

They walked by some stores with funny names like Afterthoughts and Babbage's. "I can't go in person, so can you send me a holo link to the lab?" Hana said.

Lin gave her a long look. "I'll send you the link only because I want you to talk to Ma and sort things out with her."

"Thanks." Hana ran her hands through her hair. "Tell Ma I'm okay, but please don't tell her you saw me in person."

"Contrary to popular belief, I don't hate you, Hana." Lin furrowed her brows. "I can't believe Ma would be a part of this." She paused. "You're stronger than me in a lot of ways, not going along with what's easy. I'll cover for you, and help you holo into the lab so you and Ma can talk."

Hana hugged her. "Thank you." A few pieces of her heart clicked into place. Lin may not have agreed with her, but when it counted, she was there for Hana.

That night, lying on Ink's mattress next to Chuck and staring up at the corrugated tin roof, a message beeped onto her comm.

> **Ms. Hsu:** Report to a meeting with Headmaster Zed tomorrow at eleven a.m. to discuss irregularities with your wristband data. Your teammates Charlene Cohen and Tomás Ortiz have also been asked to join.

Hana groaned. There was no way they could show up at school. If they did, the school would probably turn them over to I Ching. She poked Chuck. "Did you see the message from Zed?"

A groggy Chuck shifted. "Mmm. I'm having this great dream about swimming with dolphins. Do you really have to interrupt?"

"Yes. We're in hiding. What do we do?"

"Nothing." Chuck burrowed into her pillow and returned to her soft snoring.

Hana rubbed her temples. She tried to call Tomás. No answer.

Her mind skittered.

Chuck and half the Start-Up class were targeted for experiments. The MDD drink helped their performance and made them feel better outside the games, but Chuck and the others who'd gotten the nano pills were getting sick.

Wayman and his team might be dangerous too. The chrysanthemum tea made her challenges more difficult. And thinking of Wayman's diǎnxué moves gave her goose bumps. His actions against the JingZa could get them into huge trouble if they were caught.

And Tomás wasn't returning her calls. She needed answers about what he knew about his dad.

As she drifted off in exhaustion, her thoughts became disorganized, flighty. Bird bots and cyber bees jostled with amusement parks, historical malls, and bunnies hopping to freedom.

35

6.30.2053. *Xenobots Created for Environmental Cleanup Evolving.* The tiny machines made of organic materials known as "living machines" created to eat hazardous chemical waste have evolved, scientists say. Now these xenobots have taken a liking to the cellulose of major crops like cotton and flax. **>>> Crowdsource News Network**

Hana woke to clattering kitchen sounds. She opened her eyes, disoriented, until she remembered where she was. Ink stomped around the shack making coffee and xīfàn.

"Morning, sleepyhead." Ink waved the chopsticks she'd used to scoop the runny rice from the rice cooker.

Hana rubbed the sleep out of her eyes. They were safe from the JingZa for now, but she needed to get ahold of Ma and find out exactly what was going on. She had to stay holed up at Ink's, but she could reach out virtually with the link Lin had sent her. "Can you help me hook into I Ching's offices at nine thirty? I need to talk to my mom."

Ink nodded. "Sure."

A half hour later, Chuck stirred. She tried to sit up, groaned, and flopped back down. "I feel awful."

Chuck looked awful. Hana felt her clammy forehead. "We need to get you to Wayman's so he can start working on the antidote. Whatever's happening is getting worse."

"It's probably because I haven't had any MDD since I was last at school," Chuck said weakly. "I need to let my parents know I'm okay. I can't have them worrying about me."

"Just don't tell them where you are," Hana said.

Ink helped Chuck to her feet. "I'll take you to Wayman's." Ink tossed Hana a gray washcloth. "Do the dishes. When I come back, I'll hook you in to meet your ma."

Hana gave Chuck a brief squeeze. "I'll see you soon." She hoped Chuck would get to Wayman before she got worse.

When Ink came back, she tossed Hana the VR glasses, earbuds, and gloves, and sat in her jelly chair. "I'll join you on the inside."

Hana put on the gear and dropped in.

───────

They appeared at Ink's beach. Ghost crabs scuttled away under clouds hanging heavy and gray. Hana wondered whether the weather reflected Ink's mood or the outside conditions.

"Send me the address. We're gonna get into their system on the dark side," Ink said.

"What if they catch us?"

Ink shrugged. "Hacking and counter-hacking is part of the game. You can never stay still and think you're safe, but I keep up."

Hana had to trust Ink. "If I want to talk to my mom, can I?" She would confront Ma and find out exactly what she knew about the experiments on her Start-Up friends.

"Yes. When you want to become visible or heard, let me know. Here we go."

The beach scene slid away like melted taffy, colors and objects stretched out of shape. For a moment, the two hung in a dark void.

Their surroundings sharpened into the I Ching lab. Lin paced outside the closed door to the inner part of the lab, looking frustrated.

"She can't see or hear us?" Hana whispered.

"Nah. We're ghosts," Ink replied.

"How does this work?" Hana moved closer to Lin. Ink grabbed her arm.

"Remember you're in my house in the Bottoms. Stay close unless you want to trip over something sharp and unpleasant," Ink said. "We're tied into the same system the holoworkers use."

"Show me to my sister."

Ink did his thing and Hana flickered into holographic form next to Lin.

Lin jumped. "Yikes. Give me some warning next time, will you?"

"Sorry." Hana felt like she had to whisper, even though she knew only Lin could see and hear her.

"I didn't get a chance to talk to Ma. She was already in a meeting when I got here." Lin looked at Ink, wide-eyed. "You're Ink?"

Ink nodded. "Hold on. Let me connect with you. This will let you stream what I see, while you stay out here." He leaned close, gazed into Lin's eyes, and nodded. "You're linked. Let's go in."

The wall to the room dissolved and Hana and Ink appeared inside Ma's office.

Hana almost fainted. Ma, her grad student Julien, and Primo Zed, of all people, huddled around a desk screen. They completely ignored Ink and Hana standing a few feet from them. Hana edged closer, careful not to trip over anything on the outside, in Ink's messy shack.

"I need to put together a report for our superiors," Primo Zed said. "Tell me where we are on the experiment." Hana was shocked by his hardened expression, so different from when he would come over for dinners.

"We've been reviewing the Mice trial data, and it's gratifying to see the brain-to-brain network working so well," Ma said. "And I have the data you've been giving me for the student subjects receiving the gene therapy."

Hana felt prickly and hot all over. Ma was truly in it deep. She'd hoped Ma wasn't involved and that Pedro was the mastermind, but here she was, acting like an evil scientist in cahoots with Primo Zed.

"It's working as planned." Julien expanded a floating screen that hovered in the air between them, showing charts and numbers and vids of Chuck, Christa, the twins, and other kids scaling the mountain and passing their tests easily. "As you know, we targeted students who were drawn to the wall games on the first day of school, because they are the most addicted to the virtual world. Their minds are more likely to be successfully meshed and influenced by our gene therapy. We also picked some students who didn't choose the wall games to compare results."

Chuck had been right. Start-Up had watched them from the first day.

"For this experimental group," Julien continued, "we gave them modified versions of *Ophiocordyceps* and *Toxoplasma* genes using a virus vector to lead to the brain's ventricles. The speed protocol accelerated the process. The children who received this gene therapy are able to link more quickly together—perfect for the brain-to-brain network project."

"Get to the point," Primo said impatiently.

"We wanted to see whether the Start-Up students who got the gene therapy would be the ones who ended up in the top half of the class," Ma said. "Our hypothesis was this group would do better with the boosts."

"Is that the case, and are we ready to roll this out to the whole class?" Primo asked.

Ink, who'd been wandering around the office peering at knickknacks, paused and looked up.

Ma gave Julien a sideways glance and nodded. "We need to continue to review the safety data that you send us each week," Ma answered. "If the test group continues to respond well, we can roll out the gene therapy to all of the students by the end of July. And if that works out, we can go nationwide."

Hana's blood went cold. It didn't matter if they were in the top or bottom half of Start-Up; it was a ruse to get all of them drugged up. To make things worse, Ma appeared to be leading this effort.

An urgent message from Lin came into view. *Security is here!*

The door opened and a JingZa guard burst in. Lin followed behind.

"Lin, what's the meaning of this?" Ma demanded.

"There's been a breach in the holoware interface," the guard said. He pointed to Hana and Ink with a clicker.

The air shimmered like a mirage.

Ma, Primo, and Julien stared at Ink and Hana as they became visible to those in the room.

They were caught.

36

"**W**elp," Ink said. "Time to get outta here."

But it was too late.

The officer shot some sort of beam that pinned them in place. Ink's avatar shimmered and froze.

Hana couldn't move either. She had to get out of here, kuài. She tried to toggle her tabs to leave.

Nothing.

Her field of vision was stuck. She tried to use her arms outside the VR to tear off her glasses.

Her heart sped up. It didn't work. The guard had some-how immobilized her on the outside too. She could be having a heart attack. She was so going to kill Ink if she got out of here alive. So much for Ink's super-secret hacking tech that was in fact A Massive Failure.

"Hana! What are you doing here? Who is this person?" Ma demanded. She turned to the I Ching guard. "Let her talk."

The JingZa pointed his clicker at her. Hana didn't feel different, except now she could move around, though her controls to the multiweb were still disabled.

"Ma! How could you be involved in this experiment?" Hana said.

Ma's face blanched, but she recovered quickly and turned to Primo Zed. "Give me a few minutes to talk to Hana."

Zed gave her an impatient look. "You have fifteen minutes. I'm only letting you do this because of our long history and friendship." He and Julien left the room, followed by the guard. Ma, Hana, and Lin remained, with Ink frozen in the corner.

Ma rushed over to Hana. "You shouldn't be here." She tried to take Hana's arm, but her hand went through Hana's hologram. "What kind of program is this?"

"I gave her the address," Lin said defiantly.

"I don't understand," Hana said. "Why are you doing this to the Start-Up kids? Why are you turning us into zombies?" How could Ma's face be so full of concern even though she was capable of this?

Ma's eyes darted to the door where Primo had left. "There's much to explain. We don't have time."

Hana crossed her arms and glared laser beams. "We have fifteen minutes."

"It's hard to explain to someone who's not enmeshed, but here's the thing," Ma said. "When you're connected to the multiweb, you are changed fundamentally as a person. It took me a long time to learn this."

"What do you mean?" Hana spat out.

"Before you're enmeshed, you're one mind, in your own body, thinking your own thoughts. You try to learn things and do good, but you're basically small and powerless. You're a victim of your emotions." Ma's face grew determined. "When you're neurally connected to the multiweb, you have access to all the info humanity has ever learned. The filter that used to be your brain becomes less of a barrier."

Hana frowned. She liked the filter that was her brain. "What does that have to do with the fungi and parasites you're infecting my friends with?"

"Are you really doing that?" Lin interjected.

Ma spared Lin a glance. "We developed a protocol where we can link human minds together. It's called the Super Brain Network. We will have so much more human computing power to deal with the serious problems we face, like climate change, species extinction, famine, war, and the need to find a backup planet."

Hana's mind spun. "But what about AI? Can't the smartest computers help? And why the parasite and fungus?"

"The problem with linking minds is that it's hard to deal with all the idiosyncrasies, emotions, and psychological baggage people come with." Ma rubbed her temples. "So we found a way to soothe people's minds and make it easier for them to link together."

"Messing with kids' brains using a zombie ant fungus

and a cat brain parasite would do that?" Hana couldn't help raising her voice. "You're taking away people's free will so they can get smarter and think better?"

"We're not taking away free will. We're smoothing out the quirks that make it difficult to connect with each other. This helps people communicate and work together without the friction." Ma paced in the small space. "We don't have a choice. Humanity's existence is in danger."

"What do you mean?" Lin asked.

"It's what it sounds like. Our planet's ecosystem is in collapse. If we don't solve these fundamental problems, humans will die out. We need to do what is necessary to save our species. We can't let people's emotions and psychological problems be the cause of our extinction."

Hana shook her head. "You'd experiment on people without their knowledge and let my friends get hurt. Saving the world is more important than them?" She could hear her own voice cracking. "Than me?"

"I'm saving the world to save you. I'm doing everything to ensure the safety of you and your friends."

The conversation with Popo in the workshop popped into Hana's mind. "What about the precautionary principle?"

Ma sucked in her breath. "You've been talking to your grandma."

"She has a point. Shouldn't we be more careful when it

comes to people—kids?" Hana said. "Look at all the kids at Start-Up who've gotten so sick."

"Sick? The students aren't sick. Primo Zed sends me reports every week and the students are doing fine."

"They're not. My friend Chuck can barely stand up, Christa fainted, and the other kids who got the pills are always exhausted. It's not right."

Ma frowned and her gaze blanked out, as if reading through a report. "What you're saying is not lining up with the data I have. It would be concerning, if true. But I trust Primo. He's been my best friend for years, and we've always had the same goals and values. He's never given me a reason to doubt him."

"Ma, I'm telling the truth! Please check it out," Hana said. "Primo is lying to you. You have to believe me."

Ma rubbed her temples. "Tell you what, I'll dig into the safety data. Also, why don't you come work with me as an intern after school beginning in the fall? I'll show you what I've been working on, and you can decide for yourself what you think about it. It's more complex than you believe. I know you want to work on Popo's memory. We can carve out some research for that."

Hana glanced over at Lin and Ma. After all this time being on the outside, Ma was offering everything Hana wanted—being close to Lin and Ma and working on real science to heal Popo. Ma had also promised to investigate the safety data. Her mind was a jumble and her heart skittered.

"We're out of time. Hana. Let's talk more later. Please know I wouldn't do this to the Start-Up kids—to you—if I wasn't convinced it was safe."

The JingZa guard and Primo Zed reappeared.

"Let her go. Hana doesn't know anything," Ma said. "I'll bring her back in if we need to."

Primo Zed gave a curt nod but pointed to Ink. "Let's keep him to find out how he hacked into the system and who he's working with."

The officer brought up his clicker and pointed it at Hana.

The I Ching office scene melted sideways as Hana's avatar stretched and frazzled and was booted out of Ma's office.

37

*H*ana fell onto her butt on Ink's bedding. Her mind reeled. Ma had protected her from the JingZa for now, but Ink was still trapped.

Ink sat in her jelly chair, immobilized. Hana rushed over. She had to get her offline as quickly as possible to help her, and to prevent I Ching from tracing her link to the Bottoms. She wouldn't escape so easily if she got caught again. Hana hauled Ink from the chair. Ink slumped on top of her, and Hana buckled under her weight.

She dragged Ink's dead weight onto her mattress and shook her as hard as she dared. "Ink! Wake up!"

Ink was breathing but had a blank, unfocused stare. Waving a hand in front of her face did nothing. Hana shook Ink's shoulder again. Nothing.

Hana couldn't leave her. Only one other place in the Bottoms came to mind. She swiped an extra set of glasses and wedged herself under Ink.

"Ungghh," Ink muttered.

"You're awake! Come on, I need to take you to Way-man's."

Ink's eyes fluttered and her head lolled. She was still mostly out of it. Hana heaved them both to standing and staggered to the door. She glanced at the spot where Ink's motorcycle was hidden, but she didn't know how to drive it. Luckily, Ink supported her own weight, and Hana was able to walk with her awkwardly draped over her shoulders.

Outside, the skies had darkened to a deep gray and the rain poured. A summer squall was blowing through the nearly empty streets.

Hana gritted her teeth and dragged Ink down the street, refusing to think about her conversation with Ma. One thing at a time.

The rain gushed down, quickly soaking them.

⟍⟍⟋⟋⟍⟍⟋⟋

It was a good thing Wayman didn't live too far, because Hana was exhausted after a couple of blocks. At his house, she knocked frantically. After a brief pause, Chuck answered the door. Wayman ushered them in. Chuck helped Hana crab-walk Ink to the couch, where Hana fell into a heap next to Ink. "We got caught at I Ching's holo-office, and somehow they captured Ink mentally."

"Slow down," Wayman said. "Chuck, please hand me some towels. What happened?"

Hana gave the one-minute recap. "Can you help her?"

Chuck brought over a handful of dish towels, which Hana used to mop herself and pat at Ink's face and hair. Not fully conscious, she seemed softer, without the hard edge.

Wayman wrinkled his brow. "I can break the connection, but I need to do it quickly. They can trace her back here as long as they have her in their grips."

"I'm sorry, I didn't mean to lead them to you," Hana said.

"It's fine." He raised his hand toward Ink's brow.

"What happened? Why were we frozen?"

"You know how your muscles are paralyzed while you're sleeping and dreaming?" Wayman said. "I Ching probably sent a wireless signal to Ink's meshed brain to activate those chemicals, so I will use a small amount of qi to bring her energy back in balance."

"Will it hurt her? What'll happen to her neural mesh?" Hana remembered the bunnies in the woods.

"Don't worry, it's not a diǎnxué move. Could you bring over some tea? She'll need it when she comes to." He hovered his hands about two inches from Ink's brow and held them steady.

At first, nothing happened. Moments later, Ink shivered and blinked. She pushed herself up, her pale eyes darting back and forth. "What did you do to me?"

"I broke the mental grip they had on you." Wayman

offered the tea with its familiar chrysanthemum scent. "Drink this. It will help."

Ink took the cup with unsteady hands. After a sip, she let out a ragged breath. Her eyes lost their focus as she checked her neural connections. Her shoulders relaxed.

"What did they do to you when they had you trapped?" Hana asked.

Ink glared at Hana over the tea. "I dunno what you've gotten yourselves into. It took all my hacked software to resist that Primo Zed guy. I didn't tell him anything." She gave Hana a pitying glance. "That was your ma?"

Wayman's eyes flickered to Hana, and his expression was a strange mix of compassion and sadness.

Ink pushed herself off the couch. "I'm not doing this anymore. I'm outta here."

Hana wanted to grab her arm, but the look in Ink's eyes stopped her. "You heard what they're up to, right? We need your help," Hana said.

Ink strode to the door. "Nope. You're on your own."

"But how do we get back online if we need to? And could they catch us again?"

Ink nodded to Hana's eyepiece and the one lying on the couch. "Keep those. Stay off the Start-Up servers and you'll be fine. I'm done." She stepped out into the pouring rain, slamming the door behind her.

Hana yanked open the door to follow, but Wayman

said, "Let her go. Now, tell me again what happened. This time, slowly and in detail."

Hana considered Wayman warily. He'd roped her into this from the beginning. He might have even set Ink on her at the junkyard on Enmesh Day, but she and Chuck couldn't take on Start-Up on their own. She told Wayman what she'd learned at the I Ching holo-office—the brain-to-brain networking experiment—but left out her confrontation with her mother.

He steepled his fingers and leaned back in his chair. "We need to counteract the gene therapy with our own genetic edits."

"What do you mean?"

"It will be like an antidote. Because their genetic edits are fairly recent, we can either disrupt the replication process or go another route." He drummed his fingers on his chair. "Their gene therapy obviously uses the speed protocol to be able to affect the students so quickly. We'll have to counteract it."

"You can do that?" Chuck asked.

"I did get my PhD in molecular cellular biology and genetics." He swept his arm around the shabby room. "Despite evidence to the contrary, I have a lab and do research in it."

"How do you do research if you're not meshed?" Hana asked.

Wayman grinned. "I'm not a fossil. I have access to

the multiweb like you do. I just don't hardwire it into my brain cells." As if to make his point, Wayman took out an ancient-looking tablet and tapped on it. His look of concentration reminded Hana of Ma's when she was lost in a scientific puzzle.

"I'll contact the scientists in the Ghost Crab Nation network to come virtually to work on the antidote, and we'll all think about how to get it to the students." He rubbed his temple, then looked up as if he'd made a decision. "It's time to show you my lab." He stood up. "Come with me."

ana and Chuck followed Wayman to a narrow hallway that led to a bedroom. It was bare-bones, with a tattered quilt on the bed and a framed photo of a couple and a girl on a rickety nightstand. Wayman led them to a closet door, which slid open at his touch. He shoved aside clothes on the floor to reveal a hatch. "In here." He yanked the door open, and automated lights flicked on to reveal a descending spiral metal staircase.

Hana and Chuck exchanged glances. Going into the underground lair of someone associated with a group she'd never heard of until a few weeks ago probably wasn't the wisest move, but Wayman was the only one who seemed to have answers. She had to trust him.

He made his way down the steps, and Hana followed. Chuck came last, her knuckles white from gripping the handhold and her legs shaking with effort. Hana steadied her as they made their way down.

At the bottom of the steps, to the right was a metal door with an antique handle, and to the left was a tunnel that looked like the ones she'd use to get from the junkyard to the forest. Hana figured it must lead to a second exit.

Wayman fumbled with a key and swung open the metal door, revealing a small but well-lit underground lab about the size of the house upstairs. It was like Ma's lab at I Ching with its machines and lab counters, but more cramped.

"Make yourself comfortable. I'll be back with a bite to eat."

When Wayman left, Hana leaned against the door and sank to the floor. She let out a whoosh of air, the last day and a half of running scared finally catching up. Chuck plopped down next to her. Glancing at Chuck's pale face, she let loose a bark of laughter.

Chuck gave her a *what is going on with you* look.

Like a stranded seal, more laughter burst out. Hana's own mother was behind a conspiracy to brainwash the next class of meshed kids. She giggled uncontrollably. "It's too much."

Pretty soon, Chuck joined in the laughter.

Tears rolled down Hana's cheeks—and she began to hiccup.

Chuck put her arms around Hana. "I knew when I met you, Start-Up would be interesting, but if I'd known it'd be this interesting, I would've made friends with someone else."

Hana broke down into hiccupy laughs again and buried her face in Chuck's shoulder. After a long moment, Hana asked, "What are we going to do?"

"You mean now that we know your mom and Tomás's

dad are planning to turn us all into freaky zombies?"

"Yeah, that." Hana pushed herself to her feet. "Where is Tomás, anyway? He hasn't replied to any of my messages."

She paced around the lab. Ink had said they could use their glasses without being traced. Hana snapped the glasses on. The names of the equipment and their functions popped up—AUTOCLAVE, CENTRIFUGE, THERMAL CYCLER, NANOPLATE READERS, and more.

A red light in the upper corner of her vision flashed. Her inbox was filled with urgent messages from Ma and Lin. She found a ratty couch, sat down, and opened Ma's vid message. The worry line across Ma's forehead was even more grooved than usual. "Hana. I don't know where you are. I will try to keep I Ching security away from you, but I need you to come home. I'm going to look into what you told me, and we can fix this." Hana trashed the message and set a three-day block on any new messages from Ma. She wanted to believe Ma didn't know anything about the sick kids at Start-Up, but Ma was very thorough and conscientious, and it was hard to imagine she was so clueless.

She opened one from Lin: "Hana, where are you?"

Hana recorded a quick reply. "Keep Ma off my case for a few days. I'm safe and don't want her to worry. I'm working on a plan, and I'll be in touch."

She scrolled through the rest of her unopened messages and paused at the one Lin had sent a few days earlier with the subject *Dad's Old Vids!* What she would give to have Ba here now. None of this would've happened if he were alive. Ma wouldn't have become obsessed with her work, and she wouldn't have flung herself into a plan to change the world by genetically manipulating people, including her own kids.

She needed to see him and hear his voice. Hana clicked on the vid and let it run.

The scene was their home office. Ba sat in his office chair, laughing with his feet out, as Lin spun him around. Lin looked to be about seven and Hana six. Hana reached up the bookshelf behind them and pulled out books, letting them fall to the floor.

"Peanut," Ba said. "Let's treat these books like friends. Would you like it if someone threw you to the ground?"

Seeing Ba in the video, Hana brought a hand to her mouth and tears spilled out. She hadn't heard his voice in a year.

Six-year-old Hana was about to cry too, but Ba scooped her up and gave her a big hug.

"Baba." Lin clamored for their dad's attention while he soothed Hana.

"Walter," Ma's voice said, "remind me why I'm recording on the old vidcorder instead of using my implants?"

Ba grinned at the screen. "Call me paranoid, but I prefer having a backup somewhere outside of your head. Though it's a very beautiful head."

He picked up one of the books from the floor and a paper slipped out. He broke into a delighted smile. "Kids. Look at this photo of when I first met your mom and I visited her dad's lab." Little Hana and Lin gathered around him. "Here's her dad, your grandpa, lost in thought over an experiment, while I'm over here trying to flirt with your mom."

Six-year-old Hana giggled. "You look funny."

Ba tapped little Hana's nose. "That's cuz I didn't need to become handsome until you kids came along." He held out the photograph to the camera. "Sophia, take a look at this."

The camera zoomed in on the image and quickly panned back to Hana, who wiggled out of Ba's lap and ran to the bookshelf.

Hana stopped breathing. She only half noticed the vid continuing, her younger self inches from the camera, mouth coming in with slobbery kisses.

She rewound the vid back to the close-up of the photo and hit pause. She studied the picture of the man hunched over a lab counter.

Her grandpa when he was in his forties or fifties.

It was the same nose, same profile.

The man who supposedly died.

But didn't.

It was Wayman, as a younger man.

Wayman was her grandfather.

39

*H*ana fell back on the couch.

It all made sense now. Wayman was Anwei.

Suddenly, the little things Wayman had said and done made sense. At the woods, he acted weird after hearing her last name. He'd discouraged her from telling Ma about their findings and told her they shouldn't worry her. His strange look when Ink came out of her stupor and pitied Hana. All this time, Wayman knew who she was and hadn't told her. He knew his own daughter, Hana's mom, was involved in the I Ching plot. And he'd used Hana to make her spy on her own mom, turn against her, once again splintering their family.

Most horribly, he'd abandoned Popo and Ma about twenty years ago. Ma had lost her father, like Hana. Hana had no choice when her Ba died, but Wayman had punched a hole in his family on purpose, letting them think he was dead.

He'd made Ma suffer the loss of a dad for no reason.

She dropped her head into her hands.

"What is it?" Chuck said. "Are you all right? Did you see something on your glasses?"

"It's Wayman. He's my dead grandpa."

"He's your dead grandpa?"

"Well, he's not dead." She closed her eyes. "He's my grandpa who we thought was dead. And instead of telling me the truth, he used me to spy on Start-Up." Hana was furious at what he'd done, but most of all, she hated that despite all his lies, he was right about Start-Up.

"Back up." Chuck put her hands on both Hana's shoulders. "I don't understand. Wayman is your grandpa?"

"Yes. I have to talk to him." She yanked the door open and stalked out the small passageway. Chuck followed her as she clanged up the stairs back to Wayman's house and stormed into the common room to see Wayman at the stove, making meatwiches.

"Why?" Hana said softly. She took in his hands, long and thin, like Ma's, and his slight sloping shoulders, like Lin's. "Why did you leave Popo and Ma?"

Wayman's shoulders stiffened. His face fell, and he waited a long moment before he spoke. "I'm sorry. I can explain." He turned to Chuck. "May we have some privacy?"

Chuck took one look at Hana and hustled out of the room.

Hana faced Wayman and reluctantly slid a chair over. She found herself staring at her mom's nose and eyebrows. "You've known all this time," she said.

"Yes."

"It wasn't an accident I met Ink that day?"

"No. I've been watching over Peiwen and the family since we separated." Wayman added, "Peiwen is your pópo's Chinese name."

"But how could you let them think you'd died?" Her voice cracked.

Wayman scratched his head. "It's not what you think. It's hard to explain."

"Try."

"I thought we faced an existential threat when everyone got enmeshed. I had to take a radical step and completely unplug myself."

Really. An existential threat again. It seemed anyone could use the convenient excuse of humanity about to die out to justify whatever messed-up scheme they came up with.

"I truly believed—and still believe—having people plugged directly into the multiweb and being enhanced by AI threatens the very existence of humanity. We are no longer humans. Or we are humans plus something else, and it's not a good thing."

"But why did you leave Popo?" Hana's voice trembled. "Why did you make Ma think she'd lost her father?"

"Society was at the edge of a precipice. We could either fall off and never return or fight it. I chose to fight by joining the AntiTechs. We planned to blast the world back into an unplugged state." Wayman let out a bitter laugh. "I was naive. Sophia—your mom—wanted to be on the leading edge of the tech revolution. She was a true believer in the enmeshed world. Your pópo agreed with me philosophically, but she didn't want to abandon your mom."

"She was okay with you leaving them?"

"Of course not. We stayed in touch for a while." Wayman grew silent. "When the Infotech War heated up, I realized violence and revolution weren't the answer. Meditation, connection with nature, and qigong would be my salvation. I trained with a qigong master."

"And you let Popo and Ma think you'd died?"

Wayman shook his head. He opened his mouth, about to say something, then blinked slowly. "I could see your mother getting enmeshed and falling deeply into the multiweb. If I was to succeed in my project, I had to disconnect from her. Seeing her made it too hard."

"Too hard for you, you mean," Hana spat out.

"I thought I was doing what was best. I would learn to control my mind and qi and planned to share it with others. I moved away and traveled for many years. I went to places in the world untouched by enmeshment, like the Amazon jungle in Brazil and Venezuela.

"When I returned from my travels, I started paying attention to what was happening in the world, how the Corporations consolidated power. As soon as they got direct access to people's minds, their ability to manipulate people through data mining got more dangerous, and privacy became less and less possible. That's when I re-engaged. I restarted my lab. I trained junkyard kids like Ink in qigong and gathered like-minded scientists and activists. I found other people in the Ghost Crab Nation and organized our city's cell.

"We kept up with you and your sister as your Start-Up and Enmesh Days approached. I didn't contact you because too much time had passed. You didn't need a grandfather. But when I met you, I could see what I'd missed.

"I don't expect you to forgive me," Wayman said, "but I would like us to be friends at least."

Hana had nothing to say to this old man.

"How about we get through the next few days and work on counteracting what's happening with the Start-Up kids?" Wayman said.

Hana pushed away from the table and stormed out the door. She wanted nothing to do with him.

40

*T*he rain came pouring down. Hana stumbled through puddles, heedless of the mud splattering up her legs. She tramped through the empty streets, past the shacks and basketball courts. She wasn't worried about getting caught by the JingZa because the Bottoms was offline—there were no cameras or screen walls lining these streets—but she had to get away from Wayman. She needed space to think and rage.

She headed toward Ink's shack, the only other place in the Bottoms that felt safe. When she got there, she pounded on the door. Rainwater dripped down her neck and back, her hair limp and wet against her head.

No one answered.

Hana rounded the corner of the shack to the straggly bushes that normally sheltered Ink's motorcycle. It was gone. She ducked under the canopy to escape the rain and threw herself against the shack's wall and buried her head in her hands. A chill seeped through her, sinking into her bones.

She didn't know who to believe, or who had betrayed her worse.

Both Ma and Wayman thought they were saving humanity with their schemes, Ma with her grand plans to create a superhuman mind network, and Wayman with his fight against changing how humans thought.

Ma believed more connections between brains, and fewer messy emotions, were the answer. Wayman thought connections with nature and mental isolation were the solution.

But both forgot the actual people at the heart of it all. Ma was so concerned with her idea of humanity, she ignored her children. Wayman was so worried about his view, he ignored his family too.

Like father, like daughter.

Hana wanted so much to believe in Ma, to be connected to her, but Ma had changed. Where was the laughing and silly mother who'd made a family full of love with Ba? Lin was fading away too, drawn to Cassie and the multiweb. Hana leaned back. The leaves of the bushes fluttered with the pattering of the rain.

She closed her eyes. Images washed through her mind.

Ba sitting with her curled up in his lap on the sofa as they read together.

Lin lying on her bed with her feet propped on the wall, laughing on her comm.

Chuck jabbing and sparring on the blacktop and doing the same as a warrior in shiny black armor. Chuck's joke about rescuing her from the Tower of her *I Ching* reading.

Tomás and herself racing to the tree trunk, and him standing with her high on top of a snowy world.

Ink, tattooed and full of menace, playing with the world's data streams in the beautiful mind beach and showing them the amusement park from another time.

Popo, always busy with her hands, making dumplings and armadillos.

Ma and Hana, walking with linked arms to the mall. Ma helping Popo to her room and her constant worry over the environment.

Even Wayman, moving patiently by the stream, gathering nature's energy.

Hana sat up. Somehow, without her knowing how, the gaping hole left behind when Ba died had been stitched together with a tentative, colorful web of friends and family. The love he'd nurtured in each of them still seeped through her family, and in turn she'd spread that love to her new friends.

Now she needed her friends and her family to be okay.

She wasn't done being mad at either Ma or Wayman. She didn't fully understand the big picture and who was right, but she did know the immediate danger was to herself and her classmates.

She loved her sister and her mom, and she loved her new friends. She loved every quirky thing about each of them. She couldn't imagine a world where their personalities were smoothed out, their quirks papered over, all so they could be smarter and save the dying oceans.

It was so hard to stand up to Ma's brilliance and the force of her ideas and to go against everything Ma believed in. Going forward with saving her friends meant exposing Ma and getting her in trouble. Hana wasn't sure she could betray her mom like that.

But it wasn't hard to choose between a version of humanity that included all the oddities and weirdness and one that didn't.

A rustling interrupted her thoughts.

"Hey there." Chuck's crooked smile greeted her as she ducked under the plant's overhang.

Hana's heart swelled. Chuck was exactly who she needed at this moment—a reminder that no matter how complicated her family was, she'd made one great friend. She scooted over to let Chuck in. "How did you find me?"

"I followed you. You didn't exactly cover your tracks." Chuck crouched on her heels. "Are you all right?"

Flyaway strands from Chuck's braids stuck out at odd angles. The freckles sprinkled across her nose scrunched with her grin. Even with the dark circles under her eyes, she glowed. Hana broke out in an answering smile and flung herself at Chuck. They squished together with elbows and shoulders jabbing into each other, but it didn't matter. "I'm good. I'm really good," Hana said. "You saved me from the Tower after all."

"That's right, Rapunzel." Chuck squeezed her back. "And you saved me. Let's get back to the lab."

Hana laughed. "Yes, let's."

41

*T*hey sprawled on the couches back in the lab. Confronting both Ma and her newfound grandpa made Hana want a strawberry-banana smoothie and a nap, but there was no time for such luxuries.

Wayman sat on a stool, still apologetic. Hana knew she had to accept a brief truce, so she tried hard to wipe away her scowl.

"We need to get started right away," he said. "With Chuck's blood sample, I will synthesize a therapy to counteract the effects of the pills. It may take a couple of days."

"How will we get it to the students?" Hana asked.

Wayman's brow wrinkled. "That is a conundrum. We need a delivery mechanism that can get to all the Start-Up kids at the same time. Are you ever together in one place?"

"During our assemblies," Chuck said, "and morning breaks out in the yard."

Hana slumped. She and Chuck wouldn't be able to return to Start-Up school without being questioned. They couldn't sneak in and go around giving antidotes to everyone.

Her thoughts bounced around, trying to jell into some sense.

Hana buried her face in her hands. She needed to calm her mind to think, but the last two times she'd tried Wayman's advice to breathe had both failed—during the AI challenge and afterward when questioned by their teachers. His qigong was useless when she needed it.

Then she remembered something he'd said when he taught her at the rock. *I'm offering you a different way to be in the world.* And she, Ink, and Chuck had experienced that—being in the moment, immersed in the abandoned park ride, flying up and around.

Hana picked up her head. Trying to force herself to be calm was the opposite of qigong's philosophy. She took a deep breath and exhaled slowly. She paid attention to her lungs and heartbeat, and her mind emptied of worries. Her thoughts flowed.

The pills given to Chuck and the others. Their hyped-up reactions in the VR world. The MDD energy drink that amped it up and the chrysanthemum tea that dampened it.

Wayman's warning: *Do not trust everything you see or hear.* Popo's similar words: *Do not fall for the lies.*

The diǎnxué touch that affected the meshed bunny more than the unmeshed one.

Tomás, whose hexagram was the Raven, the trickster.

Ma and Pedro conspiring.

Lin and her stories of the Trojan War.

Some common thread held everything together. Hints of a bigger picture taunted her.

Then, like Ink's spiderweb, all the strands knitted together.

Hana gripped Chuck's arm. "I know how we can get the antidote into Start-Up!" She jumped up. "We need Tomás to help us." She frowned. "But I don't know if we can trust him."

"Let's talk to him. Where can we find him?" Chuck said.

Good question. Hana thought about where Tomás would go if he were upset. She tossed one of Ink's glasses to Chuck and pulled her over to a pair of jelly chairs by the couches. "I know where to find him."

Hana and Chuck appeared in a field in their *Way of the Warlords* avatars. Hana scrolled through a menu of past locations they'd visited until the wintry village and mountainside scene popped up.

"Ouch," Chuck said. "The scene of our first defeat."

Hana grinned wryly. "We're going to the village this time." She touched the screen, and they found themselves outside the cabin on the mountainside. Snow fell lightly, and the chill wind bit where their furs left skin exposed.

"How do you feel?" Hana asked.

"Great, of course. Over here." Chuck skip-ran down a stone path that led to a snow-covered road. It curved switchback-style down a steep slope toward the cozy village sprawled below, wisps of smoke curling from the chimneys of wooden houses.

They hiked down the path, their woven boots crunching in the snow. Puffed-up flakes whirled around their faces.

"Why do you think Tomás will be down there?" Chuck asked.

"Something he said last time we were here." She remembered him perched on the ledge high above them. *Next time we're here, let's go to the village. I bet there's a card house.*

They reached the town square, an open area surrounded by shops and buildings. Now she needed to find the gaming house. A man stumbled out of one of the wooden buildings, yelling obscenities. Hana and Chuck deftly avoided him as he lurched by. "There it is."

They pushed their way through the large wooden door and into a smoky gambling den. It was two stories tall, with a wraparound balcony on the second floor. A table of young gamblers with porcelain cups of tea glanced up as they entered.

"I guess people can see us here," Hana muttered.

"But can I Ching?" Chuck asked.

"According to Ink, these glasses are completely off the multiweb, so we should be invisible, like when she hacked into the game on the first day," Hana said.

They wended their way around the game tables. A figure in a white peasant shirt hunched over a cup of tea at the bar, a familiar set to his shoulders.

Hana strode over and tapped him.

Tomás turned around, in his Peasant4762 avatar.

"Where've you been?" She wanted to both hug and shake him.

He shook his head, eyes darting around. Hana squeezed herself into the space next to him, edging out an older woman with a leathery face and a skullcap, who sniffed and moved away.

"Are you safe and hidden from Start-Up?" she asked.

Tomás nodded. "I'm on my dad's equipment, which is off the multiweb."

That didn't make Hana feel better. Pedro could be monitoring him, or Tomás and his dad could be working together—and Tomás's dad was a part of everything happening at Start-Up.

Chuck bounded over with a huge grin. "Tomás!" She pounded him on the back and gave him a bear hug. His eyes widened as she squeezed him.

Hana grabbed Chuck by the wrist and dragged her aside, dodging the serving boys with trays of tea.

"What're you doing?" Chuck said. "We found him. Isn't that great?"

"Now I don't know. Why is he always nervous when we ask him about his dad? What if he disappeared because he's helping him?"

Chuck scoffed. "Tomás is okay. You know how he is."

"I don't know." Hana made her way back to Tomás. "Can we go someplace quieter to talk?"

He nodded. "Over there." They followed him to the back of the room. Under one of the balconies was an unoccupied huánghuālí couch, a wooden platform with carved sides and a worn silk pallet.

After settling in, Hana said, "We need your help, but you need to explain what you're hiding."

Tomás leaned back and closed his eyes. After some time, he looked at her with anguished eyes. "I promise what's going on with me has nothing to do with the Start-Up conspiracy. Please trust me."

Hana considered him.

"I believe you," Chuck said.

Hana looked at Chuck. She was a rock, like the *I Ching* predicted: *forming foundations that cannot be shaken and being sincere in word and duty.* After a long pause, she nodded. If Chuck trusted him, she would too.

Hana filled Tomás in on what he'd missed—how their parents had a plan to link the minds of their class of meshed students and how the ones who'd taken the nano pills were in immediate danger.

Tomás sat back and rubbed little circles on his temple. "What's your plan?" he finally asked.

"Cyber bees."

"What?"

"What?" Chuck echoed.

"We'll reprogram cyber bees to sting the students with the antidote Wayman is making. When everyone is in the yard on morning break, we'll send in the bees," she said.

Chuck gripped Hana's arm. "You are a genius. Cyber bees are little robots, so they can be hacked."

"And their artificial stingers are used to collect and share pollen and nectar, so they can be filled with the antidote," Tomás said.

"But I need you to help hack the bees," Hana continued. "We have a bunch we picked up at the field, and I know you have some too. Could you fix them? Or study them and hack others? We need to control the bees to make them deliver the antidotes."

Tomás furrowed his brow. "Supposing I could do that . . . we can't have the bees fly into the yard. The security force field will fry them, remember? It seems to repel anything electronic."

Hana grinned. "That's where part two of my plan comes in. We use my bird bots to fly the bees in their bellies. The bots aren't powered electronically, so they can get by the invisible fence. We glide them in with deactivated cyber bees inside. They'll be like Trojan horses."

Tomás broke into an answering grin. "'All warfare is based on deception.'"

Hana nodded. "Sun Tzu."

Chuck laughed. "And once they get into the yard"—she punched her open palm—"Bam! You turn on the bees and they sting everybody." Her face turned thoughtful. "Bees. Our secret weapons."

"That's pretty much the plan." Hana turned to Tomás. "Will you help us?"

Tomás's eyes flashed.

She breathed softly, waiting. They gazed at each other for several heartbeats, surrounded by the sounds of clacking game tiles and clinking teacups, the murmur of conversations, and occasional shouts of conversations, and occasional shouts of "Húle!" signaling a mahjong win.

His shoulders relaxed and he nodded. "Where are you?"

"We're at Wayman's lab, which is below his house, in the Bottoms."

"I'll go over now."

Hana reached out to Tomás's arm. "Thank you."

His eyes flickered, reflecting the candlelit chandelier, and he returned her grip. They stood together for another moment, trading smiles.

Outside the gaming house, snowflakes danced in thousands of tiny patterns. Hana spread her hands wide and gathered the entire scene, pulling it in and balling it into nothingness.

She and Chuck blipped out of the game.

42

Back at Wayman's lab underneath his house, Hana was startled to find it a hive of activity. A dozen people with glowing edges wearing lab coats worked at the various machines. Hana realized they were holograms, just like the people at Ma's lab who came to work virtually and were projected into the lab.

She and Chuck exchanged glances. Hana got up from the jelly chair and walked over to Wayman, pushing aside her continued anger at him. It was easier not to think of him as her grandpa.

He looked up. "Meet Isadore. She's with Ghost Crab Nation and a lab technician at Pear. We're already at work synthesizing an antidote from Chuck's blood sample." After they exchanged greetings, Wayman's fingers tapped his tablet and the holotechnicians dimmed to about 70 percent. "I've muted the sound they hear from this lab, so we can talk without them listening in."

Hana explained her idea about using cyber bees to deliver the antidote and gliding them into the school inside automatons to avoid the security force field. "So we need to make a bunch of bird automatons." She frowned. "I need my tools and spare parts from my workshop, but I can't go back home." Even though her workshop was offline, the house cameras could still capture Hana if she snuck into the yard.

"How about getting Ink or the scavengers to help?" Wayman asked.

"Ink stormed off and doesn't want anything to do with us anymore," she said.

The lab lights flashed warning of someone at the door upstairs, and Wayman motioned for them to stay in the lab while he went to see who it was. A few minutes later, he returned with Tomás.

Chuck, who had stayed on the jelly chair, propped herself up and waved.

Hana rushed over to him. Standing face-to-face, she smiled tentatively, and so did he.

Tomás dug into a pocket and brought out a handful of cyber bees, most twisted and broken from the zapping fence, but a few in decent shape. "I've been picking these up every day at school."

Hana took a bee from Tomás's hand, which twitched at her touch.

"Ink gave us these glasses." Hana broke their eye contact and handed him a pair. "You can use them to get online and see if you can hack the bees."

Tomás opened his mouth, then closed it. "Um, sure." He put on the glasses and held up a cyber bee and inspected it.

His eyes didn't dart to the upper corner to access the menu, instead focusing straight ahead. "Looks like I can get into Dowsanto's server through a back door."

As she watched his eyes, the puzzle pieces of Tomás fell into place.

Hana reached out and plucked Ink's glasses off his face. He continued to stare into the middle distance for a split second, blinked, and focused back on her.

"I know what's going on with you," Hana said.

He stiffened.

"You're good with computers and you're a hacker. You know things other people don't. In the games, you act all wonky, like your boosts don't work, but I think you're lying. You could fly a hovercruiser even though you shouldn't have been connected to the multiweb without the glasses tech."

Tomás looked like he was about to crush the cyber bee between his fingers.

"Just now, you didn't use your glasses properly, because you didn't have to. You're meshed," she said.

He sagged.

"Am I right? You're already connected to the multiweb."

He nodded slowly.

Chuck leaned forward. "What? You're already meshed but you're a Start-Up? Do they know?" She narrowed her eyes. "Are you thirteen and you're messing with us?"

"How did it happen?" Hana said.

"My dad's experimenting with enmeshment," Tomás said. "He wanted to prove that it's safe for a younger person to get meshed, and I volunteered."

"Now it makes sense." Hana sank onto the couch. "You're covering for your dad, but it's not related to this conspiracy."

"Right."

"Why are you in Start-Up? What's the point?"

"My dad didn't want me to stick out. He thought doing Start-Up would keep me under the radar." He paused. "It was hard in the games. I was meshed but had to pretend I wasn't, so I copied you."

Hana snorted. "That wasn't too bright, since my tech didn't work." Now she understood why he bumbled in the market fight, was as slow as she was climbing the cliff, and was so upset when the bunnies were felled by Wayman's diǎnxué moves. "It still doesn't make sense. You could've waited a year until everyone who is thirteen is meshed and you'd blend right in."

"He doesn't explain things to me," Tomás said. "But I'd do anything for my dad. It's how we are."

Hana let out a wavering breath. She could understand his all-encompassing need to be close with his dad. All this time, his secret had closed him off—and it explained all the times he'd been prickly or unable to explain himself.

She put a hand on his arm.

He flinched, then relaxed.

She looked into the caramel of his eyes, trying to see the filaments in his brain that made him different, enmeshed. Then it hit her.

"You used contact lenses to change your eye colors when you rode the maglev," Hana said.

"That's how I got around the iris scanners," Tomás explained. "It was like a fake ID, so the system wouldn't know who I was or that I was meshed."

She remembered another thing. "And that's why Ink acted strangely when you two met. She could tell you were meshed."

Tomás shrugged. "I don't know if she could tell, but I could see her tech was different from anything I'd come across. I was scared she'd out me."

Hana shook her head. "You lived an elaborate web of lies."

"I know."

"So can you help with the bees?"

His eyes crinkled with his smile. "Yeah, I can figure out how to call and control them." Tomás jabbed his fingers through his hair, leaving it stuck at wild angles. "At least I don't have to pretend I'm someone I'm not anymore."

Warmth for him flooded through her. Now he made sense. "Right. We have to make enough bots and have enough cyber bees to sting all the kids who are in the experimental program."

Chuck looked up. "We saw the list of those kids at Ink's beachscape. It was one hundred and fifty students, half the three hundred kids at City Center Start-Up."

Hana did some quick math. "We'll need about one hundred and fifty cyber bees, and if we can fit five bees in each automaton, we'll need to make thirty bots. We'll go to the bluff that's behind the school and release them into the field during a morning break. You do your hacker thing, and the bees will sting everybody."

"Eek. It seems awfully cruel to the kids," Chuck said.

"It seems cruel to the bees," Tomás added.

"They're robots," Hana said. "If we tried to control meshed Bees, that would be a different story."

Chuck's eyes darted up at the mention of enhanced Bees.

"It could work," Wayman said. "I'll get back to synthesizing the antidote. I'll use a biomarker that will let the cyber bees identify which students were given the pills. It should be ready in two days. Does that give you enough time?"

"We need to get more bees and more bots, but we'll figure it out," Hana said.

"Let's get to work, then," Wayman said.

The three huddled at the couch. "How do we find one hundred and fifty cyber bees and make thirty bots in two days?" Chuck said.

Hana slumped and squeezed her eyes shut. She had no idea how they'd pull this off. If only she had an expert bot-maker like . . . She sat up and messaged Lin with Ink's glasses, *Can you meet at the junkyard where we used to go, in an hour? And bring Popo.*

43

The Dragon I Ching hexagram says,
"With perseverance, all that is
undertaken shall come to pass."
—H. H. June 30, 2053

Plastic shells crunched underfoot as Hana paced around the garbage piles at the junkyard. It was a risk to come here because the JingZa might be patrolling, but it was a place nearby that Lin also knew, from when they used to scavenge together. She hoped Popo would join too. When they were young, Popo used to bring them here on their missions for treasure, but she'd been less active in recent years, disappearing to her room for hours at a time.

"Where've you been? Ma's furious you've blocked her calls."

Hana turned to see Lin and hurried over for a quick hug. "I'm fine."

"She's worried, you know."

Hana scowled. "She worries about you, not me."

"That's not true. Let's talk to her."

"We did at her office, and you heard what she said,"

Hana said. "Anyway, I need your help making some bots. We're trying to save the kids who are affected with an antidote." She explained their plan.

Lin sidestepped around an old hoverbike. "Your plan is complicated. Let's try to convince Ma to shut down the experiment."

"We don't have time. We have to save my friends." Hana wasn't even sure Ma would listen to her.

"How many bots do you need?" Lin asked.

"As many as you can make. Ten would be great."

"That's a lot to make in two days."

"Can you get Popo to help?" Hana missed Popo's smile. "Why couldn't she come today?"

"Today wasn't a great day," Lin said. "I don't think she's in a condition to make bots."

Hana's stomach churned. Popo was slipping away. "We just made bots together last week."

"I don't know," Lin said. "I have to think about it."

"Don't think too long. My friends who are sick really need your help," Hana said. "Please meet us at the bluff by the school on Thursday at ten o'clock with the bots."

Hana watched with worry as Lin headed back home. She wasn't sure whether Lin would make the bots, and even if she did, it would be hard to make so many.

The next two days, Hana and Chuck spent nearly all their waking hours putting together more bots. Wayman got Tish and other junkyard kids to scavenge for parts for them, since the JingZa could show up in the junkyard at any moment. Chuck was surprisingly good with the small parts, but she kept taking breaks to don her glasses and head into *Way of the Warlords*. Hana thought it was strange, but she supposed Chuck was still recovering.

At night, they crashed on a fold-out couch, while Tomás went back to his dad's safe house, preferring to stay off the radar there. In the lab, he spent most of his time looking like he was napping in a jelly chair while holding a couple of cyber bees in his palm. He assured them that was how he hacked their systems. Sometimes his brow would knit together, or he'd pop up and pace around. Hana hoped that meant their plan was on track.

The afternoon before their planned rescue, Hana groaned as she sat up on the couch. "These cushions are not very cushy." She leaned over and poked Chuck. "C'mon, sleepyhead. We've got some more bots to make."

Chuck didn't answer. She wasn't asleep, but she was pale and sweaty. She tried to push herself up from the couch but collapsed. "I can't move," she whispered, her eyes wide. "Since I've skipped school, I haven't had the MDD to give me energy."

"Wayman." Hana jumped up from the couch. "Something's wrong with Chuck!"

Wayman hurried over and knelt by Chuck and placed a hand on her forehead. "Get some water."

Hana scrambled to find a blister pack and brought it over with trembling hands.

"Is the antidote ready? She needs it."

Wayman sported the same black circles under his eyes that Chuck had, but he'd gotten his by not sleeping for the last couple of days. "It's ready, but we haven't had time to test it on people, only simulations."

"Is it safe?" Hana asked.

"I believe so, but it's up to you to decide if you want it." Wayman placed his hand on Chuck's arm. "There's a risk, because we had to cut some corners to get it done quickly."

Chuck swallowed hard. She took a deep breath. "Fire away. I don't want to feel like this one moment more."

Wayman hurried over to the workspace where he and his team had been working and returned carrying an injector.

"Are you ready?"

Chuck nodded.

He pricked her arm with a small needle.

"How long will it be before it works?" Hana asked.

"It might take some time," Wayman said.

Chuck sank back into the couch, and Hana paced restlessly. Tomás sat in a jelly chair, eyes closed, still working on hacking the cyber bees. Hana tried to keep her mind off Chuck by working on an automaton, but she couldn't help worrying. What if the antidote didn't work and Chuck never got better?

Three hours later, Chuck stirred and pushed herself up from the couch.

"It worked!" Hana gave Chuck a tremendous hug.

Chuck laughed. "I'm back, my péngyou. You can't keep me down." She gobbled two meatwiches, chattered non-stop, and prowled around the lab.

It was so good to have Chuck back and even more of a relief that the antidote worked. The pieces of Hana's plan were coming together. First Tomás would hijack and hack cyber bees to reprogram them, then they'd fill them with the antidote, and finally they'd pack them into the automatons and release them to the Start-Up kids. They'd already made several of the automatons, and Wayman's lab was hard at work making enough antidote to cure all the students in the experiment.

When the sky turned orange and pink, the three went by the underground tunnels to the stream in the woods. As

Hana left the safety of the lab, she worried about what would happen if they ran into the JingZa, but it was worth the risk to stop the mind-control experiments at Start-Up. Chuck grabbed Ink's glasses on the way out, and Tomás carried a large mesh bag. It was a warm summer evening and the trees rustled in the breeze.

Standing on top of the flat rock where she'd spent days practicing how to breathe, Hana surveyed the scene. A bunny bounded into the underbrush. The sunset cast a rose-gold glow on the treetops. Chuck gazed into the distance with her glasses on.

"What are you doing?" Hana asked.

"Um. Nothing." Chuck touched her eyepiece. "When Tomás does his hacking, I thought it might be cool to see it through the glasses." Hana gave Chuck a considering look. Chuck had been acting strange the last few days, but then again, she'd been through a lot. It was probably just because she was dealing with the parasite and fungus genes.

Tomás blinked and slowly swiveled his head, as if casting a beacon call to the cyber bees. Soon, a low *hum* filled the air. A few, and then more, shiny bees buzzed over.

"They're coming!" Chuck said.

Tomás held his bag open and dozens of cyber bees flew in. He powered them down as soon as they reached the bag. After hundreds of metallic bees had flown in, he closed the bag.

Dozens more cyber bees flew around their heads. The music of their drones built up and mingled with the waking crickets.

The first step of the plan was complete. They had hijacked Dowsanto's cyber bees.

The next morning, the three stood on the bluff overlooking the school's fields. The morning dew had burned off and school was in session. The clouds moved rapidly over them, giving the world a Tilt-A-Whirl feel. Below them were the two-story building and field where the students took their midmorning break.

Hana and Chuck wore Ink's hacker glasses so they could communicate with each other and with Tomás if needed.

"I wish Ink were here," Hana said.

"Guess she's gone for good," Tomás said. "She's not reliable."

Hana cut a glance at him. "Maybe." She felt terrible about how Ink had ended things, and she wondered if she'd see her again.

At their feet lay a large sack. Inside was a pile of only twenty bird automatons. Each of their metal bellies contained five cyber bees filled with Wayman's antidote, but they were short ten bots.

It was ten o'clock and Lin still hadn't shown up. If she didn't show, they'd have to squeeze more bees into each bot, but they wouldn't be able to fit them all. Wayman had worked with his Ghost Crab Nation lab staff to fill each bee's stinger, and they'd made enough bees to save the kids who'd been given the nano pills. But it wouldn't matter if they couldn't get all the bees across the security force field.

"Are you sure this will work?" Chuck asked. Her eyes tracked to the upper right. Hana wondered what she was up to.

"I'm not sure about anything," Hana replied. "The bots are purely mechanical, so they should glide through the electronic sensors." She silently thanked Lin for her fixation on Trojan horses.

"And the flight path?" Tomás asked. "How do you know the air currents are right for the bots to fly into the school-yard?"

"Have you noticed how windy it is out there? It's a wind tunnel. Look." A gust blew a flurry of leaves over to the field, proving her point.

Hana took out the bots and lined them up at her feet. Chuck and Tomás helped her unload the sack.

Ten minutes before the morning break, Lin still hadn't shown up. Hana's stomach clenched. "We're going to have to fit more bees into each bot." Hana opened the trapdoor of one of the bird bots and rummaged in a box for the extra cyber bees.

"Who's that?" Chuck said.

A lone figure walk-jogged over to them.

A wave of relief flooded over her. "It's my sister."

Lin carried a sack and deposited it at her feet. "Bird bots to the rescue."

Hana crouched down and sifted through the bag. The bird bots she pulled out were exquisite—magnificently built pigeons, robins, cardinals, and other fantastic creations. She recognized the detail and flair in each of the bots—the unmistakable genius touch of Popo.

"Popo saw me in the workshop and took over." Lin's face softened. "I hadn't been there in so long and had avoided going because I didn't want to be reminded of Ba. But it was great to sit with Popo and make bots again and listen to her stories."

"They're perfect." Hana was thrilled at hearing Popo had been well enough to make the bots. She counted them and passed them out to the others. "Now we have enough for all the cyber bees." Hana introduced Lin.

They scrambled to stuff the cyber bees into Lin's bots as the Start-Up students streamed out of the building. Some sat by the wall of the building, listlessly sucking up MDD, while others kicked around a ball or walked the perimeter of the field.

"There they are," Chuck said.

Hana finished latching one of the bots. "Let's do it."

They went to work. They furiously wound up each bird and flung it toward the field. One by one, the bird bots, powered by springs and helped by the wind, glided down to the school fields. The flying army of rattling birds swooped in, their wings glinting in the summer sun and going *plickety-snickety* in the wind.

A couple landed near the students. More winged in. One of the twins pointed up as bird after bird flew into the schoolyard. The students ran over to the fallen ones.

Nothing happened.

"What's the problem?" Chuck asked.

Hana's stomach sank. She had made the belly hatches secure, just like Lin and Popo had, because that was how they'd all learned to build them, to hold on to their secret wishes. She'd thought it would be a good thing, so the bees wouldn't fall out midflight—but they were too secure.

"The bellies aren't opening," she said. "The cyber bees are trapped."

44

Hana stared in dismay at Chuck, Tomás, and Lin.

"What now?" Chuck asked.

Hana had no idea. The whole plan was based on her idea and her bots, and it wasn't working. She had to think. The teachers would be out soon. "Can you make the cyber bees force their way out?" she asked Tomás.

"No. They're not strong enough."

Hana paced back and forth. Suddenly, the memory of her first day at Start-Up, and her *I Ching* hexagram, popped into her head. The text from the book taunted her: *To see and be seen, yet not make contact*. It had all been well and good to be an observer and a planner, but now it was time to make contact. To act.

"We've got to go down there," she said at last. "We need to manually open the bots."

"We won't have enough time," Lin said. "There are only four of us and we have thirty bots."

Hana squeezed her eyes shut. "It doesn't matter. We have to try. Turn on your glasses," she said to Chuck, "so we can talk to each other and to Tomás and Lin."

She scrambled down the bluff, and the others followed.

It was about a hundred yards to the fields and the black-top. Hana pumped her legs, her lungs and legs aching almost immediately. As they came to the field, she yelled out to the students, "We need your help. Open the birds up!" She scooped up one and clicked open the doors to show them. Her friends darted around, looking for more.

Asa dragged themself over, panting hard. "What's going on?"

Chuck projected her voice for all to hear. "Don't you feel like you're only alive in the VR? And you feel awful out here? We've been drugged."

Asa stared at her as if Chuck had sprouted new limbs. A bunch of students gathered around Chuck, while Lin and Tomás ran to the other birds. "It's because of *them*— our teachers, the Corporations," Chuck said. "They're using us as lab animals. We need to open those bird bots. Inside are cyber bees that will give us a shot to reverse the effects." She ran around. "I had no energy and look at me now. It works."

Hana added, "We don't have much time. Please help us." She spotted another bird and wrestled its belly door open.

Asa and some of the other students joined in hunting down the bots and setting the bees free.

Hana said to Tomás, "Now do your hack-the-bee thing."

He nodded.

Out of the confusion of bots and kids came a shout

here and a cry there. Following Tomás's programming and Wayman's markers, the cyber bees identified and stung each student with the altered DNA sequence.

The doors to the school building burst open, spilling out the teachers. The bees stung more kids.

Tomás pushed his way to Hana. "Something's wrong."

"What do you mean?"

"I can track how many bees delivered their shots, and there aren't enough students out here. One hundred and thirty-nine antidotes have been given. We're missing ten students."

Asa swayed dizzily as the antidote began to work. "My brother's in the infirmary," Asa said. "There are a bunch of students there."

Hana's head snapped up. "What?"

"Today after training, some kids were so weak they were taken to the infirmary," Asa said. "They pushed us hard today."

"The rest of the kids must be there," Chuck said.

Ms. Malhotra hurried over. Mr. Zoble and other teachers moved among the students.

A batch of cyber bees flew toward the school building, homing in on the remaining students inside.

Sirens blared and a copter cruiser buzzed down. As it hovered, three JingZa guards jumped from the hatch. They landed in a run and closed the distance to Hana and her friends in a few high-powered strides.

They surrounded them and pointed their millimeter wave guns. "Stop where you are."

Hana swallowed hard, overwhelmed by dread. She stopped. So did her friends.

They were trapped.

45

The JingZa pointed their weapons at Hana, her friends, and her sister. The other students huddled in knots, rubbing their necks where they'd been stung. Hana couldn't believe they'd come this far, and now they'd be taken. At least most of the kids had gotten the antidote.

Mr. Zoble strode over. "What is the meaning of this?"

As Hana was about to answer, her glasses flickered. The adults' and the JingZa's eyes lost focus as they gazed into the middle distance. Kids who had on glasses that had been powered off for the break now lifted their heads in the distinctive watching-a-screen mode.

The billboards on the side of the building buzzed to life.

Every screen—including Hana's glasses, flashed: *Real-TimeNews™: Breaking: A Vast Corporate Conspiracy!* The screens showed JingZa surrounding Hana and her friends in real time. A split screen showed earlier footage of the bird bots flying into the field and Hana and her friends running after them and opening them.

How in the world were they getting this real-time footage? It was disorienting seeing herself on the screens looking straight into the camera.

Then she spotted a cyber bee hovering in front of her face, a tiny flying camera.

As vids of the children getting stung by the cyber bees played on the screens, a news banner rolled across everyone's view: *Operation Cyber Bee Sting. Uncovered: I Ching and Nile Plot to Test Gene Therapy on the City Center Start-Up Class of 2054.*

Hana thought quickly. This was a perfect distraction, wherever it had come from.

Tomás and Chuck, she private messaged them using her glasses. *We need to get to the infirmary while they're distracted.* She caught Tomás's eye. *The bees need to get inside too.*

I can send the bees over, Tomás responded. *But this show, or whatever it is, isn't enough. We've got those millimeter guns on us.*

Chuck nodded almost imperceptibly. *I can distract them even more. I've got a plan. Tell me when, and I'll get on it.*

Hana gulped. With the JingZa guards' amped reflexes, their chances of escaping them were very small.

The news feeds broke into multiple screens.

AI talking heads spewed contradictory reports and wild theories. On one of the screens, Wayman, his face digitally masked, explained that the therapy lowered natural fear and increased susceptibility to suggestion. "In other words, these kids are being brainwashed so they can do the Corporations' bidding. They are guinea pigs for a larger nationwide project."

Hana eyed Chuck. She wasn't sure what Chuck had in mind, but she had to trust her. *Ready?*

Chuck blinked. *Heck yeah.*

Okay, GO.

A droning sound that had been part of the background noise grew louder and more insistent. Hana looked up.

Above them, a black cloud buzzed and shifted in a huge, writhing mass. The buzzing magnified to cringe-inducing levels.

"They're here," Chuck yelled triumphantly.

The buzzing cloud was made up of thousands of Bees. They shifted shape and formed a dark silhouette of a gigantic three-legged crow swooping in for an attack—it was a swarm of enhanced Bees channeling the spirit of Yatagarasu.

Hana smiled. So that's what Chuck had been doing with her glasses these past few days—communicating with and organizing enmeshed Bees.

The mass of Bees swarmed down on the JingZa, who threw up their arms. Even with their boosted reflexes, they couldn't ward off the overwhelming mass of attacking insects.

As the JingZa scrambled to get away from the army of

Bees, Hana didn't wait to see what happened next. *Come on!* She ran as fast as she could toward the school. Chuck and Tomás joined her in the dash.

They were halfway to the school doors when the JingZa closed in on them again, followed by the angry cloud of Bees.

Keep running, she messaged Tomás and Chuck.

We're doomed, Chuck answered.

Hana felt the same, but she couldn't give up now. She couldn't fail by twenty yards.

The whine of a hovercraft rattled Hana's eardrums. A gray cruiser with a crab painted on the side whirred overhead. Inside the driver's seat was a figure with spiky white-blond hair and ice-blue eyes.

"Ink!" Hana broke into a wide smile.

All the screens flickered and cut to Ink in the hovercraft.

Ink was back—both in person and projected larger than life on the school's wall and everyone's inner fields of vision. With a sardonic smile, Ink said, "This just in: the Ghost Crab Nation releases files from I Ching and Nile labs showing a widespread conspiracy to brain-jack hundreds of twelve-year-olds.

"And why are these armed guards bullying schoolkids?" Ink continued. "Let's find out with a live interview." She landed the hovercraft between the JingZa and Hana and her friends, and hopped out. Other Ghost Crab Nation members came out of the cruiser, acting as a camera crew to surround the corporate security guards.

Mr. Zoble rushed over. He called the officers to stand down, and they lowered their weapons and stepped back. Mr. Zoble waved away some lingering Bees and neatened his beard for the cameras. Some students gathered around him, trying to get on the drone bee cam.

Hana and her friends exchanged glances and put on a burst of speed to reach the school doors. The cyber bees Tomás had sent ahead buzzed and swarmed against the glass.

The doors were locked, clamped tight with the school in shutdown mode.

"Now what?" Hana asked.

46

*T*omás slammed his palms against the door. "There's got to be a way the bees can get in, even if we can't."

Hana searched up and down the building. A small pipe sticking out of the roof jogged her memory of the blueprints she'd seen on the first day of Start-Up. "There's a network of ducts and crawl spaces!" She searched the database and retrieved the blueprint for Tomás. "Can you send the bees to the infirmary?"

Tomás nodded. "Done."

The bees streamed up the side of the building toward the roof.

Tomás faced the door with a semi-blank look on his face. "These schools need to invest in better security." After a moment, he said, "I've disabled the lock."

The three ran into the building.

They burst into the infirmary and skidded to a stop. The normally quiet space was packed with students on makeshift stretchers. Ben, Christa, and others lay there, pale and out of it. A couple of automated nurse bots tended to them, checking their IV lines and med patches.

The screen walls showed the same news reports that were playing in their glasses and outside.

"Can you hack the nurse bots?" Hana asked Tomás. "We need to get them away from the kids for the bees to do their work. Where are those bees, anyway?"

He frowned, his eyes half focused. "The nurse bots are under triple layers of security. I don't have time to get through them." He let out an exasperated breath. "I can't do it."

Chuck stepped forward. "Here's how I hack things." She crouched in a fighting stance and rushed the nurse bots. With efficient kicks and chops, she bashed one and leveled the other, reducing them to whining hunks of metalloid.

Hana laughed. "That works too." She peered at the ceiling. Grabbing a chair, she clambered up the check-in counter and pushed one of the ceiling tiles up. A bunch of cyber bees streamed into the room through the crack.

As the bees found their marks, the students yelped with surprise and pain.

"Ow." Christa rubbed her neck.

"The sting's an antidote," Hana said. "Check your vid feeds. It's being explained on the news."

On the screen wall and in their glasses, Ink continued reporting. "The Corporations are saying zip." He held up his hands, a wrist flashing the crab tattoo, and waved his fingers like anemones seeking plankton and prey. "People. Information wants to be free. Take charge of your own brain." Ink pointed at the camera and winked, seemingly right at Hana. "Ghost Crab Nation—big and splashy today only—out."

Hana grinned and raised her hand to Ink's hologram. Ink had listened to her, and now Ghost Crab Nation was visible to the world. She had a sneaking suspicion they wouldn't be big and splashy for only one day.

A hush descended on the room.

The door hissed open, and Primo Zed rushed in with Mr. Zoble. "Hana, children, you don't know what you're doing," Primo Zed said. "You're interrupting an important scientific experiment. We're going to detain you for further questioning, especially regarding your connections with Ghost Crab Nation."

"That won't be necessary."

Ma stood at the door, eyes flashing. Pedro stepped into the room too, followed by Lin. "Primo, you doctored the reports of these sick children," Ma said. "We would've shut this down had I known."

"I knew you would, which is why I didn't send the real data," Primo said.

"Why?" Ma's voice wavered with pain. "We're a team. You know how important this project is to me, and how important it is to get right. This was a trial for the whole country, and eventually the world. You endangered these kids, including my daughter."

"Sophia, you're naive if you don't realize this is how corporate politics works," Primo said. "I Ching doesn't have patience, and we need to show results, or we're done. I know you agree the world needs this project." He glanced at the kids in the beds. "I was keeping a close eye on all of the students. No one is seriously ill yet."

"I'm responsible for the experimental protocol, so I need to make that determination. I'm shutting it down." Ma stepped over a crumpled nurse bot and leaned over Christa and picked up a cyber bee lying on the cot. "What's going on here, Hana?"

"I've been working with that group that was just on air, the Ghost Crab Nation," Hana said. "There's a man named Wayman who came up with a shot to counteract the effects of the pills you gave the kids."

Ma gave Hana a sharp look. "We have a lot to talk about."

Mr. Zoble stepped forward. "The more pressing issue is to get ahead of the news. We need to spin this before it gets out of control and damages I Ching's and Nile's reputations. The other Corporations are circling like gleeful vultures."

As if to punctuate his point, the screens flickered and a spokesperson for Plex said, "We are shocked, I repeat, shocked, by the nefarious activities of our fellow Corporations. We will bring them to the Council of Corporations."

Mr. Zoble opened a screen and set it to record. "Citizens, let me assure you the images you have seen don't tell the whole story. I Ching, Nile, and City Center Start-Up will be fully transparent and explain what is going on. If you upgrade your I Ching and Nile apps, we'll stream the latest direct to your brain." He gestured Primo Zed to join him. "In fact, we have an ask-and-answer session with the headmaster of Start-Up right now."

While they broadcast, Pedro came over to his son. "Tomás. What are you doing? You have to stay under the radar."

"They know, Dad."

Pedro's face darkened. "What?"

"My friends know I'm meshed. I don't have to hide it anymore." Tomás's voice was filled with a joy Hana hadn't heard before.

Pedro scanned Hana's and Chuck's faces. His frown disappeared, but his frame remained tense. He pulled Tomás into a bear hug. "I'm glad you're safe."

Tomás pushed away, scowling. "Why were you involved with these experiments? Look at those kids."

Pedro's gaze landed on the sick kids and he gripped his son's arms. "I'm sorry." He turned to Hana. "I've been helping your mom with her project. I was the go-between working the backchannels because Nile and I Ching can't be seen working together publicly. I didn't realize the extent of the side effects."

Pedro and Ma both seemed sincere in their shock at the state of the kids, and Ma had said she'd shut this down.

"Ma, I need to tell you something, but it's better if we do it at home."

Ma gave her a long look. "That's fine. We'll talk then." She turned to the others in the room. "I've pinged all your caregivers, and they will pick you up. You can go to I Ching's medical facilities at City Center to recover." She darted a glance at Primo. "We'll close down Start-Up school until we get to the bottom of this."

"I'm ready to go," Hana said to Ma, "but I need to stop at the Bottoms to get someone you need to see. I'll meet you at home."

"Hana, you've been gone for three days. I don't want you disappearing again," Ma said.

"I just helped save these kids. Please trust me, Ma," Hana said. "It's important."

Ma pressed her lips together and sighed. "Fine. There's some follow-up I need to do here," Ma said. "Lin, will you help me contact this list of media outlets?"

"Call me soon," Chuck said.

Hana nodded. "How did you get those enhanced Bees to do that Yatagarasu impression?"

"Once I got the translator app from *Way of the Warlords*, it wasn't hard to convince them to help. As I told you, I have a way with animals."

"I'm going to call you the Bee whisperer."

Hana and Chuck laughed and hugged a good long time. She glanced up and waved Tomás over. He grinned and joined them in a fierce group hug.

47

An hour later, Hana stood outside the front steps of her house in the Vistas. Behind her, on the walkway, twisting his cap, was Wayman.

"This might not be a good time," Wayman said, looking ready to bolt. When Hana had barged into his lab and demanded he follow her, he'd taken one look at her and agreed. It was time for him to make amends to the family he'd abandoned.

"You're right," she said. "It's a terrible time. It's about twenty years too late." Her voice caught in her throat. "It might be forever too late. Popo might not know who you are."

A strange look flitted across Wayman's face, almost a smile. "You'd be surprised."

Hana opened the door. Dramatic music came from a screen wall in the living room, where Popo sat in a comfy chair. On the screen, a handsome man, played by the heartthrob actor of her era, brought a pair of kids to a woman with puffy blonde hair. She rushed to his arms. Popo recited the lines along with the woman on the screen. "No sé como agradecerte por arriesgar tu vida para salvar a mis hijos." *I don't know how to thank you for risking your life to save my children.*

When the actor said the next lines, Wayman's voice joined in. "Son mi vida, como tú." *They're my life, like you.*

Popo turned and smiled. "Anwei. What are you doing here? I thought we were only supposed to meet at the Bottoms."

Hana's mind churned. Popo had to be lost in the past, thinking Wayman hadn't been gone for almost twenty years. Why else would she act so casually?

Wayman sat down beside her, a broad smile on his face. "Hana knows about me. I thought it was time to let Sophia and Lin know I'm alive."

It slowly dawned on her. "You knew he was alive?"

Popo said calmly, "He's always been alive. He just couldn't live with us."

"But you let Ma, Lin, and me believe he was dead?" Hana blinked back furious tears. How many secrets did her family have?

Popo hung her head.

Wayman took Popo's hand. "I'm ready to come back. Spending these last few weeks with Hana made me realize how much I've missed."

"What's going on?" Lin stood at the doorway. "Who's this?"

Wayman sprang to his feet. "Lin!"

Lin's brows furrowed.

"He's our long-lost, not-dead grandpa," Hana said bitterly. "A fact Popo apparently knew."

Lin stared from Hana to Popo, and back to Wayman, her face a mask of confusion. "What are you talking about?"

"Father."

Hana froze at the sound of Ma's ice-cold voice. Trembling, Ma stepped into the living room.

Wayman reached for Ma.

She backed away. "You. You're with that Ghost Crab Nation that broadcast all our business."

"Let me explain."

"No. You don't get to explain," Ma said in a clipped voice. "You abandoned us, and for what? Scuttling around in the shadows and blowing up buildings?" Ma glanced at Hana, her face tightening. "And you dragged my daughter into your schemes."

Hana moved away from Wayman, standing halfway between him and Ma.

Wayman pleaded to Ma, "We're not violent like the AntiTechs were. I stayed away because I couldn't live in an enmeshed world. I've followed your career for the past two decades and I am proud of what you've accomplished."

"Gee, Dad, thanks for your support," Ma said. "It would've been nicer to have had a father all my life. And you left Mom too."

"He didn't leave me," Popo said.

Ma gaped.

"Your mom and I stayed in touch," Wayman said. "We met every month."

Ma sagged onto the couch. "Why did you lie to me?" she asked Popo.

Popo's face twisted. "I watched you suffer when he left us, and I didn't want to put you through that twice if he should leave again." She swiped at a tear. "Sometimes, I forget things too, so it felt like he was always here, or always gone."

Ma stared at Wayman with a mix of curiosity and anger.

"Sophia, you haven't needed me, and I don't deserve to be in your life," Wayman said. "You've raised two wonderful daughters, taken care of Pei Wen, held a powerful and influential job, tried saving an indifferent world, all while dealing with tremendous loss."

Ma's face crumpled for a second, then she pulled herself together. "And yet you managed to sic your underground organization against my life's work."

"I didn't realize you were behind the trials at Start-Up, but I don't apologize for my beliefs. I'm proud of you for sticking to yours, and I'm glad you shut down the program when you found out it was unsafe," Wayman said. "We have a lot to discuss. We have more in common than you think."

Ma sighed heavily. "I can't right now. It's too much."

Wayman slumped.

Popo put her arms around Ma and leaned her forehead against hers. "Why don't you get some tea?"

Ma finally nodded and moved to the kitchen as if weighed down by the world.

Lin said to Hana in a low voice, "Go to Ma. I'll stay with Popo." Lin glanced over to Wayman. "And our grandfather."

Hana followed Ma to the kitchen. This was not the family reunion Hana had expected.

Ma sat wearily at the kitchen table. Hana went to the hot water pot and poured a couple of teas.

"It must be such a shock for you," Hana said.

Ma let out a deep breath and darted a look at Hana. "How did you meet him? When did you know?"

"I didn't know he was Grandpa until a few days ago, but I met him in the woods right after Enmesh Day." Hana's words tumbled out as Ma's stare bored through her soul. She explained how she'd met him and Ink and how they'd unraveled the mystery of the DNA code.

"Why didn't you come talk to me?" Ma said.

"I tried," Hana said. "Remember all those messages? And then when I had the chance, I guess I didn't ask, maybe because I was afraid of the answers I'd get."

"Honey, so much gets lost in e-messages. I know I'm the worst culprit, always brain-messaging and onweb, but maybe both of us can remember to reach out in person." Ma brought her hand out and Hana put hers in it. Her warmth was a balm.

Hana felt connected to Ma now but wondered if Ma would've taken the time out of her head to truly listen to her. "Whenever you were at home, you were distracted when I needed you."

Tears sprang to Ma's eyes. "Hana, I'm here now. I know I let my work get in the way of us too often, but I promise to be more present. It was my way of coping with Ba's death and keeping everything together." She paused. "Not letting my emotions get in the way was how I got my work done."

Hana's heart melted thinking of how Ma was abandoned by Wayman, lost Ba, saw Popo drift away, and supported the family. "What's going to happen now?"

"It's complicated." Ma's fingers rummaged through her hair. "The Council of Corporations has already called me in for disciplinary hearings. I may lose my job."

Hana had turned off the news links on her comm after leaving school, but she glanced at them now. The uproar over Ink's exposé was spiraling, but the counter-spin was in full gear too. It was too soon to know how it would all shake out.

"It's not what you think. I'm trying to make this right."

Ma set down her cup. "I'm very sorry. I thought the risks we took were justified, because I truly believed it was safe, and I didn't have the real-time info from Primo Zed. You know I wouldn't have put you in danger."

Hana wanted so much to believe Ma, and she could see Ma was trying.

"Start-Up has postponed the early enmeshment of your class," Ma continued. "They'll go back to the normal schedule of a yearlong, slower program to get you ready for enmeshment. I've called off the experiments, and I will accept whatever consequences the Council of Corporations levies against me."

"What about us?" Hana asked, thinking of her friends. "Will we return to Start-Up? Are we going to be punished?" She wasn't sure she wanted to be a Start-Up or even meshed anymore, but she didn't want to be in trouble either. The world was organized around people getting meshed at thirteen, and all the ways she could think of making a difference in society was through gaining power and influence in the Corporations. The system was rigged to give the elite few from Start-Up that kind of power. Stepping outside that system was scary, but meeting Ink and Wayman and seeing their way of life had opened her eyes to new possibilities. She wanted to make the world more fair and wondered whether she would do most good from inside the system like Ma or outside like Wayman.

"I'll sort it out," Ma said. "Your friend Ink is right—

whoever tells the story shapes the world. You three did the right thing to bring light to something dangerous that I inadvertently created. I'll do what I can to set it right and keep you and your friends out of trouble."

A weight lifted from Hana.

She wouldn't understand Ma completely, and she worried what would happen to Ma, but she and her friends had done it. They'd stopped a dangerous plot against their classmates. She had a year to figure out what to think about getting meshed, and she wouldn't have to worry about being brainwashed with a zombie fungus or a cat brain parasite.

One more thing bothered her. "Can you also help someone else?" Hana asked.

"Who?"

"There's a guy at the junkyard who was taken off the streets by I Ching. His name is Guille. I'll get you his last name. I want to help pay off his fine." Hana would've liked to overturn the whole system of Corporations kidnapping people for their labor, but helping one person was a place to start.

Ma nodded. "I'll do what I can to track him down." Ma took Hana's hands in hers. "I'm so sorry. Things will be different from now on."

Hope surged through Hana. Things felt different already.

Ma stood up. "I'm ready to talk to my father now."

Hana got up too. Ma put her hand to Hana's face, and they came together in a hug. They stood as one for a wonderfully long time.

"My strong girl," Ma breathed. "I should pay more attention to you. You always teach me something new. I love you."

"I love you too." Hana blinked away a tear.

48

Turns out I can fly with my friends.
—H. H. July 11, 2053

Hana, Chuck, and Tomás hiked a trail through the cypress swamp a few miles from the Vistas. With Start-Up summer school canceled and the regular program not yet begun, they'd spent the last week exploring the nearby wild areas. Ma had been good to her word and had kept Hana and her friends out of the public eye. The Ghost Crab Nation took the credit for exposing the conspiracy, and their continued reporting captured the nation's attention. I Ching's and Nile's rivals Maskbook and Plex took full advantage of the outrage and scheduled corporate council meetings to investigate the scheme. I Ching and Start-Up could not retaliate against the kids for breaking their rules. In fact, they were in full spin mode to cover up and explain themselves.

Now the three stood at the edge of a marshy pond and checked out the cypress trees in the water draped with scraggly Spanish moss.

"Do you know what I want right now?" Chuck half jogged and half danced on the trail between them.

"What?" Hana loved seeing her friend back at full power.

"I'd love to have some of the Miraculously Delicious Drink."

Hana burst into laughter. "Don't you think it's worth giving up the elixir of the gods to avoid being brainwashed?"

Tomás kicked at a loose stick. "Definitely. I like my mind the way it is."

"So what happened to your dad?" Chuck asked. "And your mom, Hana?"

Hana glanced at Tomás. "Ma's been spending all her time shutting down the experiment, following up on the students who got sick, and preparing for the council hearings."

Tomás pressed his lips together. "My dad was called for a hearing too."

"I've been wondering, how did Start-Up not realize you're meshed?" Chuck asked.

"My dad's tech is cutting-edge advanced. It doesn't register as a neural mesh. They don't know about me, and I'd like to keep it that way." Tomás stepped back.

Hana smiled inwardly. There was always a new secret with Tomás. She took a deep breath. "Race you to the top of the hill."

She took off, crashing through the path along the marsh's edge leading to a shrubby area.

Chuck sprang forward. "You're on!"

Tomás put on a burst of speed and passed both of them.

"No fair!" Hana yelled. She dug deep and caught up with her two friends.

The three ran up the uneven path, their feet pounding over branches, sandy dirt, and pebbles. They jostled to a stop at the crest of the small hill, once an ancient sand dune now buried under trees and bushes. Pushing their way past the tree, they took in the view below.

The wind whipped their hair into their faces. The white-caps of the bay crashed against the distant shore. Trees and old streetlamps jutted out from the mini-lagoons and lakes that dotted the drowned landscape.

A flock of tiny birds winged their way over the surface of the water, their reflections blinking a thousand silver jewels.

Hana put an arm around each of her friend's shoulders. She'd never felt more connected to them and to the world than this moment.

It was wild and wonderful.

Acknowledgments

This story is a love letter to all the books I devoured as a kid—from science fiction to fantasies, mysteries, thrillers, and more. Reading was a conversation I had with authors across space and time that lit up my mind, and I can't believe that readers can have the same experience with *Hana Hsu*. I couldn't have done it without the many people who helped bring this story to life.

Thank you to my agent, Jennifer March Soloway, for always encouraging me, from the time we met at the Big Sur in the Rockies Children's Writing Workshop to our ongoing partnership. I am so grateful for your support, insights, and friendship.

I've been lucky to work with two amazing Razorbill editors. A million thanks to Julie Rosenberg for understanding and loving this story and for your expert editorial guidance. Thank you, Gretchen Durning, for your smart and insightful edits and for shepherding the book to its final form.

The cover is epic, and for that, I can't thank artist Fiona Hsieh and designer Jessica Jenkins enough. You are superstars.

I'm grateful to the entire Razorbill team for supporting and launching this book, including Casey McIntyre, Simone Roberts-Payne, Lizzie Goodell, Summer Ogata, Jayne Ziemba, Krista Ahlberg, Marinda Valenti, Delia Davis, Christine Ma, Michelle Millet, and Abigail Powers.

My messy words would not have been turned into a book without help from early readers and fellow writers.

I'm forever grateful to Tae Keller for mentoring me through Author Mentor Match. Your editorial eye is unsurpassed, and I couldn't have done this without you. You inspire me. Thanks, Alexa Donne, for creating such a supportive program, and Kristen Schroeder, for encouraging me to apply.

I wrote and revised *Hana Hsu* in workshops at The Muse Writers Center in Norfolk, Virginia, led by brilliant teachers Ellen Bryson and Lydia Netzer. I learned so much from you both. Thank you, fellow Muse writers, for your invaluable feedback: Hannah Capin, Jessica Grace Kelley, Kimberly Engebrigsten, Chris Braig, Elaine Panneton-Pollard, Bernadette Bartlett, Brittany Page, Michelle Ross, Lauren Blackwood, and Suzanne Burns. Thanks to Michael Kandelwhal for creating a space for creatives to thrive.

Thank you, Elaine Kiely Kearns, Julie Abe, Kim Tomsic, Teresa Robeson, Victoria Warneck, Ann Mesritz, Megan E. McDonald, Katy Schuck, and Margee Durand for your critiques. Special thanks to Timothy Warneck, Brooke

Richardson, and Jackson Meddows for test-driving the story when you were the target age. Others who shared valuable expertise are Kate Brauning and Margo Dill.

Special thanks to Kathryn Ault Noble, for the wonderful illustration you made while the story was a work in progress. You are an inspiration for living a life dedicated to art and creativity. Many thanks to Michelle Mohrweis for an amazing teacher's guide with STEAM-focused projects involving paper birds, automatons, and more.

A writer doesn't exist in a vacuum. Huge hugs to my original writing group, the Penguin Posse: Renée La-Tulippe (poet extraordinaire), Yvonne Mes (inspiring us from Down Under), Victoria Warneck (a grounded and wise soul), Elaine Kiely Kearns (my Kidlit411 coconspirator), and Teresa Robeson (joint owner of our single brain cell). And to my wonderful book club friends, who sustain me with conversations and great food: Janet, Sam, Kendall, Heather, Sally, Mia, Katy, Anna, Andrea, Lilly, and Kelly.

Publishing during a pandemic led to incredible connections with authors in #The21ders and #22Debuts; thank you for your camaraderie, accountability, and friendships (shout-out to Alysa Wishingrad and Kate Albus). Thank you, Annette Hashitate, Isi Hendrix, and Konstantinos (Kos) Kalofonos, for inspiring me with your powerful stories. I can't wait for the world to enjoy them, too.

I am grateful to my teachers at Escuela Campo Alegre

and Colegio Internacional de Caracas. You instilled in me a love of learning and made me believe anything was possible. Thank you, (the late) Marion Buchanan, Janet Steinmiller, Suzanne Hill, Jack Delman, Carlos Berrendero, and Linda Mishkin, to name a few. Thanks, Tal Abbady and Alona Martinez Abbady, for the Spanish copyedits, and Patty Caballero for our lifelong friendship.

Hana Hsu is about family, and my family is my bedrock. This book is dedicated to my parents, Bernard and Terry, and my sister, Vivian. From Chicago to Caracas and beyond, you are my foundation. All my love and gratitude to my husband, David, and my daughters, Sammi and Sarah. You are my favorite people in the world, and my life is full because of you. No thanks go to Apollo, who obstructed my keyboard and distracted me with his fluffiness.

Finally, thank you, readers, for spending your valuable time with this story and getting to know Hana, her family, and her friends.